ALL THE WOUNDS IN SHADOW

THE HEALING EDGE - BOOK TWO

ANISE EDEN

DIVERSIONBOOKS

Also by Anise Eden

Diversion Books
A Division of Diversion Publishing Corp.
443 Park Avenue South, Suite 1008
New York, New York 10016
www.DiversionBooks.com

This is a work of fiction. Names, characters, places and incidents either are the
product of the author's imagination or are used fictitiously. Any resemblance to
actual persons, living or dead, events or locales is entirely coincidental.

For more information, email info@diversionbooks.com

First Diversion Books edition August 2016.
Print ISBN: 978-1-68230-287-3
eBook ISBN: 978-1-68230-286-6

To UZH, for always.

CHAPTER ONE

In my dream, only the crabs' lives were in jeopardy. Mom and I chose a spot on the pier that was shaded by a nearby oak, hoping for some relief from the humid heat. The buzzing and clicking of crickets and cicadas swelled as the summer afternoon ripened.

"Hold it perfectly still, Catie," Mom whispered. "We want them to think it's just a strange-looking plant."

"I'm trying." But after an hour, my arm ached from holding the crab net steady. "Maybe the bait isn't rotten enough to attract them."

Mom jiggled the string with the chicken neck tied to the end, making it dance just beneath the water's surface. "Should I pull it out so you can check it?"

"Ew, gross!" I grimaced. "No thanks. I believe you."

Suddenly, her whole body tensed. "Look, there's one!"

The water was green and nearly opaque with algae. Staring down, I could just make out the ghostly limbs of a blue crab swimming up toward the bait.

"Wait until he's really absorbed in what he's doing and then scoop him up," she murmured. "Not too quickly, though. You don't want to scare him."

"Right." Once the crab started attacking the chicken neck, I slid the net beneath him and slowly lifted it to the surface.

"You got him!" Mom jumped to her feet. "Pull him out, and let's have a look!"

"He feels really heavy!" We exchanged smiles of victory as I raised the dripping net up to eye level.

"Oh, no," Mom said. "It's beautiful, a great catch. But we have to throw it back."

"Don't say that!" I moaned. "Why?"

"It's a female. It's poisonous."

I examined the crab. She was right: it had a full, rounded apron. With a sigh, I tossed the crab back into the water. "Females aren't poisonous, Mom, just illegal to catch. You know that."

"Whatever you say." Mom walked over to the edge of the pier and turned around to face me. "I have to go now. Don't follow me." Before I could even grasp what she was doing, she had folded her arms across her chest, closed her eyes, and tilted her stiffened body backwards into the water.

"Mom!" I leapt forward, reaching the edge of the pier just as she hit the surface with a sharp splash. Remembering my lifeguard training, I got down on my belly, lay on the wooden planks, and thrust my arm into the water. But she was already out of reach.

I grabbed the crab net and plunged the handle down towards her, but she kept her arms folded, eyes closed. "Mom, grab the handle!" I cried out, but she kept sinking. Within seconds she was nothing more than a whitish blur.

"Don't worry! I'm coming!" *Screw lifeguard training*, I thought as I kicked off my shoes and prepared to go in after her. But just as I was about to dive, something dragged me backwards by the waist.

I looked down to find a man's arm wrapped around me—a man's arm in a blue suit jacket. A familiar voice said, "Oh no you don't."

"Ben, let go of me!" I struggled to free myself from his hold. Then I realized that I was yelling out loud, awake and in bed, thrashing about and wrestling with the python of sheets tangled around me. My cell phone beeped and vibrated along the surface of the bedside table as the alarm went off. Meanwhile, my heart pounded in my throat. In my mind's eye, all I could see was my mother sinking further and further into the river.

Goddammit, I thought, vigorously rubbing the tears from my eyes. Would my dreams ever stop transforming into nightmares— reminders that I had failed to see that my mother was in crisis, that I had failed to save her?

I strained to hear Ben bounding up the stairs to see what the yelling was about, but there was only silence. Had I only cried out in my dream? "Ben?" I called, loudly enough for him to hear me if he was awake. Still no response.

So he was still asleep. That was odd. Ben told me he'd never lost the early-riser habit he had developed in the Marine Corps. I turned off my cell phone alarm, put on my robe and slippers, and padded down the stairs. But he wasn't on the sofa, where I'd left him the night before. In fact, he was nowhere.

I scanned the first floor of my tiny row house and found a note he'd left on the coffee table. "Had to go in early. See you at work. Bring a bag packed for a few days."

Well, that's cryptic, I thought as a bud of irritation formed. I flopped down on the couch and breathed slowly, trying to bring my heart rate back down to normal after the dream I'd had. "Bring a bag packed for a few days." But packed for what? Given how focused he was on my training, I somehow doubted that Ben was planning a romantic getaway.

I tried Ben's cell. No answer. I tried Pete's cell. Again, no answer. Whatever was happening at the office, it must have been keeping them both occupied.

At least I had another way to find out what was going on with Ben. I sat cross-legged on the couch. With my hands resting on my knees, I closed my eyes and took a few slow, deep breaths. Then I pictured the filament of light that connected my heart to Ben's, and focused my mind.

In an instant, the psychic portal between us opened. As my consciousness reached out and touched his, I fell back against the couch, struck by the intensity of his emotions. He was worried about something or someone, and there was a definite sense of urgency. Still, there was no actual fear. That told me that while some kind of crisis was going on, at least Ben was safe.

Then his feelings for me crashed through the portal, flooding me. Whatever else he was dealing with, I was on his mind. Once again I was overwhelmed by the strength of his feelings. Although I knew the portal only flowed one way, I tried to send my own feelings back in his direction. I pulled my consciousness back into my body and opened my eyes.

My gaze immediately settled upon my right hand, and the exquisite ring Ben had given me the day before. The gold band was carved to look like two birds in flight, holding a luminous round piece of Scottish agate with their beaks and the tips of their wings. He'd wanted to give me something concrete to remind me of how he felt about me when he wasn't there, to reassure me when I had worries or doubts. A soft warmth bloomed in my chest as I twirled the ring slowly around my finger, admiring its craftsmanship. We'd agreed that I would decide when to tell people that the ring was from him—and that we were dating. In the meantime, we were keeping both things a secret. I wasn't quite ready to go public with our new relationship, and Ben didn't want me to feel any pressure.

As I went upstairs and laid my suitcase open on the bed, I thought about my disturbing dream. My mother's fall into the water was obviously a reference to her suicide three months before. But the poisonous female crab? And Ben stopping me from saving someone's life? I knew he didn't like it when I put myself in danger, but he'd never just let someone drown.

Then again, maybe there's nothing to decipher, I told myself. *Sometimes a dream is just a dream.* I tried to content myself with that thought as I showered, dressed, and packed in a hurry. I was anxious to get to the office and find out where we were going—and what crisis had made Ben leave that morning without so much as giving me a kiss good-bye.

• • •

ParaTrain Internship, Day One

It was a beautiful October morning, crisp and clear with the trees still wearing their brilliant fall colors. As I drove my beat-up red hatchback through the streets of Baltimore, vibrant neighborhoods slowly gave way to block after block of empty, boarded-up row houses. Once I reached the church, I punched my code into the security gate panel and entered the parking lot. Ben and his mother, psychiatrist Angeline MacGregor, had renovated the majestic old building after it fell into disuse, transforming it into an alternative healing clinic. The church was also home to ParaTrain, their paranormal skills training program. Having just completed my first week of training and graduated to intern status, I was both excited and nervous to start working directly with clients.

But something unusual was going on. The parking lot was buzzing with activity. The back of the company Land Rover stood open, half-filled with suitcases and boxes. Next to it sat Pete's white pickup truck with the pair of steer horns on top of the cab. The back of the truck was also nearly full. Ben's 1936 Jaguar was gone— parked at home for safekeeping, I assumed.

I spotted Vani arranging various items in the back of the Land Rover. Even dressed for physical labor, our aura reader could pass for a Bollywood starlet. She was dazzling in dark green leggings, a black velvet tunic, and a perfectly coiffed ponytail.

"Hey, Vani."

"Oh, hi, Cate," she said in her clipped English accent. "Perfect timing. Could you hand me that box?"

I passed her a small box that was sitting on the ground. "What's going on?" I asked, craning my neck to examine the other boxes she was shifting around. I caught glimpses of crystals, candles, and incense holders.

"Packing for a trip, somewhere near Rockville. We're going to see that sick colleague Ben and Eve visited the other day. Apparently he's worse, not better."

"Oh, I'm sorry to hear that." I wondered how Ben was handling the bad news. But before I could ask for more details, I spotted the youngest members of our group, Eve and Asa, struggling to carry a metal footlocker. Eve was a few inches shorter than me, and Asa was tall and lanky. The difference in their heights had them lurching across the parking lot.

"Thanks," Eve said breathlessly as I rushed over and grabbed one of the footlocker's handles. She wore her hair in its usual black-and-purple spikes, and her multiple facial piercings flashed as she smiled.

Asa's shaved head was damp with perspiration, even though he was only wearing a T-shirt over his khakis. "Yeah, thanks, Cate. You're stronger than you look!"

But once we reached the vehicle, we couldn't quite raise the footlocker high enough to slide it inside. Out of nowhere, a long arm appeared, pushing our burden up from the bottom and giving us the extra lift we needed.

I recognized the plaid sleeve. "Thanks, Pete." I turned around to find myself face to face with the man who was quickly becoming my favorite cowboy. He had left his family's Wyoming cattle ranch to serve in the Marines, where he'd met Ben. Now he helped run the MacGregors' clinic.

From his great height, Pete tipped the edge of his ever-present ten-gallon hat at me. "No problem. Kai would kick my ass if I let our newest member strain a muscle. Besides," he added, "it's time to take a break. Ben wants us in the lounge so he can give us the lowdown."

"Finally!" Eve exclaimed. There was a collective sigh of relief as everyone dropped what they were doing and headed towards the church's side door.

• • •

Ben was already in the lounge, staring out the window. The white sunlight illuminated his face—all squared-off edges with straight, dark brows and light brown eyes. I was startled by how my heart leapt at the sight of him.

Fatigue and worry lined his face like country roads on a map. Still, he stood with his back and shoulders straight, projecting his usual air of confidence. It was obvious that he'd left my house in a rush that morning. He was wearing his usual office attire—dark blue suit, white shirt—but his clothes were rumpled. His jaw was dark with stubble, and his hair looked as though he'd combed it with his fingers.

It took everything in me not to run up, grab him, and kiss him until he forgot about everything but us. Instead, as the others settled onto couches and armchairs, I walked up beside him. "Good morning."

He looked down at me and moistened his lips with his tongue. I could tell that he was thinking about kissing me, too. "Morning. I'm sorry I had to take off so early."

I inhaled the scents of old leather, cotton, and wool that clung to his skin. I longed to step in close and lay my hand on his chest. Although I was growing more comfortable with the idea of telling everyone about us, it clearly wasn't the moment for romantic revelations. "I'll work on forgiving you."

Flecks of gold flashed in his eyes. "I've done some hard things in my life, but leaving your house without you this morning..."

I bit back a smile, still not quite believing how much he cared about me. "You know, you could have woken me up earlier. I would have liked to come in and help—"

"I know you would have," he said, the lines around his eyes softening. "But we had enough people here. It was more important that you got some rest."

I couldn't argue with him there; I *had* been exhausted the night before. "I was a little worried when I got your note. What's going on?"

He gave me one last look of frustrated desire and took a step back. "That's what I'm about to explain to everyone. I'm going to ask for volunteers to go on a trip." He looked down, brow furrowed.

"I heard—your sick colleague." More silence. "And?"

"My guess is that the others are going to say yes, but I want to make sure you don't feel any pressure. Whatever you decide, it'll be fine. Okay?"

"Hmm." My eyebrows slowly rose. "If that's true, then why did you leave a note for me to pack a bag this morning?"

"We're leaving straight from here. I wanted to make sure you had what you needed—just in case."

"That makes sense," I said. "Okay, I won't let myself feel pressured, I promise." It was obvious that he wanted me to go, but I appreciated being offered a preliminary opt-out.

"Good." Ben cleared his throat and squared his shoulders, indicating that he was shifting into manager mode. "Tea? Coffee?"

Following his lead, I gave him a businesslike nod. "Thanks. I'll help myself." As I walked over to the teacart, I heard the familiar *clip-clip* of high heels in the hallway.

"Kai!" We all greeted him nearly in unison as Kai rounded the corner into the lounge. His strong Greek features were flawlessly made up as usual, and he wore a fitted pantsuit in designer camo with high-heeled combat boots.

Kai was a man of many talents—ancient rituals expert, psychic medium, and jewelry craftsman. He'd made the protective pendant that I wore around my neck 24/7, a beautiful silver disk covered with concentric circles that was designed to protect me from absorbing other people's energy. Kai was also our meditation instructor; in fact, he'd planned to teach me a special technique that morning. But now that we were going on a trip, I imagined that mindfulness lessons would be put on hold.

Kai gave the room a graceful finger wave and winked at Pete. Then he joined me at the teacart and shot me a knowing look. "Morning," he murmured, gesturing towards Ben. "Looks like Rumpled Stiltskin over there didn't sleep at home last night."

I felt the heat rising in my cheeks, and decided it would be best to change the subject. "You look fantastic as usual," I said, giving his outfit a good once-over. "What's with the military theme?"

Kai's eyes widened as he leaned down close and whispered, "Pete says we're going on a top secret mission."

"Oh, really?" Pete must have been pulling one of his pranks. I pointed at Kai's stiletto boots. "You're *definitely* ready then."

"Smart ass." He mock-smacked me on the back of the head. "At least I don't look like I just rolled out of bed and into a haystack.

You know, you could really turn some heads if you put any effort in at all. Do you even *own* anything other than jeans and yoga pants? Vani and I are going to have to take you shopping."

I couldn't help but smile at Kai's ribbing. When I'd started the ParaTrain program the previous week, he had been the first member of the group to really make me feel welcome, and his friendship hadn't wavered since. But before I could reply, Ben clapped his hands.

"Okay, everybody take a seat. I hate to rush you, but we are under some time pressure."

Kai and I took our mugs of tea and joined Pete on one of the couches. Pete slung his arm around Kai's shoulders and gave him a kiss on the cheek. Once we had all settled in, Ben moved to the front of the room and addressed the group.

"You all know that Eve and I went to visit a sick colleague last week." Ben rubbed the lines on his forehead. "Well, he's worse. In fact, they're giving him about a fifty percent chance of making it."

"Oh no," Eve moaned. "I thought—"

"I know," Ben said, "we all thought. But as it turns out, it's more than a bad case of food poisoning. Someone tried to kill him."

There were several gasps. My hand flew up to cover my mouth.

"And the murder attempt may still succeed," he continued. "The doctors are doing everything they can for him, but they're hoping that with our combination of skills, we can help maximize his chances."

Everyone nodded their assent—everyone except for me, that was. The others all had skills that could be useful in such circumstances. Pete was a paramedic, Eve an acupuncturist, and Asa a Reiki master. Vani's aura-healing skills would no doubt prove helpful. Even Kai could talk to the dead; maybe the spirits could give him some pointers on how to cure the patient. But as an emotional empath, what could I possibly do? Tell them how their colleague felt about the fact that someone had tried to kill him? Crappy, I imagined. What if Ben was only inviting me to come because he didn't want me to feel left out? I didn't want to be excess baggage, or worse, a burden. I raised my hand.

Ben pointed to me. "Cate?"

"I'm so sorry, Ben. That's horrible news, and of course I'll do whatever I can to help. But I'm just wondering what that might be. I don't want to come along just to get in the way."

"You're a part of our team. You could never be in the way." A muscle in Ben's jaw twitched. "To be honest, though, you *are* plan B."

My confidence dipped even lower. "What's plan B?"

"I'm very sorry, Cate—everyone—but I have to wait until we get there to explain further." He ran a hand quickly through his hair. "Due to security clearances, I can't say anything more until we arrive. After they figured out that it was an attempted murder, our colleague's protection became a military operation. Once we get where we're going, we'll all be staying in a locked facility for the duration. No one leaves—not until we've cured him, or he dies."

So Pete hadn't been kidding, after all; it *was* a secret mission, and a man's life hung in the balance. A shudder passed through my body.

"Oooh!" Kai exclaimed, pressing his hands together as though in prayer. "Are you saying it's going to be *dangerous*?"

"Not for us." Ben turned and gave me a look freighted with meaning. "There will be no risk to anyone here—as long as we follow any and all instructions we're given to the letter."

If my stomach hadn't begun to flip-flop, I would have rolled my eyes at him. So I'd disregarded some of his instructions in the past. Did that make me an outlaw for life? The suspicious part of me began to wonder if "plan B" was just an excuse for Ben to keep me under his watchful eye.

"If I thought there'd be any danger, I wouldn't even have considered asking you to come." Ben walked slowly around the room, impressing his words on each of us individually. "Having said that, no one here is under any obligation. This is on a strictly volunteer basis. I know it's a lot to take on faith; Eve is the only one here who even knows who the patient is. If it helps, I have called our usual backup team. They will be on standby to handle any of our clients who need help while we're gone."

"Oh, please. Do you really need to ask?" Kai looked expectantly around the room. "Of course we're going! That's what we do, after all—help people, whether we know them or not. Right, everyone?"

Asa's face was alight with excitement as he turned to Eve. "How cool will it be to give our professors notes excusing us from class because we have to go on a top secret mission?"

Eve grinned back. "Totally. I'm *so* in."

"My bags are already in the Land Rover," Vani said, tossing her ponytail to one side.

Since Pete went everywhere Ben went, his participation was a given. Apparently, I was the only question mark.

Kai patted my arm, presumably because he was sitting close enough to hear my heart pounding. If there was anything I could do to help save someone's life, of course I wanted to do it. But attempted murder? A military operation? A locked facility? All of those things were far outside of my experience—and Ben *had* taken pains to make sure that I didn't feel pressured to go.

On the other hand, a mere day had passed since I'd agreed to leave my old job and come to work for the MacGregor Group. I didn't want to start things off by rejecting my first chance to demonstrate solidarity. I also didn't want to look like a chicken. After all, Eve was just a college student, Asa was in grad school, and Vani was a marketing executive. Kai might have had some experience dealing with dicey situations, but I was pretty sure that none of us civilians were used to playing cloak and dagger. But if the others were scared, they weren't letting on. *And there's no reason to be scared, anyway,* I reassured myself. Ben said we wouldn't be in any danger, and security *was* one of his areas of expertise.

Besides, when I thought about staying behind, every cell in my body cried out in protest. Although Ben and I had just started dating, I was already loath to be away from him, even for a few days.

Well, that settled that. I could feel everyone's eyes on me. "I'm in, too," I said. Kai squeezed my hand.

"You're sure?" The question was for the group, but Ben was looking at me.

There was a chorus of affirmations from the others. I gave Ben a sideways smile. "Plan B, reporting for duty."

His posture visibly relaxed. "All right, then. Thanks, everyone. I hate to rush you, but we'd better load up. Time is not on our side."

Pete and Kai climbed into the pickup while the rest of us loaded ourselves into the Land Rover. And that was how we ended up traveling south on I-95, careening into the mouth of the unknown.

CHAPTER TWO

Ben drove the Land Rover and invited me to ride shotgun. Complaining about how early she'd had to get up, Vani stretched out in the backseat, put on noise-canceling headphones, and announced that she'd be catching up on her sleep. Eve and Asa took the third-row seats and began to play a zombie apocalypse game on their tablets.

The trip started out quietly. The only sounds were the whoosh of the tires, the low hum of the engine, and occasional exclamations of victory of defeat from Asa or Eve. Since the rest of the team seemed content to wait until we reached our destination to ask any more questions about the mission, I figured I should follow their lead.

I tried to distract myself by examining Ben. He had a quiet but powerful presence—one of the first things I'd noticed about him. His strong jawline set off what I'd discovered were very skilled lips, while the dark ridge of his eyebrows contrasted with the bright gold flecks that flickered in his eyes whenever he was energized about something.

In the business suits he usually wore, Ben looked to be of average build, but I knew from experience how strong he was. After all, he had carried me up a staircase without breaking a sweat, and I'd witnessed Ben and Pete handily taking down a group of armed men. I did find it endearing that, as put-together and in control as he liked to appear, Ben's short, wavy hair was always slightly unruly, no matter how hard he tried to tame it.

His right hand rested on his thigh as his left kept a loose grip on the bottom of the steering wheel. One minute his movements were firm and decisive; the next, impossibly gentle. I wondered if he'd learned that range of touch from restoring classic cars—a hobby that I imagined would require working with everything from hard metal to soft leather.

Overall, Ben appeared alert but relaxed behind the wheel. He seemed to be in his element. I made a mental note to suggest we go for a ride the next time he looked like he needed a break. I marveled at the fact that Ben and I were actually dating, and that I was learning the little things that made him happy. Just like two people in a normal relationship.

"That's not fair, you know."

I started at the sound of Ben's voice. "What?"

The corners of his mouth turned upwards. "I have to keep my eyes on the road, so I can't stare back."

Oh hell, I thought as my cheeks prickled with heat. I'd been caught. I quickly turned my eyes to the windshield. "Well you have to admit, there's not much else for me to do."

"You're right." He released a measured sigh. "I haven't been very good company."

Of course he'd hadn't. He was probably preoccupied with top secret life-and-death issues. My blush deepened. "I'm sorry. I shouldn't have distracted you."

"Of course you should've," he said emphatically. "I'm the one who should apologize. This is a tense situation, and driving in silence can't be helping." He gave me an incisive glance. "How are you doing with everything?"

"Okay, I guess." I twisted my fingers together in my lap. "A little nervous, maybe."

"I'd be surprised if you weren't. You've been through a lot of changes over the past week, and now I'm throwing you another curveball." He cast a sideways glance my way. "Why did you decide to come?"

He was right; since I'd started their training program, nearly every aspect of my life had been upended and rearranged. "Well, I'll admit that the idea of staying at home on my couch, eating ice cream, and playing online poker *was* pretty tempting. But you said it yourself—I'm plan B. What'll you do if plan A doesn't work?"

"You have a point there." His features grew soft with affection. "You never stop surprising me, Cate."

I felt my cheeks redden again. It was time to change the subject. "Let's talk about something nonserious for a change. It sounds like it's going to be all serious all the time once we get where we're going."

"Good point. Let's shorten the road. What would you like to talk about?"

Suddenly, I couldn't think of anything but the mission, which I knew we couldn't discuss further until we arrived. I racked my brain. "Twenty Questions is kind of a road-trip game, isn't it?"

"Hmm." For the first time that morning, he appeared upbeat. "I should warn you, I'm really good at that game."

At the prospect of playing a normal, lighthearted game with Ben, happiness flitted through me like a tiny fish. Still, I shook my head at his overconfidence. "Is there anything you *aren't* good at?"

"Plenty of things," he said, "but absolutely no advantage will accrue to me if I tell you what they are." A smile played across his lips. "Ladies first."

We played a few rounds. It was obvious that we were trying to make it easy for one another. I was pleasantly surprised to find that Ben took the same approach to games that I did—that their purpose was fun, not serious competition. Still, after I guessed his Jaguar in eight questions and he guessed Vani in six, it was starting to get a bit ridiculous.

I glanced around for inspiration. It wasn't hard to find. "Okay, I have something. Go ahead."

"Animal, vegetable, or mineral?"

"Mineral."

"Is it your ring?"

My mouth fell open. "You know, being telepathic is the kind of thing you're supposed to disclose to the person you're dating!"

"Not telepathic, just observant." He nodded at my hand. "You looked down at your ring right before you said you had something."

I gave him a lengthy glare. Then I put some real thought into my next answer. "Okay, ready."

"Animal, vegetable, or mineral?"

"Animal."

"Is it bigger than a breadbox?"

"Yes."

Ben glanced in the rear view mirror, presumably to make sure that Vani was asleep and Asa and Eve still had their headsets on. Then he asked, "Is it the incredibly distracting woman who's *wearing* your ring?"

I pressed my lips together. "You know, for someone who's so fond of following rules, you're certainly playing fast and loose with Twenty Questions."

"You're right, I apologize," he said, with no sincerity whatsoever. "Give me one more chance. How many questions do I have left?"

As much as I was enjoying Ben's playful side, I tried to look stern. "Seventeen."

"All right." He frowned in exaggerated concentration. "Is it a mammal?"

"Yes."

"Hmm." He rubbed his jaw and murmured, "Is it the woman I kissed last night—the one I can't stop thinking about kissing?"

A fresh blush splashed across my face as I recalled our prolonged session on my couch. "You can't stop thinking about that either?" I whispered.

His smile was triumphant. "So I guessed right?"

"No, you did *not* guess right!"

"Oh, too bad." He arched an amused eyebrow. "And no, I can't stop thinking about it. I'm thinking about it right now, in fact."

My breath caught in my throat as Ben's eyes flashed up and down my body like a sultry searchlight. "You're not even playing the game at this point."

"You're right. I'm sorry. In my defense, though, it's hard to concentrate on Twenty Questions when you're sitting this close to me."

I tried to disguise my stirring arousal with an eye roll. "Says the master of self-control."

"Only when I'm able to concentrate fully on that task," he admitted with a crooked grin. "Right now, at least half of my brain is occupied with driving."

"I see." It occurred to me that this information might come in handy sometime. "I'll have to remember that."

He shot me an inquisitive look. "Tell me what the answer was, at least?"

I only kept him in suspense for a minute. "It was Tank, the dog from your old Marine Corps unit."

"Tank!" He leaned back, stretched, and tucked his free hand behind his head. "Well, I was in the right neighborhood, anyway."

I was in the same neighborhood as a *Rottweiler?* "Meaning *what*, exactly?"

"Well, Tank used to kiss me all of the time," Ben said. "Of course, his kisses were more slobbery...."

Choking back a laugh, I warned, "I'd stop talking *right now* if I were you."

Ben held his hand up in a gesture of surrender. "Fine, but that means you have to come up with something else for us to talk about."

"No problem." I tried to think of a subject that would bring the heat between us down a notch. After all, Vani could wake up at any moment, and as an aura reader, she didn't miss much. Fortunately, the perfect topic occurred to me. "Oh, I know!" There was something I'd been meaning to ask Ben, even though I knew it might be a touchy subject. "Okay, truth time. You never really told me what you think about all of that Bronze Age origins stuff."

Learning about the origins of paranormal abilities had been one of the weirder experiences in my first week of training. According to those who studied the history of sensitives—a term for people with paranormal gifts—the oldest mentions of those gifts dated back to the Bronze Age. Since that time, the gifts appeared to have been passed down via heredity. As to how and why paranormal abilities appeared in the first place, however, there were opposing theories.

Some thought that our abilities had evolved naturally, Darwin-style, while others believed that they were spiritual gifts bestowed by a higher power upon certain ancient civilizations.

I'd gathered that when it came to the "spiritual gift" theory, Ben was a skeptic like me. However, his mother seemed quite open to the possibility, and Vani and Kai were true believers. But Ben had never come right out and told me what he thought, and the question had nagged at me—especially after he admitted that one reason his mother had taken an interest in me in the first place was that by bringing me on board, she completed the MacGregor Group's collection of paranormal gifts, which she believed would have spiritual as well as practical consequences.

"I believe I *did* tell you." Ben put both hands on the wheel. "I'm focused on running the clinic, not settling historical questions. And since I don't believe that how or when paranormal gifts developed is relevant to our work, I don't give it much thought."

"Okay, yes, you did tell me that much," I acquiesced, "but you're still not answering my question. Surely you have an opinion on the subject."

Somehow, Ben managed to erase his face of all expression. His tone, too, was perfectly neutral as he said, "I think it's important that you make up your own mind about it, Cate."

I gave him a look that I hoped was scalding. "I fully intend to make up my own mind, but that doesn't mean I don't want to know what you think. You're a psychologist, and you've been around this paranormal stuff a lot longer than I have. What if Vani or Kai asks me to help them replicate some ancient animal sacrifice or something? *While* I'm making up my own mind, it would be helpful for me to know whether you think it's all hokum!"

There was a pause, followed by, "I don't want to unduly influence you."

"Oh my God, you have *got* to be kidding me!" I threw my hands up. "You spent *all last week* trying to influence me. Now, all of a sudden, you're Switzerland?"

Ben's shoulders tightened. "It doesn't matter what I think,

because I'm not a sensitive. Whether the spiritual theory is true or false doesn't affect me, at least not directly. However, if it turns out that there's something to it, then it may very well affect *you*. I don't want to poison the well."

And I *was* a sensitive, so if he was afraid of poisoning the well for me, that could only mean one thing. "So you don't believe it."

Frustration flashed across Ben's face, but he quickly regained his composure. He paused to rub his forehead. "All right, look. At first, I thought the spiritual origins theory sounded like, as you put it, hokum. However, it's only practical to keep an open mind in our line of work. My mother, Vani, and Kai are people for whom I have a great deal of respect, so when they embrace something, I'm inclined to remain flexible on the subject until all of the evidence has been gathered. As of now, it hasn't, so as far as I'm concerned, the jury is still out."

His answer seemed honest and thorough, if not decisive. "Okay, that's fair."

"I know that's not what you wanted to hear...."

"I wanted to hear what you thought, and that's just what you told me." I sighed. "But you're right; it would have been nice to be able to cross at least one thing off of my 'weird new ideas' list."

"I'm sure it would have." His shoulders relaxed a bit. "I hope you realize how rare you are, Cate. I don't know anyone else who would be capable of taking in all of the new concepts you've embraced over the past week."

Annoyance rumbled inside of me like the beginning of an earthquake. "It wasn't like I had a choice, remember?" At the behest of my former boss, Dr. Nelson, Ben had cooperated in coercing me to stay through the entire first week of training, even when I'd wanted to leave. While I'd come to accept that they'd done so with my best interests in mind, I would never be okay with their methods. "Speaking of undue influence...."

Ben checked on the other passengers in the rear view mirror again, then slid his free hand onto my thigh and gave it a quick squeeze. In a low, intimate voice, he said, "I was trying to pay you a compliment, not start an argument."

The heat of his touch stole so much of my concentration that I couldn't form a pithy comeback. He left his hand on my leg just long enough to turn it into molten lava. It was all I could do to keep from squirming in my seat. Still, I didn't want him to remove his hand; it was a delectable torment.

For what must have been the millionth time, I cursed the ParaTrain program's "no sex during training" rule. According to Vani, that level of physical intimacy caused the auras of the people involved to comingle, tainting each other's energies for a week at least—and my aura had to remain spotless, or I wouldn't get the full benefit of the training exercises. However, Ben's hand on my leg was putting all kinds of images in my mind that made me want to take the rule book and throw it violently out the window.

Suddenly, a reckless sedan cut us off and Ben had to return both hands to the wheel in a hurry. I sucked in my cheeks to silence a half sigh, half moan as his touch left me.

Ben had been jolted out of relaxation mode and was back on full alert. When he spoke again, his voice was tight with worry. "Look, while we're on this mission, I want you to tell me immediately if you run into any problems or have any questions—really, if anything at all makes you uncomfortable. Also, tell me if you need anything— anything at all, at any time. All right?"

A fist of anxiety formed in my stomach. I hated walking into the unknown and not being able to ask any specific questions. I wondered why the others seemed so calm about facing real-life secrecy, mystery, and danger. Eve and Asa might be too young and inexperienced to know that they should be scared. Vani seemed to have a preternatural confidence, an unshakable belief that nothing bad would happen to her. Maybe Kai had simply been with Pete long enough to trust his judgment (and Ben's) when it came to safety. But I couldn't help it; I was on edge, and there was no use denying it to myself.

After all, the only real job I'd ever had was working as a

psychotherapist at a community mental health clinic. True, we dealt with serious crises and even life-and-death situations at times—but only our clients', not our own. Ever since Ben and Dr. Nelson had convinced me to leave my former job and work for the MacGregors as an empath healer, my concerns had centered around how hard it was going be to leave my existing therapy clients and my old career behind, *not* around how dangerous my new job might be.

I slid my hands under my legs so I wouldn't bite my nails. "Are you *expecting* me to run into problems and feel uncomfortable?"

Ben considered my question for a moment too long. When he glanced over to answer me, he must have seen that I was on the verge of panicking. "No, I'm not," he said firmly, "but it's going to be a different world down there—one that I'm simply more familiar with than you are. If you do run into any problems, we'll deal with them. I just need you to tell me right away instead of trying to deal with things on your own."

I swallowed hard. "A different world—you mean, because of the military?"

"In large part, yes," he said, "but also because you're still in training, and we may need to use some paranormal healing techniques that will be new to you."

He had a point on both counts. First of all, everything I knew about military culture came from a few clients who were veterans, news stories, and a handful of movies—and that had been enough to intimidate me. And the one time I'd tried to use a new paranormal skill on my own—in spite of Ben's explicit instructions not to—I'd ended up going into cardiac arrest. I would have died if Ben and Pete hadn't saved me. Not at all anxious to repeat that incident, I nodded. "Okay, I'll tell you if anything comes up."

"Good. I'm glad that's settled." Ben returned his focus to the road.

I looked out the side window and tried to ignore the knot in my stomach. As I watched the trees rush by in a blur, I thought of my best friend and former supervisor, Simone. She had a tendency to worry about me, especially after the breakdown I'd suffered following my mother's funeral. I'd been basically homebound for over two months, and Simone had been my only real link to the outside world. After everything she'd done for me, the least I could do was let her know I'd be gone for a while so she wouldn't freak out if she couldn't get ahold of me. I told Ben, "I'm going to let Simone know that I'll be away so she doesn't get worried."

"Good idea."

I sent Simone a text saying that I'd be out of town for a few days. She immediately texted back a bunch of questions I couldn't answer, so I made up a cover story that was technically true: Ben and I had started dating and were going away together. After I dealt with her complete shock about the fact that I was dating someone, reassured her that Ben wasn't a psycho, and promised that I wasn't being kidnapped, Simone gave me her provisional blessing—but only after extracting a promise that I would tell her every detail when I got home, and letting me know that if she didn't hear from me after a week she was "coming to get me." Although I knew that she was joking, in light of the grim mystery we were facing, I found her rescue vow oddly comforting.

"That was a long text," Ben observed as I put my phone away.

I smiled to myself. "She wanted reassurance that you weren't kidnapping me and taking me to a remote hideout off the grid somewhere in the mountains of West Virginia."

"Hmm." He frowned. "A locked facility near D.C. doesn't sound much better."

"Don't worry. I was delightfully vague."

We rode in silence for a few minutes before Ben spoke again. "It's not too late to change your mind, you know."

I twisted around to look at him. "What?"

With his brows locked into a dark, straight line, his eyes shifted between the road and me. "You said yourself that you're nervous. If you decide you don't want to a part of this, when we get where we're going, I can put you in a taxicab and send you back home. No questions asked."

I appreciated the fact that he was willing to put my comfort ahead of the perceived needs of the mission. But by being so damn thoughtful, he'd made it even more difficult for me to even think about being away from him. "You said we'll be safe, right?"

"Right."

"And we're going to help your colleague, an innocent man whom someone is trying to kill?"

"Yes."

"Well then." I tilted my head sideways and folded my arms across my chest. "I said I'm in, and I'm in. So unless you don't want me there, stop trying to give me outs."

One corner of his mouth pulled upwards. "Yes ma'am."

"Good. I'm glad that's settled," I said, smiling as I repeated his words back to him.

Suddenly, loud cheers from the back row filled the vehicle. Asa and Eve had conquered some treacherous zombie foe. With Vani awakening, and our gaming warriors regaling us with a blow-by-blow description of the battle, Ben and I shared one last stolen glance. Then I turned to face the others and he fixed his eyes on the road ahead.

CHAPTER THREE

It took us less than an hour to reach our destination. The National Institutes of Health, or NIH, looked like a cross between a wealthy college campus and a high-tech business park. As Ben navigated the maze of roadways, the rest of us leaned toward the windows to get a glimpse of our surroundings. We drove through a seemingly endless array of huge brick buildings and manicured landscapes interspersed with old-growth trees. All of that disappeared suddenly, however, as we approached the largest building we'd seen so far and entered its underground garage, driving in a dark, downward spiral for what seemed like an eternity.

"We're under the NIH hospital," Ben said. The interior of the Land Rover flashed light and dark as we passed beneath the overhead bulbs. I glanced behind us at Pete's truck, relieved to see that there were several inches of clearance between the steer horns and the parking garage's ceiling. We must have been at least six or seven stories underground by the time we finally stopped.

We parked the cars next to a set of elevators. Two men and a woman were waiting there for us. They wore short-sleeved khaki shirts, olive green pants, and matching caps with straight sides and top creases from front to back.

We followed behind Ben and Pete as they greeted our welcome party. Their handshakes with the two men turned into brief embraces and warm greetings. Then Ben and Pete turned to the woman, who opened her arms wide to each of them and hugged them tightly.

The two uniformed men began poking Ben in the arms and chest. "Damn, Rottie, there's nothing left of you!" one of the men exclaimed, referring to Ben by his old Marine Corps nickname.

The other man hooked his thumb at Pete and added, "Yeah, man, Slim here was always a lean dog, but this desk job has got you wasting away!"

Ben grinned. "And I see you two still have nothing better to do than pump iron."

"Jesus, you guys," said the woman, laughing. "Save it for after we get everybody settled in, at least! And where's everyone's manners?" She waved to the rest of us. "Hi, Kai! And welcome, MacGregor Group."

"Hello, Ness!" Kai stepped forward and hugged the woman, then the two men in turn. "So good to see you all again."

"I'm surprised you remember the last time," one of the men teased.

Kai opened his mouth to defend himself, but Pete stepped in. "Come on, now, we both know that was Kai's first time drinkin' Jäger, and none of us were exactly at our best the next mornin', so…."

"You can say that again," one of the men said, rubbing his forehead to the sound of snickering.

"Allow me to introduce the rest of the MacGregor group." Ben urged me to step forward. "This is Cate Duncan. Cate, this Corporal Perez."

"Hector," the man corrected, extending his hand. He murmured to Ben, "Captain told us to use first names only so the civilians will feel more comfortable."

"Ah, okay." Ben led me down the receiving line. "In that case, Cate, meet Kevin and Nessa."

I shook both of their hands as Vani, Asa, and Eve followed behind me. Hector and Kevin were both well over six feet tall and did look like they spent a substantial amount of time lifting weights. The woman, Nessa, was close to six feet tall—around Ben's height—and moved with graceful strength, like a dancer. She had sharp, refined features sprinkled with freckles, and her red hair was pulled back into a ponytail.

Once introductions were done, Hector grinned and nodded

towards our vehicles. "Since Rottie's turned into a weakling and all, it's a good thing we volunteered to come help unpack your gear."

More jovial trash talk ensued as we unloaded the contents of our vehicles onto rolling carts. Beneath the marines' relaxed exteriors, however, I recognized something I'd also seen in Ben and Pete—a certain taut readiness, and a firm core of competence. The confident quality of their presence was reassuring, but it also made me acutely aware that I was a mere civilian—and that I had almost no idea what I was stepping into. I focused on trying not to bite my lip as we crowded into the large cargo elevator and headed even further underground.

I was sure that NIH's hospital had nice parts, but we weren't in one of them. Instead, the elevator door opened onto a long corridor that could have been the setting for any one of the horror movies I'd seen in high school. The bare cinderblock walls matched the grey concrete floors, whose high-gloss finish had dulled over time. Low ceilings of white foam tiles buzzed with the sound of ancient fluorescent bulbs. One of the bulbs flickered erratically, crackling like an insect caught in a zap trap. I half expected a masked villain carrying a rusty power tool to come around the far corner and charge us.

"Cozy," I whispered to Kai.

He leaned down and murmured, "Don't worry, honey. We'll warm it up." Then he gave me a conspiratorial wink and steered me back toward the elevator to begin unloading.

I reached over to take my suitcase from the rolling cart, fearful that if I didn't have my hands on it at all times, it might get lost in the maze of concrete, never to be seen again. But just as I reached for it, so did Nessa. We both glanced down as our hands simultaneously grasped the handle. I began to explain that I'd take care of it myself when she exclaimed, "Oh my God!" After recovering from a fleeting moment of surprise, Nessa looked up at me and smiled. "Ben didn't tell us you two were an *item*!" she exclaimed, glancing over at Ben as her words echoed through the corridor.

My jaw dropped. "What?"

Everyone stopped what they were doing. I shot Ben a desperate glance.

Nessa's eyes widened. "Oh, was I not supposed to say…?" She clapped a hand over her mouth and turned to Ben. "I'm sorry, I just saw the ring and assumed…."

"Of course you did." Ben walked over and stood beside me. "It's fine. It's just—"

It was just that somehow, Nessa knew the significance of the ring I was wearing. But when the other members of the MacGregor group had asked about it the day before, I hadn't told them that the ring was a gift from Ben, much less what it signified. Ben's expression was pained, and I could tell that he was searching for what to say next.

But since I was the one who had wanted to keep our relationship a secret in the first place, I felt like it was my responsibility to deal with the situation. And with the cat at least partially out of the bag, I knew that if I lied, I'd be seen through. I decided to bite the bullet. "It's just that we haven't told everyone yet," I explained, smiling up at Ben. "We haven't had a chance, really. We only started dating yesterday, and then we were busy getting ready to come here…." I shrugged.

"Oh, okay," Nessa said a little too loudly. She cleared her throat and looked at the floor. "Well, I'm sorry for jumping the gun on you there."

Even as self-consciousness pumped blood into my cheeks, I also felt sorry for Nessa, who looked truly mortified. "It's no problem, really," I said—graciously, I hoped—as Ben's arm slid around my waist.

"Cate's right, it's no problem," Kai said, giving me a sly smile. "Most of us already had our suspicions."

"Except for Asa," Eve announced. "Pay up, loser!" She gleefully collected five bucks from Asa, prompting a light outbreak of laughter.

With the tension broken, Ben and I accepted everyone's good wishes—which they delivered as nonchalantly as possible, to my relief. I was surprised to find myself feeling more relaxed. Then realized that I had been reluctant to tell our friends partially because I was concerned about how they'd take the news. "I'm glad that you're all okay with this," I admitted. "I was afraid you might be weirded out."

Asa smirked as he pointed at Pete and Kai. "*Puh-leez*. It's not like we're strangers to having couples in the office."

"That's right," Vani said. "Not to mention that we're all happy Ben is finally dating someone. We'd just about given up on him."

"What do you mean, just about? We gave up on him a long time ago," Hector said.

Kevin nodded. "We had him written off as a total lost cause."

"All right, all right," Ben said, but I knew that he was bringing the conversation to a close more for my benefit than his own. "Now that the soap opera's over, can you show us where to put our gear?"

Kevin made a dramatic show of turning on his heel, grabbing a cart, and rolling it down the hallway. "Five minutes in, and Rottie's already giving orders."

There were several appreciative chuckles as we followed behind.

Nessa slid in beside me. "I'm really sorry, Cate."

"It's okay." I gave her the most reassuring smile I could muster. "I promise."

"All right, if you say so. Thanks."

We traveled down the long hallway to an identical hallway, then another, and another. Finally we trundled to a stop. Hector turned to address us.

"Okay, everybody. You've been divided into rooms according to your functions," he said. "This will cause the least disruption in your routines. Ben and Pete, you're over here, closest to our barracks." He nodded towards a door, then walked further down the hallway. "Kai and Asa, you're on the right. Eve and Vani, across the hall. Make yourselves comfortable, and if you need anything, don't hesitate to ask anyone wearing Charlies."

"Charlies?" Vani asked.

"These uniforms." He pointed to his shirt. "Cate? You can follow me."

I wanted to kiss Ben when he took my suitcase and accompanied us. We turned every which way through a maze of corridors. "Sorry you're so far away from the others," Hector said over his shoulder, "but space is tight around here. We didn't have much to work with." Stopping in front of a door, he said, "Here we are, home sweet home."

"Thanks," I said, trying and failing to sound grateful.

"No problem." He addressed Ben. "We have a briefing at 1400. I'll come and get everybody."

"Got it. Thanks, Hector." Ben opened the door and we walked inside. The room was small and starkly utilitarian, with a set of bunk beds, a dresser, and a desk with a chair. Everything was steel and tile, hard and cold. Someone had painted the room yellow at one point, but the color had faded into a depressing tan. Rough-looking white sheets and towels were stacked on the desk. I stepped over to an open door that led into a bathroom. It was small and spare, containing a bathtub but no shower.

Seeing the look on my face, Ben put my suitcase on the desk and drew me into a tight embrace. "I'm sorry your room isn't closer to the others. It's only for sleeping in, though. You won't be spending much time here." He placed his hands on my cheeks and kissed me tenderly on the forehead. My body warmed as though I'd been standing on a cold, overcast beach and the sun had just come out. Ben slid his fingers down and tucked them behind my neck, his eyes searching mine. "I'm really sorry about the way things played out back there. Are you okay?"

The whole situation had put me in something akin to a mild state of shock. I had no idea how I was going to feel when that wore off. "Yeah, I'm okay," I replied, with the same uncertainty I'd felt when I first tried sushi.

"You don't look it. Let's sit." Ben sat on the bottom bunk. I joined him, conscious of the lumps in the plastic-covered mattress.

He took my hands in his and began stroking my palms with his thumbs. Some tight thing inside of me began to loosen. I scooted closer to him and rested my head against his shoulder. "How much time do we have until Hector comes back for us?"

"Not enough," he said in a low rumble. He tilted my chin up and pressed his warm lips firmly against mine. He lingered there just long enough to send me to the edge of squirming—and to make me feel that the universe was a cold, unfair, and uncaring place when he pulled away. "Never enough."

I dropped my head against his shoulder again and nestled in closer. Ben had always been so secretive about his time in the Marines, but given the circumstances, I decided to venture a question. "So how do you all know each other, anyway?"

"Pete and I were in boot camp with Nessa, Kevin, and Hector."

"Oh." I tried to hide my amazement that he'd actually answered me. "Well, I *was* surprised when Nessa outed us."

"Yeah." Ben looked down and slowly rubbed his jaw. "Actually, that's my fault."

"What?" I jerked away from him. "How?"

"I completely forgot that she knew about the ring." Ben slid closer to me until our legs were touching. "I used to keep that ring in a box with my personal effects. Nessa spotted it and asked me about it once. It was just so long ago that I forgot."

The mystery deepened. Once again stunned by its beauty, I twirled the ring around my finger. "What did you tell her?"

"That it's a family heirloom, and that my mother gave it to me in case I ever met anyone really special."

We both sat perfectly still, the meaning of his words vibrating in the air between us. I swallowed hard. "A family heirloom? How old is it?"

"We're not sure exactly, but it's been in the family for at least four or five generations. My grandmother gave it to my mother when she left Scotland to come to school in the States. My mother only wore it on special occasions, though. She said it wasn't her style."

I could imagine that. From what I'd seen of Dr. MacGregor, she went for a classy but understated look. The ring wasn't ostentatious, but it was memorable, as Nessa had demonstrated.

As though anticipating my next question, Ben took my ring hand in his. "You're the only person I've ever offered this ring to, Cate—or *wanted* to give it to."

"But, Ben...." Suddenly self-conscious, I felt my breathing quicken. "Your mother said if you met anyone really special. I'm not.... I mean, are you sure?" I stammered. "It must mean a lot... and it must be worth, I don't know.... And we practically just met...."

Once I ran out of words, I began to slide the ring off of my finger. Ben stopped me, taking a firm hold of my hand. I looked up and was astonished by the passion I saw swimming in his eyes. His voice was soft but intense. "Cate, you *are* special, so much more than you realize. Not only are you incredibly special among people in general, but you're also special to me, in particular. And you're the one I want to wear this ring—the *only* one. Do you understand?"

As his words washed over me, I felt my own emotions rising to meet his. "Yes," I whispered. He released his hold on my hand, and I slid the ring back to the base of my finger.

"I'm not sure you do, but I'll keep working to convince you." The gold flecks in Ben's eyes flashed like firecrackers. He slid his hand behind my neck, leaned down, and kissed my temple. His lips were like the source of a waterfall pouring warmth into my body. I felt his chest expand as he took a deep breath, nose buried in my hair. "I'm very sorry, Cate. I wanted you to be in control of when, where, and with whom we shared our relationship."

"I know you did. There's no need to apologize, though. It's not your fault." Given what Nessa knew about the ring, I understood why she'd jumped to the conclusion that she had. "Part of me was nervous about how our friends would react, but obviously that wasn't an issue."

"Yes, they seemed quite happy," he said wryly. I smiled, remembering the ribbing they'd given him.

We sat in silence for a few moments. When Ben spoke again,

there was devilment in his tone. "Well, at least now you don't have to worry about any of the guys down here hitting on you."

I gave him my driest smirk. "Right, because I was *so* worried about that." I made a sweeping gesture that took in my rumpled outfit and unruly braid. "No one's going to hit on me, Ben. No one will even notice that I'm here."

Ben arched an eyebrow at me. "I'm certain the guys will notice little else."

I shook my head and laughed. Ben was definitely delusional if he thought I was that much of a man-magnet. "There is a positive side, though."

"What's that?"

I stretched out my arm and tilted my head to one side, casually examining my fingernails. "At least we got to tell everyone that we just started dating so they know there's nothing serious going on."

"True." Ben ducked past my arm and placed an archipelago of kisses along my neck, starting just below my ear and heading south. I suppressed a moan as his lips on my skin set off a chain reaction throughout my body, an explosive reminder of the chemistry between us. "Definitely nothing serious," he murmured.

Even after I cleared my throat, my voice came out as a husky whisper. "Good. I'm glad we're agreed on that."

I could feel Ben's lips smiling against my neck. I groaned in complaint as he pulled away. "Right now," he said, "all I really want to do is focus all of my attention on how incredible it is to kiss you. However, I'm afraid that if I do that, we'll never leave the room."

My sigh was wistful. "That's a reasonable fear."

"And Hector's going to be back any minute." Ben put his hands on my shoulders and began to massage. "Listen, Cate, in spite of everything, I'm really glad that you're here—not only because we might need you, but also—and I know this is selfish on my part— because it would have made me very unhappy to spend any time away from you."

"Same here," I quietly admitted, as the warmth from his hands spread through me.

There was a knock at the door. As though on cue, Hector's voice asked, "You guys ready?"

"Be right there," Ben called out. He placed his hand gently on my cheek, locked his eyes onto mine, and whispered, "Thank you for coming." Then he stood up and offered me his hand. It was time for the briefing.

CHAPTER FOUR

Stepping into the briefing room was like slamming into a wall of high-octane energy. It reminded me of the transformation Pete and Ben had undergone the night they came to my house to protect me from my client's gun-toting boyfriend. All at once they had become sharp, focused, full of purpose—on a razor's edge of readiness for anything that might happen. Now I was entering a room with about ten people wearing Charlies seated around a large conference table, and the effect was multiplied exponentially. Our welcoming party was there, all busily engaged in conversations.

The other members of our group sat along one side of the table, but Ben pointed me toward two empty chairs near the front of the room. Among the parade of spotless uniforms, I felt utterly schlumpy. There was nothing creased, pressed, or remotely businesslike in my suitcase. I was wearing yoga pants, sneakers, and an extra sweatshirt Ben had brought along. It was way too big for me, not to mention navy blue, which wasn't my best color. But the subbasement was chilly, and in my hurry to pack, I'd forgotten to bring a sweater.

Vani had used our few free minutes to freshen her make-up and let down her cascade of long, black hair. Asa hadn't changed, although I noticed for the first time that his T-shirt read Triple Nerd Score. Eve was punk-gothed out with clothes worn in artistically torn layers of black, grey, and red. Several people stared openly at Kai, who basked in the attention. He had put on dramatic black eyeliner and changed into leather pants and an emerald green silk blouse—definitely a peacock amongst pigeons. Kai preened and chatted while Pete sat back and pretended not to notice that his boyfriend had become the star attraction.

Maybe because the military had a reputation for being such a macho group, I'd worried that Pete and Kai might get a cool reception from some corners. But I sensed nothing in the room but camaraderie. "No one seems to mind that Pete and Kai are together," I murmured to Ben.

"No, they wouldn't," he replied in a low voice. "These guys never cared about that kind of thing. Besides, Pete's saved the lives of enough of the people in this room that he gets maximum respect no matter what they might think of his lifestyle. And Kai is well respected and somewhat feared in his own right. He's pretty vicious in a bar fight."

Bar fights? I took another look at Kai as he flipped his hair back. I tried unsuccessfully to imagine him doing anything that might risk breaking a nail.

All at once, the significance of something Ben had said dawned on me. "Wait a minute, Pete saved their lives? Is this *your* old Marine Corps unit?"

But before he could answer, someone shouted, "Atten*tion!*" Everyone in uniform instantly shot to their feet and stared straight ahead.

"As you were," a gruff voice said. A large tree trunk of a man passed behind us and took his place at the front of the room. His skin was tanned, his features chiseled and hard, and he wore the same khaki-and-green uniform as the other marines, but with silver bars on his collar.

Everyone else settled back into their seats. The tree trunk shook hands with a pale man in a white lab coat and tortoiseshell glasses who was sitting across the table from us. He had the easy confidence of a salesman, and although he appeared to be in his fifties, he had a boyish face. I hadn't noticed him before, but when our eyes met, I felt a strange connection between us. He gave me an odd smile as he sat back down.

Tree-Trunk Man stood at the head of the table and glanced

sharply around the room as though taking inventory of every wrinkled shirt, every hair out of place. Hands clasped behind his back, he filled the air with the gravelly power of his voice. "For those of you who don't know, I'm Captain Abbott, the officer in charge." I didn't doubt that for a second. Authority rolled off of him in waves. His penetrating blue eyes turned on Ben and me, and my breath caught in my throat. "For the benefit of the MacGregor Group, who recently joined us—" to my relief, he looked away again—"I will remind you that while this officially became a military operation several days ago, we are trying to keep the environment as casual as possible so that the civilians feel comfortable in their work. Nonetheless, no one is to leave this floor without my express permission, a marine guard, and a damn good reason. Is that understood?"

"Yes sir!" the marines barked. Captain Abbott gave Ben a questioning look, as though inquiring as to whether the members of the MacGregor Group understood. Ben nodded, and Captain Abbott continued. "All of the civilian personnel in this room have undergone the necessary background checks and been given limited Top Secret clearance strictly confined to the purposes of this mission."

As Eve and Asa quietly high-fived one another, I glanced nervously at Ben. I hadn't heard anything about a background check.

"Yes, you too, Miss Duncan," the captain said. "Your clearance came through this morning, in spite of the questionable company you keep." He gestured toward Ben, who rubbed his face to hide a smile. "Ben will fill you in on what your security clearance means, but here's the short version. Rule number one: whatever happens here, stays here—forever. Rule number two: if a marine gives you an instruction, you follow it immediately. Your lives and the lives of others may depend on it. Understood?"

I took my cue and murmured, "Yes sir," with the rest of the staff.

"Very good. I'll turn the time over to Dr. Gastrell so he can give us an update on the patient's situation."

Captain Abbott took his seat as the man in the white lab coat stood up. "Hello, everyone. I'm Rex Gastrell, but everyone calls me Skeet." He gave me a strange smile again, making me even more uneasy. "I'm head of the Paranormal Division of the National Institutes of Mental Health, or NIMH, which is a subdivision of NIH. In other words, I'm in charge of everything here that the Marine Corps isn't. Is that fair to say, Captain?" Captain Abbott nodded.

The answers to questions I hadn't been allowed to ask until then began to coalesce in my mind. Ben had told me the previous week that the MacGregor Group had an ongoing relationship with NIMH. NIMH quietly did research on sensitives, and the MacGregors treated their subjects when the need arose. So they were all colleagues, in a very real sense; at least that explained what we were doing there.

Skeet continued, "As most of you know, five days ago, one of our visiting neuroscientists, Dr. Braz Belo, collapsed in his lab. At first, the doctors at Walter Reed Medical Center thought it was a simple case of food poisoning. But when his heart rate slowed and he developed convulsions and trouble breathing, it became clear that something else was going on. On Tuesday, they began to suspect aconite poisoning and administered an antidote. It had some positive effect, and we believe that Dr. Belo should live for several more days. Unfortunately, unless a miracle happens, we were too late to save his life."

There was a heavy silence in the room. Skeet looked down and shielded his face with his hand for a moment before continuing. "We've brought the MacGregor Group in for additional assistance. Vani and Eve are here to help support Dr. Belo's health through aura healing and acupuncture. Test results have led us to believe that Dr. Belo's mental faculties may be completely intact, along with his hearing and his sense of smell, so we have been keeping him abreast of his medical situation. Asa, of course, will be the key there. If Asa can communicate telepathically with Dr. Belo, then we can discern his level of cognitive functioning, and hopefully learn as much as possible about what happened to him. Meanwhile, Kai has been working with some Buddhist meditation experts, putting the finishing touches on a trance state that, once achieved, should allow Asa to work without getting the migraines that the use of his gift usually causes."

Kai reached over to rub Asa's head, but Asa quickly ducked to the side.

"Thank you for the update, Dr. Gastrell," Captain Abbott boomed as he and Skeet changed places again. "And now, MacGregor Group, allow me to introduce the hard-charging marines of Yankee Company!"

His words inspired a shout of "Oo-rah!" from the marines, a sound so forceful that it nearly blew me out of my chair.

"This elite Marine Corps Security Force unit is tasked with the highly sensitive mission of protecting whistleblowers and other individuals believed to be at risk from elements within the United States government. A warm welcome to Pete and Ben, our former members."

I glanced at Ben and Pete with new respect and a little awe. So *that's* what they had done in the Marines—guarded whistleblowers? That certainly fit much of what I knew about them, like their willingness to put themselves in harm's way to protect people who were under threat, and their strong sense of integrity. A knot that I didn't realize had formed in my stomach began to untie itself. I glanced across the table at Kai, who cast me a sly wink. I had asked him once what Pete and Ben had done in the Marines, but they'd kept it a well-guarded secret, and Kai hadn't known a thing. I could tell that he was just as glad as I was to finally learn something about our partners' mysterious pasts.

Still, it was shocking to hear that the Marines had to devote a unit to protecting people from our own government in the first place—especially whistleblowers, people who were presumably trying to do good. I would have to ask Ben about more that later.

"You may be wondering how Yankee Company came to be a

part of this mission," Captain Abbott said. "Dr. Gastrell, would you like to give us the background?"

"Certainly." Dr. Gastrell leaned forward, resting his elbows on the table and speaking intently. "At first, foul play was not suspected. Aconite is a common remedy for nerve pain in traditional Chinese and Ayurvedic medicine. Aconite poisoning most often happens via accidental overdose. However, I knew that Dr. Belo was a hard-core skeptic when it came to herbal remedies. He wouldn't even take melatonin for sleep due to what he believed were inconsistencies and lack of oversight in the manufacturing process. Doubtful of the accidental overdose story, I asked the FBI to investigate."

"Thank you, Dr. Gastrell." Captain Abbott cast his eyes about the room, giving us a moment to absorb that information. "The FBI found that Dr. Belo was, in fact, the victim of a murder attempt. A tiny injection site was discovered on his neck behind the ear. Its size and location on the body, combined with the type and concentration of poison used, pointed to one of the CIA's signature methods for making an assassination look like an accident. That's when Yankee Company was called in. Our CIA contacts claim to know nothing about the attack. Either they're lying, or the attack was carried out by a rogue agent or cell. To ensure Dr. Belo's safety, we transferred him here, while a decoy Dr. Belo remains on Walter Reed's roster as a patient who can't receive visitors. However, whoever poisoned Dr. Belo may have tracked his movements. If they discover his true whereabouts, they may try to finish what they started. And if they find out that we've managed to get him talking, so to speak, everyone working on this project could become a target."

The hair on my neck prickled again as Captain Abbott swept his hand through the air. "You have nothing to fear down here, however. This subbasement of the hospital is secure. Although this location has served many purposes over the years, officially, it doesn't even exist. Neither does Yankee Company, for that matter. But we don't know how much the attackers know, and if they are CIA, we can't be too careful. That's why we need to keep security airtight."

I'd read enough about U.S. history to know that the CIA had a long and spine-chilling history of assassinations. But why would they want to kill a scientist, of all people—especially a neuroscientist at NIMH? I looked around the room. While everyone appeared grim, my surprise and confusion were mirrored only in the faces of Vani, Eve, and Asa. They weren't asking any questions, however—and I didn't blame them. Captain Abbott seemed like the type of person who was used to doing the asking, not the answering. But I couldn't help it. The accumulation of mysteries was making me nervous. I slid my hand into the air.

Captain Abbott's head whipped around. "Yes, Miss Duncan?"

"I'm sorry, I don't understand," I began tentatively. "Why would the CIA want to kill Dr. Belo?"

Ben, Captain Abbott, and Skeet all exchanged glances. Then Ben turned to me. "That's what we're here to help them figure out."

"Oh." Suddenly feeling the weight of that responsibility, I slouched back down into my chair. "Can I ask what Dr. Belo was researching?"

"An excellent question!" Skeet's face lit up. He glanced at Captain Abbott, who gave him a nod. "Dr. Belo is originally from Brazil," Skeet said, "but we invited him here on a special grant to do research on the brain's pineal gland."

I reached back into my grad school memories. "The pineal gland—the seat of the soul?"

"Yes, indeed! The seat of the soul, according to Descartes." Skeet practically glowed. "Of course, we now know more about the functions of the pineal gland. It produces melatonin and possibly DMT, a compound that may be instrumental in producing near-death experiences. Dr. Belo is fond of saying that he's spent most of his career asking the question: what came first, the soul or the pineal gland?" When Skeet realized that he was the only one in the room chuckling at his joke, he cleared his throat and continued. "Being a spiritual man, Dr. Belo believes that the soul came first, and that God created the pineal gland as a gateway to allow us to experience the divine presence. He's done quite a bit of research on this theory."

"Like the third eye study," Kai chimed in.

"Yes!" Skeet pointed at Kai. "Dr. Belo was part of the team that discovered that the pineal gland contains photoreceptor cells, the same type of cells found in our eyes—an odd thing to find in the middle of the brain, you must admit. This discovery, of course, has given spiritually-minded folks more reason to believe that the gland is, in fact, a third eye—a pathway to communicate with God. And that's just one of the interesting aspects of Dr. Belo's research."

Skeet walked around the room like an energized professor in front of a lecture hall. "He came to NIH on a special grant to work with the National Cancer Institute. They're investigating outcomes in patients whose pineal glands are damaged in the process of treating some very rare tumors that can develop in that part of the brain. Dr. Belo is studying what effects this damage has on a person's sense of themselves as a spiritual being, their sense of morality, and their conscience." Skeet's face fell. "Or he *was*, that is."

I felt a rush of compassion for Skeet. It was obvious that in Dr. Belo, he was losing a respected colleague, if not a friend. "That sounds fascinating," I said—and to me it was, even if it didn't shed any light on why Dr. Belo might have become a CIA target.

"Yes, quite," Skeet said, but he appeared to be lost in his own thoughts.

"Any other questions?" Captain Abbott barked. No one spoke. "In that case, marines, it's time to get back to work. Ben, a word."

Within moments, everyone wearing a uniform had left the room. Ben gathered our crew by the door. "Why don't you all go back to your rooms for a few minutes before we get started? We might not get many more opportunities to relax." He nodded at Hector and another marine who were standing in the hallway. "They offered to walk you back. Apparently it's easy to get lost down here."

I glanced over at Captain Abbott and Dr. Gastrell. They stood in the far corner of the room, conferring. "Do you know what Captain Abbott wants to talk to you about?"

"No idea." Ben shrugged. "Something security-related, no doubt." Then he looked at each of us one by one. "Thank you for being here. As you've heard, it's an important mission, and they need all the help they can get."

"Well, somebody's got to cover your ass," Pete drawled.

Kai punched Pete's arm lightly. "No need to thank us. We're all glad to be here—right, people?"

Ben smiled as everyone nodded and murmured their assent. "All right, then," he said, "I'll come and get you as you're needed."

Ben and I were the last ones in the line out the door. Dr. Gastrell slipped in front of me, blocking my exit, and extended his hand. "Cate, it's such a pleasure to meet you. May I have a quick word?"

I shot Ben an anxious glance, feeling awkward about being singled out.

"It doesn't have to be in private," Skeet quickly added.

"Okay." After a brief handshake, I said, "It's nice to meet you, too."

Skeet took off his glasses and cleaned them with the corner of his lab coat. "In preparation for your arrival, I was speaking with Dr. MacGregor—the elder, that is." He put his glasses back on and gave Ben a quick nod. Then he turned to me, his expression pained. "She told me that you recently lost your mother. I'm so sorry."

My mother. In an instant, everything in the room seemed to disappear except for the space surrounding Skeet, Ben, and me. My breathing sounded loud and ragged to my ears, and my pulse pounded in my head. My eyes could see every worry line on Skeet's face as though through a magnifying glass. I felt the heat of Ben's body on my own as he drew closer to me. "Yes. Three months ago."

Skeet nodded as if in slow motion. "I just wanted to extend my sincere condolences."

I swallowed hard. Ben laid his hand on my lower back, steadying me.

"I also wanted to say that I hope this situation won't prove to be too difficult for you. If it does, however, we will all certainly understand."

At first I was unable to piece together what he meant, but then I realized what he was getting at. He hoped it wouldn't be too hard for me to be around another dying person so soon. Someone else was giving me an out.

Thankfully, the stubborn part of me shook itself awake and helped me pull myself together. I took a deep breath and exhaled slowly. My tunnel-like experience faded and my breathing and pulse returned to normal. "Thank you, Dr. Gastrell," I said, reaching behind me and grasping Ben's hand at the small of my back. "That's very thoughtful of you. But I'm here to help Dr. Belo, and I'm confident that I'll be able to handle any personal issues that may arise."

"Of course." Dr. Gastrell bowed his head to me. "Well, while you're here, any time you'd like to talk about Braz's research, I'd be more than happy. And please call me Skeet; everyone else does."

"Thank you." I mustered up a professional smile.

"I'll be right with you and the captain," Ben told him. Skeet headed back toward the other side of the room. As he walked away, that sense of connection struck me again. Was it his walk, or his cologne...? Something about him seemed familiar. I had no idea where I could have met him before, though.

"Are you okay?" Ben asked me quietly.

"Yeah," I said, "I guess that was just sort of unexpected."

"I can imagine," Ben said, his voice edged with irritation. "My mother must have brought it up with him because she was concerned about you. I'm surprised she didn't mention it to me, though."

"Me, too." I thought about telling Ben that Dr. Gastrell had already been making me uncomfortable, but "Skeet's smiling at me weird" didn't sound like a very worthy complaint. "It's okay, though. It was kind of them to be concerned."

"Cate." Ben's hand cradled my elbow. "You know I'm here if you need anything."

As I looked up into Ben's eyes, the strength of his caring flowed into me, setting everything right again. I placed my hand over his and squeezed. "Yes, I know. You've only told me like a hundred times."

"Good," he said, squeezing my hand back. "We won't need you for a while at least. Try to relax this afternoon, maybe get some more rest. You might need it. And I'll see you soon, I promise."

CHAPTER FIVE

Buzz, snap, buzz. The sound of another failing fluorescent bulb in the hallway. The light under the door flickered. Fantastic; the horror movie had moved right outside of my room.

I pulled myself up into a seated position and stretched. The clock read 3:43 p.m. I was beginning to wonder if Ben was ever going to come for me. But I knew that I was plan B, and they probably hadn't exhausted plan A yet. I'd been trying to relax, but my brain just kept chewing on what I'd learned in the morning briefing.

I knew I'd been raised in something of a bubble, thanks to my mother's well-intentioned efforts to shelter me. But I'd made it a point to educate myself as much as possible since leaving home, and had shed much of my naïveté. Still, if the Marine Corp had an entire unit dedicated to protecting whistleblowers from our own government…. I'd watched enough movies and TV shows about crime and espionage to suspect that there were occasional territorial wars between federal agencies. But the existence of Yankee Company made it seem like there was an actual internal *war* going on. Between that revelation and everything I'd learned recently about the paranormal, it seemed likely that there was an endless number of dimensions to the world that I didn't know about—and might never know about.

I pondered all of the ways in which being a part of Yankee Company must have shaped Ben, and how radically different our worldviews must be given his experiences. I wondered if I would ever really be able to understand certain aspects of him as well as the other marines did. Would crucial parts of who Ben was forever remain inaccessible to me? If so, what did that mean for us as a couple? Just raising the question made my stomach feel like lead.

Being alone with my thoughts wasn't helping me relax at all. I decided that if I didn't get out of that room, I was going to go stir crazy. There had to be coffee available somewhere in that subbasement; I would go on the hunt. After quickly rebraiding my hair, I layered two fitted tunics over my jeans to see if I could keep warm without resorting to Ben's oversized sweatshirt. Then I left a note on the desk saying that I'd be back soon, just in case anyone came for me.

The hallway was empty and silent. It occurred to me that I had no idea where anything was. Ben had been right; in that maze of duplicate hallways it would be easy to get lost. I needed breadcrumbs. I went back to the room and scrounged a handful of pennies from the bottom of my purse. I figured I could leave one on the floor against the near corner each time I took a turn.

After exploring a few empty corridors and seeing no one, I began to think my coffee hunt might be in vain. Then, just as I passed by an open door, a woman's voice called out from the room. "Cate!"

I stood in the doorway of what appeared to be a small gym. The floor was lined with mats. The lights were low, and the room smelled of stale perspiration and old socks. I recognized some of the equipment from my few short-lived gym memberships. There was a bench press, a set of free weights, a medicine ball, and a blue exercise ball. I didn't see any people, however.

"Hey!" the voice called again. I looked up to find Nessa close to the ceiling, holding on to a rope. Someone had removed one of the ceiling tiles and tied the rope to some fixture higher up. Nessa climbed down halfway and jumped to the floor, every motion appearing effortless. She straightened up and wiped her forehead on the sleeve of her T-shirt. "Do you have a few minutes? I want to lift some weights but I need a spotter."

"Um...." My eyes darted about. I did have a few minutes, so I couldn't exactly say no. On the other hand, I hadn't touched weights in years, and I didn't know what she expected me to do if something went wrong.

Nessa walked over and sat on the bench. She toweled off and took a few swigs from a water bottle. "I won't need you, I promise," she reassured. "It's just a safety regulation."

"Oh!" I forced a smile. "Well, sure, in that case."

"Thanks." She began to adjust the weights on the bar. "I hope I'm not keeping you from anything."

"Well, no. I mean, I was just trying to find someplace to get coffee."

"Coffee sounds good, actually. We can go to the staff lounge after this." Nessa placed the bar on the bench press frame and laid back. "Okay, all you need to do is stand behind my head. If I kill myself, just yell down the hall." She tilted her head back so she could see me and grinned.

"Got it!" I gave her the thumbs-up.

Nessa lifted the bar and began a series of slow, repetitive bench presses. Apparently, she wasn't even winded, because she started up a conversation. "Hey, I'm sorry again about this morning. I have a tendency to put my foot in my mouth."

"Please don't worry about it," I said, trying not to stare. Nessa handled the weights as though they were feathers. "Ben explained everything. It was perfectly natural for you to assume what you did. There was no way for you to know it was a secret."

"It was a *secret*?" She tilted her head back again and gave me a curious look. "I thought you just hadn't got around to telling everyone yet."

I felt a blush creeping up my neck. "Right. That's what I meant—that we hadn't told anyone." I hoped that Nessa wasn't an experienced poker player or an interrogator or something, because I knew from experience that I was a horribly ineffective liar. I cast about quickly for a change of subject. "So you and Ben served together in Yankee Company?"

"Yeah. Ben, Pete, Hector, Kevin, and I started together on Parris Island. Almost as soon as we got there, somebody leaked that I was a failed ballerina. You can imagine the grief I got. But those four guys defended me—until I started kicking ass in training exercises, that is. No one gave me a hard time after that." As though for emphasis, she dropped the bar back onto the bench press frame with a loud *clink*.

That sounded like Ben and Pete, all right. "A failed ballerina? Were you injured?"

"No, nothing like that." Nessa sat up and toweled off again before walking over to the collection of hand weights and selecting some intimidatingly large dumbbells. "Ballet is just very competitive. No matter how hard I worked, I was never more than decent, passable. I didn't have what it took to make a career out of it. The wrong body type, not enough raw talent. It was always going to be a hobby. And since dance was my major in college and I didn't really have a fallback…."

I squinted at her. "You joined the *Marines*?" It wasn't until after the words were out that I realized how rude my question must have sounded. "Sorry," I muttered, "I guess you're not the only one with a foot-in-mouth tendency."

"Don't sweat it! It's a reasonable question, and one I've been asked a lot, believe me." She lay back on the bench and began pressing the dumbbells towards the ceiling. "My father's a marine, and my two older brothers." This time, she spoke with some effort between lifts. "They always made it sound like a life of adventure. Not to mention job security. Plus, having grown up surrounded by marines, I knew I enjoyed their company. I guess you do, too, huh?" she asked with a knowing smile.

"Well, Ben and Pete, yes. But they're the first marines I've really hung out with, and I've only known them for a little over a week, so—"

Her eyes widened. "A week? Really?" She appeared to be puzzling over that piece of information as she extended the dumbbells out to her sides and then brought them overhead in an arc. "You must be experienced in that paranormal stuff, then."

"No, actually. Before I got involved with the MacGregor

Group, I was a psychotherapist. I knew I could do some things that I couldn't really explain, but it never occurred to me that they might be—you know. Paranormal." I shrugged. "Until Ben and his group explained how it all works."

"Oh, wow." She looked frankly dumbfounded. "And Ben brought you down *here*?"

Wondering what she was getting at, I said, "Well, I volunteered."

"Oh." Nessa sat up and placed the dumbbells on the floor. Then she examined me as though she were seeing me for the first time. "I'm sorry, I didn't mean to sound so surprised. Obviously Ben is confident that you can handle all of this."

"All of what?" The muscles in the middle of my chest grew taut. "Ben said—I mean, Captain Abbott told us we wouldn't be in any danger."

"There's no reason why you should be." She began cleaning off the weight lifting equipment with a spray bottle and towel. "But there are always risks on a mission like this. And Ben told us there are also risks in the kind of work you all do, although I don't really know anything about what those are."

Unfortunately, I did. My whole body tensed as I thought back to my cardiac arrest experience of the week before. My growing anxiety must have showed, because Nessa added, "I'm really sorry if I worried you. I was just surprised. Ben's usually so conservative when it comes to safety."

With a subtle eye roll, I said, "I kind of picked up on that."

"Already?" She smiled broadly. "Well, anyway. Being a psychotherapist—that sounds like a great job. It must be really satisfying to help people like that."

"It was," I said, trying to keep the disappointment out of my voice.

She frowned. "Was?"

"I had to quit to come to work for the MacGregors. I was told that I can't do two types of helping jobs at once or I'll get burned out."

"Oh, I'm sorry." As she spoke, Nessa unzipped a gym bag

against the wall, took out her ponytail, brushed her hair, and replaced the band. "Is that because you're—an empath? Did I get that right?"

"Yes. How did you know?"

"Ben told us a little bit about what everybody's abilities are. I'll admit, I'm still a little foggy on what you all do, but it's clear that you're a pretty amazing group. I'm starting to understand why Ben didn't come back to the Corps."

"Were you expecting him to?"

She tossed her linens into a plastic trashcan that doubled as a laundry basket. "Kind of. I mean, everybody understood why he left after his dad died. We all figured he'd go home for six months, maybe a year, however long it took to get his mom situated. But the Corps was his real home. He fit in so perfectly here, it was like he was born to it. None of us could imagine him truly being happy being anywhere else, doing anything else." Looking pensive, she added, "I guess we were wrong."

It was a question I hadn't thought to ask before. Ben seemed so dedicated to his role managing the MacGregor Group. But did he really enjoy it, or was he just making the best of it because he knew his mother needed his help? The way Nessa talked, it sounded as though the Corps was his true calling—a calling from which he'd been wrenched away by tragic circumstances. The mere thought of that possibility made my heart sore. I decided that whenever a good moment arose, I would find a way to broach the subject with him.

"You ready for coffee?" Nessa asked.

"Sure, thanks."

"Thank you for spotting," she said as she grabbed her gym bag and led me into the hall.

"You're welcome, although the way you handled those weights, it was obvious you didn't need me."

"Thanks, but that was just a light workout—trying to keep from turning into jelly while we're stuck down here." She shot me a playful grin. "So, dating after a week? That must have been some week—and Ben must have been on his best behavior."

I laughed lightly, unsure how to respond. "I guess when you really connect with someone, things can happen quickly."

"That's true," she said warmly. "I hope everything goes well for the two of you. We joke around about him, but Ben's one of the good guys."

"Thanks. I hope things go well, too."

I sensed a slight but definite downshift in her mood. I wondered for a moment whether there had ever been anything more than friendship between her and Ben. But when I focused on Nessa and opened up my empathic senses, I knew immediately that she was a what-you-see-is-what-you-get type of person. Her energy was refreshing, like windows thrown open. Her statement about Ben being "one of the good guys" had been completely straightforward; I sensed no underlying romantic emotions or hints of a hidden history. So they really had been just friends. Maybe what I'd picked up was simply Nessa's sadness that her good friend hadn't returned to the Corps as she had hoped.

Still, watching her work out had drawn my attention to the contrasts between Nessa and me. She was physically fit and strong; I got winded going up more than one flight of stairs. She was tall and lithe; I was of average height with a surfeit of curves. Since she was a marine, I figured she was capable of handling just about anything, whereas I had fainted the previous week after Vani did some basic maintenance work on my aura. Nessa was the kind of woman I would have pictured with Ben, not me.

Cut it out, I told myself as my heartbeat wobbled. I closed my eyes and noticed the weight of the ring on my finger, the talisman Ben had given me just for those moments of doubt. I needed to pull myself together. "Do you think I can get my coffee in a to-go cup? I left a note saying I wouldn't be gone long, and they might need my help with Dr. Belo anytime."

"No problem," Nessa said, opening a new door. "We've got some travel mugs."

• • •

I was shaken out of a shallow sleep by a series of knocks. "Cate?"

Instantly alert, I jumped up and opened the door. Ben was leaning against the doorjamb. His drawn, tight expression softened into a half smile when our eyes met. "Hey."

"Hey." I resisted the temptation to leap at him, seeing that every one of his gestures telegraphed fatigue. "Come in."

"Thanks." He collapsed into the chair and leaned his elbow on the desk.

"What's going on?"

He blew out a heavy breath. "We're just not having much luck with Dr. Belo. We've all been working with him, trying various things. I wish we had more time to experiment, but his condition is deteriorating. I think we're going to have to move on to plan B after all."

"I'm so sorry, Ben. What do you need me to do?" I moved to stand, but Ben held his hand up.

"Nothing right now," he said. "Braz is sleeping at the moment, and he needs his rest. Our group will meet after dinner to work out a plan."

"Okay." The silence of the room was broken as my stomach rumbled. "Excuse me. I think it was your mention of dinner…."

"No need to apologize. You must be starving. I was coming to take you to the mess hall, in fact…" But his expression dimmed as he examined me. He came over and sat next to me on the bed. "Something's wrong. What is it?"

I'd been trying to keep my expression neutral, but Ben was getting better and better at reading me. "Well, nothing, really," I said, but that didn't stop the worry lines on his brow from gathering together. "I just hung out with Nessa for a little bit this afternoon."

"What happened? Didn't you two get along?"

"Of course we did. That's not it. It's just…" I shrugged. "The way Nessa talked, it sounded like you really loved being in the Marine Corps, like you were at home there. I made me wonder why you never went back."

"Oh, that." Ben looked down and ran his fingers over his

jawline. "Well, Nessa's right; I did love being in the Corps. If my mother hadn't needed my help, I likely never would have left. A part of me will always miss it, and in truth, a part of me will never leave. Once a marine, always a marine." Ben smoothed a lock of hair away from my face. "But once I'd been out for a while, talking with my mother about her work, I realized how much the idea of running the clinic appealed to me, as well. For one thing, I would be in charge, which suited me."

I bit my lip to keep from smirking. "You don't say."

A smile played across Ben's lips. "I readily admit that I like to be in control of things. And the work itself is similar. Both in the Corps and at the clinic, I'm able to help people in real ways—protecting those who are vulnerable, and teaching them how to protect themselves. Throw in my interests in healing and the paranormal— thanks to my mother's research—and while it wasn't an easy choice, I'm confident that it was the right one."

He looked so certain that I was inclined to believe him. It was hard to think straight, though, because Ben had begun stroking my hair, igniting me like a slow-burning furnace. I closed my eyes and took in the sensations. "So, even being with your old unit again— no regrets?"

"None. Cate, look at me." Ben's hands cradled my face, holding it inches from his. "I'm exactly where I want to be—in the right place, doing the right work." As though he had sensed my secret insecurities, he added, "And most importantly, now I'm with the right person. Why would I ever want to leave?" He searched my face. "Do you understand what I'm saying?"

I wanted to; I really wanted to. I willed the portal between us to open, inhaling sharply as his passion for me crashed through—and his determination that I acknowledge it. "Yes," I whispered.

The gold flecks in his eyes shimmered. "Good."

A longing to be as close to Ben as possible wended its way through my body. I slid my fingers around the back of his neck and pulled him toward me until our lips were nearly touching. Mesmerized, we stared into each other's eyes for a few more seconds, not speaking or moving. Then I placed my lips gently against his, pulled his lower lip into my mouth, and gave it a soft bite.

I both heard and felt his sharp intake of breath. As my tongue traced the inside of his lip, he emitted a low growl. I opened my mouth ever so slightly, inviting him in.

That was all the encouragement Ben needed. First, he savored my lips, and I sighed as a flush of heat made my whole body go weak. He slid an arm around my back and another beneath my knees and swept me onto his lap, pulling away from our kiss just long enough to allow me a gasp of air. Then, his mouth returned to ravage mine, swallowing each whimper that escaped my throat and pushing fire through my limbs.

As my longing sharpened, my body began to do things without first consulting my mind. Of their own accord, my arms wrapped themselves around Ben's shoulders and my fingernails dug into the hard muscle of his back as his tongue plundered me. The searing heat that filled my body spread outward, sensitizing every square inch of my skin.

Suddenly, Ben broke the kiss. Moving his lips against my earlobe, he murmured devilishly, "Your eyes are turning from green to grey again." It was a reminder that he had learned my "tell"—how my eyes change color when I'm aroused—and that he knew exactly what state I was in.

The fresh heat of a blush splashed across my cheeks, but as I turned my head to reply, Ben's mouth covered mine again. Another current of desire shot through me and my back arched, pressing my chest against his, asking. It was the agony of a promise I knew wasn't going to be fulfilled for some time. Still, it was a delicious agony.

I slid one hand down to his waist and tucked my fingers into his belt. Ben started slightly at this new touch. Then, much to my dismay, he began to slowly extract himself from my embrace. Eventually we were both looking down, nearly panting, with our foreheads pressed together.

Between breaths, Ben said, "If we keep this up, we're going to be late for our meeting."

Our meeting. Of course. I felt a painful stab of guilt for sitting there making out while a man was lying nearby in a coma. For a few selfish moments, I'd forgotten entirely why we were there. I took a few slow, deep breaths in an effort to get my vital signs back to normal.

Ben was the first to find the conviction to stand. "We still have time to grab some dinner."

All at once, I was reminded of the work I'd done with Ben the week before to help him overcome his fear of eating in front of other people. Concern needled me. "Are you going to eat, too?" I asked, trying to sound casual.

"I already did, doctor," he said with mock gravitas. "Don't worry. This place is full of marines. I'll be fine."

"Oh, right." I'd forgotten—his fellow marines were the one group of people with whom Ben had always felt comfortable breaking bread. His phobia caused him to believe that if he ate with anyone else, they would die afterwards. Using empathic healing techniques and mealtime therapy, I had managed to get Ben comfortable eating with me. I was relieved, though, that as long as we were in the subbasement, there were plenty of people around with whom Ben could enjoy a meal. It wasn't entirely clear why his phobia was dormant around his fellow marines, but Ben figured it had something to do with the fact that they all accepted a certain level of danger just by joining the Corps.

Ben stood and held his hand out to me. "Ready?"

"Always." I plastered on a fake smile to cover my nerves. "Let's go."

Chapter Six

We were the last ones to arrive for our meeting in the conference room. Pete and Asa played cards while Vani, Eve, and Kai decried the lack of mirrors with decent lighting in our underground home.

When they spotted us, the room fell quiet. There were several broad smiles. I could feel the blood rising to the surface of my cheeks. Kai shot a warning look around the room like a boomerang. "Come on people. We talked about this, remember?" He rolled his eyes at Ben and me. "They promised to try to act normal—normal for us, anyway."

"And to not make a big deal out of the fact that you're an item now," Vani added with her signature diplomacy.

Kai shielded his eyes with his hand and shook his head. "You see what I'm dealing with here."

Eve began to giggle, but stifled it immediately when Kai glanced her way.

Ben slipped a protective arm around my waist. "Thank you, everyone, for *trying* to act normal, at least," he said. "We appreciate it."

As self-conscious as I felt, their positivity was contagious, and I couldn't help smiling. "Thank you for being happy for us."

Kai came over and gave me a quick hug. "Of course, baby. We all love both of you." Then he looked off into the distance and tapped his finger against the side of his mouth. "Well, we love *you*. Ben's all right."

"Thank you, Kai," Ben said dryly, then slipped into manager mode. "Okay, folks, what do you say we fill Cate in?"

"Yes," I said, eager to cement the change of subject. "I'd really like to hear what you've been doing with Dr. Belo and what I can do to help."

Much to my relief, that was all the rest of the group needed to hear. We congregated at the front end of the conference table and they filled me in on the situation.

Dr. Belo had a pacemaker and was on a ventilator, so Eve had given him acupuncture to help support his heart and lung functions. Under Kai's watchful eye, she had also ventured into one of her precog trances, which had yielded the sight of Dr. Belo in a casket. Then her vision had speared off into disturbing images of enormous dark armies marching across the globe—this despite the fact that their hearts had been torn out, leaving open wounds in their chests. Her vision had confirmed that Dr. Belo wasn't going to make it, but no one had yet figured out what significance the other images held. Eve sheepishly suggested that her subconscious might have brought in the dark armies from the zombie apocalypse video game she and Asa had been playing on our trip to NIH. But given the accuracy of Eve's previous visions of the future, the others weren't willing to be so sanguine.

Vani had cleared Dr. Belo's aura of negative energy, thereby strengthening his immune system. Then, using a special crystal and something called Tibetan singing bowls, Kai had put Asa into the new trance state he'd learned about from the meditation specialists. It had been a success; while in trance, Asa was able to channel Dr. Belo's thoughts without getting a headache. Asa effectively became a conduit, even using Dr. Belo's body language and speaking his thoughts in the first person. As it turned out, the doctors had been correct; Dr. Belo's cognitive functions remained fully intact, with one crucial exception. He was completely unable to recall the day of his poisoning or the day prior. Since no brain damage was evident, they concluded that he was suffering from a psychological block, probably trauma-related.

Ben and Skeet had tried every technique they could think of to help Dr. Belo overcome the block: hypnotism, progressive relaxation, visualization—the works. They'd even had a phone consultation with Dr. MacGregor to get her ideas about what might be effective. Ben figured that if they'd had a few more weeks with Dr. Belo, they might have succeeded.

But we only had days at best, not weeks. Skeet thought it was time to bring me in, hoping that my skills could speed the process along. Ben was initially reluctant, but Skeet had worn him down—with Kai's help, apparently. Kai was confident that I could handle it.

"I'm starting to get it now," I said. "You want me to submerge into him?"

Ben nodded. "We know it might not work, but it's all we've got left."

Empathic submergence, or the ability to enter someone else's consciousness, was one of my paranormal gifts. Ben said they hoped I could combine my submergence technique with psychotherapeutic skills to resolve whatever psychological block was causing Braz's memory loss. They wanted *me* to do this—a person who hadn't even known what an empath *was* until the week before.

No pressure, I thought, *I'm just their last resort.* To distract myself from a rush of anxiety, I asked, "So what's Dr. Belo like?"

Vani rolled her eyes dramatically and flipped her hair back. "He's a horrible flirt, for one thing."

Asa nodded in agreement. "He isn't exactly appropriate all of the time—although his argument is that since he's dying, he can say whatever he wants."

That sounded like a fair point. "And his mental faculties are really intact?"

"Definitely," Ben said. "He's sharp as a tack."

"Yeah, but you have to catch him while he's awake," Asa said. "He fades in and out of sleep, and he has really weird dreams."

"Okay," I said, "one last question. The only way I've ever been able to submerge into people before was by making eye contact. How am I going to submerge into someone who can't open his eyes?"

"We're way ahead of you," Ben said. "We got our hands on a device that's used in eye surgery. It holds the eyelids open while dropping in artificial tears at regular intervals."

I tried not to wince. "Wow, you've thought of everything." Everything except for the fact that I had no idea whether I'd be able to submerge into a terminally ill man who was in a coma. And that I'd be communicating with him exclusively through a proxy. And that I had no idea how—or if—any of that would work.

From his seat next to me, Ben slid a comforting arm around my shoulders and murmured, "Look, no one is expecting you to work a miracle here. This is an unprecedented situation. No one really knows what's going to work and what isn't. All we can do is try."

I looked around the room at the optimistic faces of my friends, all of whom had already done their best. The least I could do was put my own fears aside and give it a shot. "So when do I get to meet him?"

"How about now?" Asa suggested. "I'm up for it. He's always pretty calm, so if it's just a short visit, I can read his mind without having to go into the headache-prevention trance."

"All right, if you're sure," Ben said. Although he was trying to sound confident, I could hear the worry creeping into his voice.

We got up, gathered our things, and headed towards Braz's room. As we walked, I pulled Ben toward the back of the group and whispered, "Don't worry, I'll be fine."

Ben slid his arm around my shoulders, squeezed gently, and kissed the top of my head. "I know you will, because I'll be right there with you."

CHAPTER SEVEN

Mom.

That was my first thought, and it stopped me cold in the doorway. Dr. Belo's was a standard hospital room, and he was lying motionless on his back with tubes everywhere—just like my mother had been when I'd finally reached the hospital after her overdose. I recognized the constant beeping sounds of the monitors; the smell of various antiseptics and bodily fluids; the thin blankets and thinner robe; the blue and white everything.

My breath caught in my throat. *It's not Mom*, I told myself. *Look again.* Dr. Belo was a stocky man with tawny skin and a full head of salt-and-pepper hair. He appeared to be in his mid-sixties.

Ben rubbed my lower back as the rest of the crew filtered past me and into the room. He turned to Asa. "Is he awake?"

Asa screwed his eyes shut in concentration. "Well, he is now, and he wants to know why we woke him up. He says he was having a... *good* dream." Then Asa turned to Dr. Belo and stage-whispered, "No, I'm not going to tell them that. There are ladies in the room."

Ben nudged me closer to the bed. "Dr. Belo," he said, "I'd like you to meet therapist and empath Cate Duncan."

The whole situation felt uncomfortable, like a shirt put on backwards. But as Ben wrapped his arm around my shoulders and traced circles on my upper arm with his thumb, a sweet sensation slid through me. Instinctively, I tucked my body into his.

Ben gave my shoulders a light squeeze and continued, "As we discussed, Cate is going to be working with you to help overcome this memory block of yours. We're hoping that she'll be able to succeed where Skeet and I have failed."

"Ben," Asa said, "he wants her to say hello. He wants to hear her voice."

Dr. Belo's request pulled me out of the funk I was in. I pushed past the strangeness of talking to a man in a coma and said, "Hello, Dr. Belo. It's an honor to meet you."

Asa blushed deeply.

"What is it?" I asked.

"Umm…." Asa hesitated, but Ben gestured for him to proceed. "He said your voice is sexy, and you smell sweet, so he's sure that the pleasure will be all his."

Pete and Kai snorted with laughter. Vani threw her hands in the air and said, "I told you he was a flirt!"

Eve leaned towards Dr. Belo and said sternly, "Don't even go there, Braz. She's dating Ben."

Asa sighed. "He says, 'Ah, I should have known that someone who sounds so beautiful would already be taken.'"

A blush tore across my face. "I'm not *taken*," I began, but then realized the absurdity of explaining my relationship status to Braz. I felt the vibration of Ben's body against mine as he chuckled silently.

Asa shook his head. "Ben, he wants to know if you'll be sitting in on his therapy sessions, or if you're brave enough to leave him alone with your girlfriend."

Ben looked down at me. "Cate? It's up to you."

I considered. It would be nice to have someone there for moral support, but I wasn't used to people observing me while I worked. "I think it might make me less nervous to try it on my own first."

"Understood. I'll be available if you need me; we all will. But don't worry, Braz," Ben warned playfully, "I trust *her* completely."

Asa grinned. "Well, we can't start right now. He's asleep again. Or at least he's thinking, 'snore, snore, snore.'"

Pete guffawed and slapped his knee. "I guess we'd better leave him alone so he can get back to that good dream of his."

We all filed out of the room, and Ben closed the door behind us. "So that's Dr. Belo. What do you think?"

My sadness at Dr. Belo's situation mingled with hope. He

obviously had a strong will, a good sense of humor, and a unique personality. "I think I'm going to enjoy working with him."

"Glad to hear it." Ben slid his arm around my waist. "Cate, I was hoping we could get started tonight, but Braz clearly isn't up for it, and you look tired."

"I *am* tired, but I have no idea why. I had a nap this afternoon."

"Don't underestimate the stress of the situation. Even if you're not conscious of it, it can take a lot out of you. That goes for everyone, by the way," Ben said to the group.

"You do look a bit worn out," Vani said, draping her arm around my shoulders. "If you're going to do your best work, you should be well-rested. We don't exactly have time for trial and error."

"My best work?" I felt a wave of despair. "But I have no idea what I'm doing!"

"Of course you do," Ben said firmly. "It's the same empathic submergence technique you used with me at your house, and the same skills that you've been using with your therapy clients. Don't worry. I know this situation is strange, but once you get started, you'll be fine."

I guessed it was possible. I did use the submergence technique regularly, and it had been effective when I'd used it to help Ben with his eating phobia. "I just hope you're right."

"I am," Ben said. "We'll all meet again in the conference room after breakfast."

I could barely keep my eyes open as Ben walked me back to my room. Once I hit the mattress, I floated off.

• • •

ParaTrain Internship, Day Two

"Do we have any more paper towels?"

Mom tossed me another roll. "Do you need spray?"

"No, I'm okay." Mom and I were situated on either side of my Great-Aunt Edith's kitchen. She had just moved into an assisted-living facility and decided to sell her house. We'd known that her memory was failing, but it wasn't until we went to clean out the house that we realized how much Aunt Edith had declined over those last few months.

"What's with the plates of food?" I asked as I picked up another small dish of cheese and crackers. It had been laid out and never touched, left to mold and attract flies.

"I'm not sure," Mom said, "but the neighbors said that whenever she heard people talking outside the house, she thought they were visitors coming. I guess she put the food out for them."

"Oh my goodness." I laid my hand over my heart to soothe a sudden ache. "That's sad, but it fits. She's such a good hostess. Poor Aunt Edith."

"Yeah. I'm glad she's going to be well cared for now."

But Aunt Edith had passed away years ago. It was then that it dawned on me: I must be dreaming. Kai had told me that when the spirits of the dead came to us in dreams, we could sometimes ask them questions. Well, I had plenty of questions, but I didn't know how skittish spirits were, so I decided to start off light. As I sprayed another layer of cleaning fluid on the counter, I asked, "So what do you think of Ben?"

She waggled her eyebrows at me. "Pretty hot, honey!"

"Eww, Mom!" I flicked some bubbles off of my yellow rubber gloves at her. "You're not supposed to say that. That's just gross."

She threw her head back and laughed her musical laugh. "Sorry, I couldn't resist. In all seriousness, though, I like him a lot. And I can tell that you two connect on a soul level. But please don't ask me for any relationship advice. That's not exactly my area of expertise."

The whole question-and-answer thing seemed to be going smoothly. I decided to go a little deeper. "You never did tell me what happened between you and my father." All I knew was that my father had left us both when I was almost a year old. I'd asked her about him once, but it was clear that even thinking of him caused her deep pain. I'd never mentioned him again, and neither had she.

As a consequence, I didn't know anything else about him—his name, where he was from, or even if he was still alive.

"You're right. I never did, did I?" She looked out the kitchen window, the sun filtering through the white lace curtains and lighting her face. "I loved your father in that dreamy-eyed way that young women do. He was a little older, dashing, and impressive, so his interest in me was pretty flattering." She went back to scrubbing the counter. "Eventually, though, I started to wonder whether he was more interested in me, or in what I could do."

I squinted at her. "What you could *do*?"

"Being an empath, I mean. He was fascinated with my gift."

"Why? I mean, how did he even know?"

"He had a job like Ben's." She turned away from me to scrub a different part of the counter.

My father had been… what? A psychologist? Had he run some kind of paranormal clinic? No, that would have been too much of a coincidence. My real life must have been bleeding into my dream. Still, her words planted a small seed of anxiety deep in the pit of my stomach. I could feel her energy pulling away from me, so I tried to draw her back. "Is that what drove you two apart?"

"In part. But that's a story for another time." She turned back around and placed one of her rubber-gloved hands on mine, using the other to push an escaped strand of hair behind my ear. Then she pointed at the counter in front of me. "Now get back to work. That's not going to scrub itself."

I closed my eyes defensively as she flicked some bubbles back at me. When I reopened them, she was gone, Aunt Edith's house was gone, and I was staring up at a mesh of springs holding up a grey mattress. I was back in the subbasement—had been there the whole time.

To distract myself from the pain of losing her all over again, I tried to focus on breathing, and on the fact that my mother liked Ben. That was a comforting thought. And I knew intuitively what she meant when she said that Ben and I connected on a soul level. It felt as though our bond was about who we were at the root, not about a lot of the other things that often drew people together. For example, I'd been physically attracted to people before, but Ben had only to be near me to fill my senses and ignite an overwhelming process in my body, a chain reaction of heat and longing. I knew that kind of intensity couldn't just come from physical chemistry; it had to be a consequence of who he was, his character, his heart—his soul.

At least that was how it felt to me. But what if it was different for Ben? What if he *was* primarily interested in me because I was an empath?

Up until then, I had tried not to look too closely at why someone as smart, capable, and unreasonably sexy as Ben was dating someone as messed up as I was. After all, a mere two weeks before, I couldn't leave my house without taking anti-anxiety pills. And at twenty-six years of age, I'd never even had a real boyfriend.

I didn't count Sid, my former friend-with-benefits, because our physical connection hadn't been normal, either—something I'd learned during my first week in ParaTrain. As an empath, I absorbed too much negative emotional energy, which eventually reached toxic levels. And Sid was what they called a catalyst, someone who had the ability to draw the toxicity out of empaths like a poultice. So our attraction had been paranormal, two magnets of opposite charges.

But the more important reason that Sid didn't count was that we'd never been in love. The few other relationships in my past had never lasted beyond the "fledgling" stage. They'd ended when I became overwhelmed by irrational fears and ran away as soon as things got serious—another common side effect of being an empath, I'd been told. With nothing but romantic failures to my name, I had become convinced that romance was something that happened to other people. Ben, Kai, and Vani promised that they could teach me how to have a romantic relationship without getting overwhelmed, which was the only reason I'd decided to risk pursuing something with Ben in the first place.

If Ben's attraction to me was rooted in my gift, at least that made some kind of sense, and provided an answer to the question of why he was interested in me. For some reason, though, the mere thought made me feel light-headed, and my stomach began to churn. I'd have to push that idea and the dream about my mother out of my mind, at least temporarily.

Once I'd managed to clear my head, only one thought remained: coffee. I needed it, and I knew where to get it. The clock read 7:02 a.m. Ben and I hadn't decided on a meeting time, but I was pretty sure no one would be coming for me before 8:00 a.m. at the earliest. I did a quick job of making myself presentable in case I ran into anyone, then grabbed my handful of pennies and headed to the staff lounge Nessa had shown me.

In answer to my silent prayer, I could smell coffee brewing. As I rounded the corner and approached the open door, I heard familiar voices. I picked up my pace, but then stopped dead when I got close to the door and heard the end of a sentence spoken in Kevin's Southern drawl: "...Cate's just not the kind of gal I would've imagined he'd go for." Following an instant impulse, I ducked behind the propped open door and hid.

"Nice, you mean?" Nessa asked jovially.

"Maybe that's it," Kevin said.

Hector's voice chimed in. "Yeah, Ben's so stubborn, I always figured it would take a hard-as-nails harpy to keep him in line."

"Yeah," Kevin agreed. "She seems kind of soft, like he could roll right over her."

"You never know," Nessa said. "Cate might be tougher than she looks."

Hector chimed in, "Well, you know he's got a kink for that paranormal stuff."

His words felt like fingers poking a bruise. I covered my mouth before any sound could escape.

Nessa quickly scolded, "An intellectual interest and professional commitment is not a 'kink,' you moron."

"You know what I mean," Hector said. "He's into that stuff. And she's a what, a telepath?"

"Empath," Nessa said.

Kevin asked, "What's an empath?"

"Somebody with the magical ability to put up with Rottie," Hector said.

"Now that's a rare gift," Kevin agreed.

Nessa said dryly, "I don't even know why I bother trying."

I heard footsteps coming down the hallway towards me—fortunately from the direction that wouldn't reveal my hiding place. I peeked out through the crack between the door and the wall to see Ben heading our way.

Hector chuckled. "Well, she must be supernaturally tolerant, at least. I mean, they've been together a whole day and he hasn't blown it yet."

"Who hasn't blown what yet?" Ben asked as he breezed into the lounge. I slowly released the breath I'd been holding.

There was a cacophony of warm greetings. Then Kevin said, "We were just talking about you—trying to figure out how you got a woman to stay with you for a whole day without screwing it up."

"Yeah," Hector joked. "I mean, I don't remember you ever getting past one date. You been going to charm school or something?"

"Nobody's more surprised than I am." It was nice to hear Ben sounding lighthearted.

Nessa laughed. "Well, whatever you're doing, keep doing it. Don't listen to these two love doctors. They're both still single, you'll notice."

"Which means we have lots of failure to learn from," Kevin said earnestly.

Ben guffawed. "Now, there's a selling point."

"Unfortunately for you," Hector interjected, "the love doctors have to go on duty. You'll have no one but Red here to keep you company."

"We'll manage," Ben said.

As mugs clinked into the sink and boots headed for the door, I flattened my back against the wall. "See ya, bro," Kevin called over his shoulder as he and Hector proceeded to walk away from me down the hallway.

I considered joining Nessa and Ben, but then realized that they would wonder why they hadn't heard me coming, and I'd be busted. I'd just have to wait it out—not for too long, I hoped.

"They're in the top drawer," Nessa said.

"Thanks," came Ben's reply. I heard a drawer slide open, followed by the jostling of silverware. There was silence except for the sounds of coffee being prepared: liquid pouring, a spoon tinkling inside of a mug. Finally, Ben said, "Cate told me you two spent some time together yesterday. Thanks for keeping her company."

"I appreciated her company, too," Nessa said. "I like her. She seems like a really nice person, if a bit preoccupied. Of course, I would be, too, under the circumstances."

There was an unusually long pause. "What circumstances?"

"Oh, you know. Finding herself in the middle of a mission like this when she's only been at the whole paranormal thing for a week—and with a guy she just started dating. No offense."

"Is she all right?" Ben asked urgently. "Did she tell you something was wrong?"

"No, and calm down," Nessa said. "She didn't say anything was wrong, but it was obvious that she was tense. And honestly, after I found out that she's basically new to every aspect of this, I was surprised that you brought her here at all, especially given how overly cautious you usually are. From what I gathered, this is nothing like the world she's used to."

Ben sighed audibly. "I debated about whether to ask her. But I figured that since I was going to worry about her no matter where she was, I'd leave it up to her. Honestly, I was relieved that she decided to come. At least while she's here, I can protect her."

"A-hah!" Nessa exclaimed. "So you *were* being overly cautious— true to form. Okay, well, at least that makes some sense. What do you have to protect her from back home?"

Ben hesitated. I nibbled on a fingernail, wondering myself what his answer would be.

"This lowlife bastard was after her last week," he finally said. "We got him thrown in jail, along with some of his crew. But there's no way to know who else he might have told about Cate. I wouldn't put retaliation beyond him, and I'm sure he knows plenty of bottom feeders."

A single, cold bead of sweat trickled down the back my neck. Ben was talking about Don, the boyfriend of Elana, one of my therapy clients. When Elana was thinking of breaking up with him, Don somehow decided that it was my fault. So he came to my house, threatened me, and told me to stay away from her. Later, when I thought Elana might be in danger from Don, I'd gone over to her place, but I'd been hopelessly ill prepared to protect her. Ben and Pete ended up having to rush in and save us both from Don and his colleagues, a group of armed drug dealers.

Now Don was in jail, and I'd assumed that was the end of it—or would be for a long time, anyway. But—retaliation? From behind bars? That thought had never occurred to me. I felt hopelessly naïve.

"Damn," Nessa said. "I'm sorry to hear that. I'm glad Cate's here, too, then. Like you said, she's safe. We'll all look out for her." With a hint of amusement, Nessa added, "If you want, we can put her in bubble wrap. Perez found these huge rolls in one of the storage rooms. He tore some off and put it in his pocket; he's been popping it incessantly. Slim's going to snap his neck any minute now."

Ben chuckled. "I always knew one of them would kill the other eventually."

"That's all we need—another attempted murder on our hands."

"I'll keep Slim in check if you'll get the bubble wrap away from Perez."

"Deal." I heard a chair pull away from the table, and the crisp rhythm of Nessa's steps as she headed toward the door. "See you later."

"See ya."

I held my breath again as Nessa walked out and turned away from me. The sound of her footfalls disappeared down the hallway.

It occurred to me that I should slip away, but I couldn't quite bring myself to leave. After all, my body was still screaming for a cup of coffee. But it was still true that if I appeared out of nowhere, Ben would know I'd been eavesdropping—something that, unfortunately, I had a history of doing, if completely unintentionally. I had resigned myself to waiting behind the door until Ben left when I heard him turn on the sink. That was the cover I needed. After a minute, I could walk in and Ben would assume that the running water had drowned out the sound of my approach.

As soon as he turned off the water, I prepared to emerge— but then I heard him approach the doorway. *Dammit*, I thought, watching through the crack as he stopped suddenly and looked both ways down the hallway. I screwed my eyes shut, willing him to either go back inside or leave.

"Good morning, Cate," he said, peering at me through the crack. "Eavesdropping again?"

"Ow!" I was so startled by the sound of his voice that I jumped and hit my knee against the doorknob. He pulled the door away from the wall, exposing my hiding place.

"Are you all right?"

"Yes," I said, rubbing my knee. "And I didn't *mean* to eavesdrop. I came to get some coffee, but I didn't want to interrupt your conversation."

"How long were you back there?"

I shrugged.

"I see." He gestured toward the staff lounge. "Well, there's plenty of coffee. *Inside*."

"Right. Thanks."

He followed me into the lounge and closed the door behind us. The staff lounge was small, with one wall covered with kitchen-style cabinets and a sink and counter beneath. On the counter sat a coffee brewer and all of the fixings; the pot was still half full. In the middle of the room stood a small round table and three chairs. Ben sat at the table while I went to the counter and poured myself a mug.

"You would have been welcome to join us, you know."

"I almost did," I said. "I will, next time."

"Good." Ben rested his elbows on the table and clasped his hands behind his neck. His tone threaded with worry, he said, "You heard what I said about Don."

"Yeah." I sat at the table and looked down, circling the rim of my mug with my fingertip. "I guess it was stupid for me to feel safe—"

"It wasn't—isn't—stupid," Ben insisted. "The chances of anything else happening are incredibly slim."

"Slim isn't zero, though."

"Well, no."

An optimistic thought skittered through my mind. "But you can't be *that* worried. I mean, you left me home alone yesterday morning, and you and Pete didn't even answer your cell phones when I called."

"I meant to apologize for that," he said quickly. "I was on the phone finalizing arrangements for us here, and since I knew that you were safe at home—"

"Wait, how did you know that?"

Matter-of-factly, Ben said, "I checked the cameras."

"*What* cameras?"

"The ones on the exterior of your house—oh, right." Ben nodded as though a realization had just hit him. "I may not have told you about those."

I felt as though there was a surly bear hibernating inside of me, and Ben was poking it with a stick. "Then you should tell me now."

"Of course," he said, suddenly wary. "Pete and I put them up after Don threatened you—standard security procedure. Of course we shut off the video feed after you told us that you didn't need us anymore. But we hadn't got around to taking the cameras down yet—which turned out to be a good thing yesterday morning, since I was able to keep eyes on your place until after you left."

My inner bear emitted a low, dangerous growl. "You were *spying* on me, on my house?"

"No, of course not." Ben flattened his hands on the table. "Not on *you*. On anyone who might try to *get* to you."

"Oh for God's sake, Ben!" I threw my hands up. I couldn't tell whether he really didn't see the problem, or he was being purposefully obtuse. "You do realize this is the kind of thing that might make someone think that you're creepy, or a stalker—or at the *very* least, that you have no idea what appropriate boundaries are. Or worse, that you *do* know what they are, but you choose to disregard them whenever you think you have a good enough reason!"

"Fair enough." Ben gave a conciliatory nod. "I apologize. That was an oversight on my part. I intended to fill you in on all of the precautions we were taking, but other things kept happening that took priority."

I took a couple of slow, deep breaths and tried to coax my inner bear back into hibernation. It was true that the past week *had* been pretty chaotic. We'd been running from crisis to crisis, it seemed. While that didn't excuse the fact that he'd put up surveillance equipment at my house without asking me first, at least I could understand how it might have happened. "Okay, it was an oversight. And I appreciate that you turned off the video feed when you stopped guarding me. That was the *right* thing to do. Which is why I'm completely baffled by the fact that you decided it was okay to just turn it back on yesterday without my permission!"

Ben clasped his hands together on the table and looked me in the eye. "In order to ask your permission, I would have had to wake you up, and you were exhausted. Also, I didn't want to worry you unnecessarily about the Don situation."

I leaned forward and looked him in the eye right back. "So in other words, you knew you were crossing a line, but you did it anyway. For your own reasons."

He glanced towards the ceiling for a moment. "You could say that, yes."

My fingers curled into fists and my nails bit into my palms. "If you were really that worried about Don, what would you have done if I hadn't volunteered to come down here?"

Staring at the tabletop, Ben pursed his lips. Finally, he said, "I would have asked Pete to stay behind."

I couldn't believe what I was hearing. "And you didn't *mention* that?"

"Well, no. You decided to come with us."

I narrowed my eyes at him. "No, I mean *before*, when you were offering me those opportunities to stay home, why didn't you see fit to mention that they came with a condition—having Pete *tail* me?"

"Not *tail* you," Ben said, "make sure you were safe. And if you had decided to stay home, we would have talked about it. But you didn't, so I didn't think it was necessary to bring it up." As his brows gathered together, he added, "I also didn't think it would be controversial."

"Of course you didn't!" I was sorely tempted to let loose on him with the full force of my indignation. But while I would never admit it to Ben, if there really *was* a chance that I might be in danger, I felt a little bit relieved that someone was on top of it. Still, I couldn't let him think that it was okay to "keep eyes on" my house, or on me, without my permission. "For the record, the next time you're contemplating invading my privacy, talk to me about it first, even if it means *waking me up*," I said, trying to sound as icy as possible. "And I want those cameras taken down as soon as we get home!" After a fear-fueled, lightning-quick second thought, I added, "Probably!"

Ben's confusion only lasted for a moment. "Of course, whatever you like. But at some point we should talk about installing a state-of-the art security system—"

"Benjamin!" I shouted.

He held his hands up in a gesture of surrender.

I stabbed the table with my finger. "No more talk about security measures for me—not until we have a serious conversation about the concept of informed consent!"

One of Ben's eyebrows slowly arched. "You know I'm always happy to talk about anything with you, Cate. But if you don't mind, I'd prefer to table that discussion for now."

"Why?"

"Because there's something else we need to talk about that can't wait."

"Of course there is," I leaned back and folded my arms across my chest. "What is it?"

Frowning, he sat back in his chair. "You know now that I was relieved when you decided to come down here with us, and why. But seeing the situation through Nessa's eyes has reminded me how unfamiliar all of this is to you, and that it might be stressful in ways that I hadn't thought about." As our eyes met, he slid his hand across the table, palm up. "How are you holding up?"

The weight of Ben's concern pushed the portal doors to open, and all of his worries flowed into me. Given that we were in such a safe place, his emotions seemed inappropriately intense. I knew that something else must have been amplifying them. In that moment, though, he needed reassurance, not analysis. Fortunately, that was something I could offer. Of all of the things weighing on my mind at that moment, the mission itself wasn't one of them.

I put my earlier frustrations with Ben aside and made an effort to sound calm. "I don't know what I said to Nessa that worried her, but I'm fine. Really. And as for this situation being new and stressful, I volunteered to come, remember? We all did, as a matter of fact, but I don't see you obsessing over the others and whether or not *they're* stressed out."

"Of course I worry about them, but not as much as I worry about you. They're all seasoned members of this team. They have more practice using their skills and gifts; they have a better understanding of how paranormal healing works; and they have much more experience working together. Meanwhile, you just started your internship."

"Be that as it may, I also have a few years as a therapist under my belt. This isn't the first time I've had to deal with risks, or adapt to a situation that was tricky and unfamiliar. And there were no marines guarding us at the clinic," I added. "Down here, I feel positively relaxed by comparison."

The deep lines that had formed on Ben's forehead began to soften. "That's true. I'd forgotten that your past experiences would have prepared you somewhat."

But the way he held his shoulders still broadcasted tension. I had to figure out what else was fueling Ben's fears. After a moment, the answer dawned on me—something so obvious that I felt like an idiot for not seeing it sooner. "Is it possible that your worries about me are disproportionate because of... you know?" I waggled the finger that bore his ring.

"Yes, that's part of it."

After a series of startled blinks, I asked, "It is?" I hadn't expected him to concede that point at *all*, let alone so quickly.

"Naturally. You're the woman in my life. Of course my concerns for you will be more intense."

"I'm the *what?*" A feverish sensation flashed through me. I drummed my fingers on the edge of the table. "Ben, that sounds so... *serious.*"

"I'm a serious person," he said frankly, "and so are you. There's no point in pretending otherwise, no matter how slowly we decide to take things." His eyes shimmered gold. "Is there?"

Dammit. He was right; there was no point denying it. Neither one of us lived life lightly—particularly when it came to matters of the heart. I had experienced his emotions through the portal, and just thinking about his feelings for me made my stomach flutter. Meanwhile, my feelings for him were already much deeper than I wanted to admit. "Well, no," I acquiesced, "but that doesn't mean you have to say it out *loud.* I mean, we could at least *pretend* that we're keeping things light for a while longer."

The corners of Ben's eyes crinkled with amusement as he reached across the table and took my hands in his. "Keeping things light isn't really my forté," he admitted, "but for you, I'll give it a try." He began stroking the backs of my hands with his thumbs, lulling my body into a warm trance. "Just promise me again that while we're here, you'll talk to me right away if you have any problems or questions. If you can do that, I'll promise to try not to worry so much."

For a fleeting moment, I considered telling him about my mother's dream and the questions it had raised. Was he primarily interested in me because I was an empath? But I knew that even if he was, he might not be fully aware of it—and if he *was* aware, and answered "yes," I wasn't ready to hear it. I pushed the thought away as my eyes rose to meet his. The depth of caring I saw there made my doubts seem inconsequential, pulling me back into the moment. "Like I said, everything is fine. But if something comes up, I promise to tell you. Okay?"

"Okay. Thank you."

"Will you stop worrying now?"

He gave me a self-deprecating smile. "Like I said, I'll try."

"Good lord." I rolled my eyes. "Nessa was right; you *are* overly cautious."

"I'd be careful about cosigning everything Nessa says." Devilishness crept into his voice. "After all, putting you in bubble wrap was also her idea—an idea not without merit, I thought."

I gave him my best glare. "You know *exactly* what you can do with your bubble wrap."

"Well, not *exactly*," he murmured suggestively. "I'm still sorting through ideas."

Baffled as to how one could possibly debauch bubble wrap, I struggled to formulate a sufficiently scathing comeback. Fortunately, there was a knock at the door. Ben got up and consulted with the marine outside.

When he returned moments later, his expression was grave. "It's Dr. Belo. His kidneys are failing. They're putting him on dialysis, but this means he might not have as long as we'd hoped."

His words poured through me like ice water. "Oh no, Ben. We should go."

"Yeah." He squinted and looked me up and down. "You're sure you're ready for this?"

"Yes, I'm sure. Let's go." I pushed my chair back, stood up, and followed Ben to our next destination, keeping my hands clasped together so he wouldn't see them trembling.

CHAPTER EIGHT

A mesmeric ringing emanated from Dr. Belo's room as Ben and I approached. Different musical notes layered one on top of the other, becoming quite loud by the time we reached the door. Inside, Kai was sitting at a small table filled with what appeared to be about a dozen brass bowls of different sizes. He was using a wooden mallet to alternately tap them or circle their edges, making the air vibrate with sound.

Asa sat in an armchair with his eyes closed and his hands resting on his knees. He looked so relaxed that I thought he might be asleep. He wore a camo baseball cap with a long clear crystal affixed to the underside of the lid. It stuck out from his forehead like a unicorn's horn.

I leaned down and whispered to Kai, "How does this work?"

"These are the Tibetan singing bowls. Each makes a sound that activates a different chakra," he explained. "I'm tuning in each of Asa's chakras to Braz's so Asa can act as his proxy."

"What about the hat?"

"The crystal is a special seven-sided piece of quartz that opens the channels of spiritual communication," Kai said. "Some say it activates that pineal gland Braz was studying. That's why Asa's wearing it on his forehead, where the third-eye chakra is located."

"Wow, that's amazing," I whispered as I approached Dr. Belo. He appeared unchanged except for the medieval-looking metal device that was holding his eyes open. It hummed for a few seconds as it administered drops of liquid into his eyes.

Ben and I stood by quietly. After Kai wound down his bowl

playing, he went over and placed his hands on top of Asa's. "To whom am I speaking?" he asked.

"That was beautiful playing, my dear Kai," Asa said, but in a register slightly lower than his usual voice. "And this is Braz, of course. Asa is very generous to let me speak through him."

"Yes, he is," Kai said. "Ben has brought Cate over for your session."

"I know," Braz said through Asa. "I caught the scent of her lovely soap—coconut, is it?"

"Coconut milk," I acknowledged, marveling at his keen sense of smell.

"Ah, yes. Well, greetings, Amada. That means beloved, and I can tell that you are, so that's what I'll call you. And please call me Braz."

"Are you going to be okay?" Ben whispered.

"I'll be fine," I said with more confidence than I felt.

"There are two marines at the end of the corridor," he added as Kai tugged at his arm. "If you need help, just holler, and they'll come get us."

"Got it. I'll let you know as soon as we're done." I did my best to sound reassuring.

"Ta ta." Kai closed the door behind them.

My nerves began to fray around the edges. I looked at Asa, sitting there with a Mona Lisa smile on his face, and this man I didn't know in a coma with his eyelids being forced open. Panic rose in my throat. I swallowed it down, but then jumped as Braz again used Asa to speak. "Amada? Is everything all right?"

A man in a coma was asking me if I was all right. My anxiety was making me horribly self-centered. I needed to focus on him and concentrate on the task at hand.

I pulled a chair up near Dr. Belo's head. "I'm fine," I said, "just a little nervous. I want to help you, but I'm sort of new at this. I want to make sure I do it right."

"My dear, don't worry. I am going to die; at least you can't make things worse." Asa broke into a throaty laugh very different from his own. Then he said in a more serious tone, "I'm sorry. This must be very uncomfortable for you. But please don't be nervous. You have a God-given gift, this ability to submerge into other people. Ben told me about it. All you have to do is open yourself up, and your gift will do the rest. It should be effortless. Surely you have experienced this?"

I nodded. Then I remembered that he couldn't see me and said, "Yes."

"Then do what you do, my dear. Look into my eyes. I only wish I hadn't lost my vision, so that I could look back into yours."

I clasped my hands so that I wouldn't bite my nails. "Are you uncomfortable? I mean, with that contraption holding your eyelids open?"

"Not at all. I can't feel a thing, only your presence. I am perfectly comfortable and in no pain."

Somewhat reassured, I tried to slip into therapist mode. "Well, the way this works is that I'll ask you some questions to get us started. You simply answer them. Then at some point I'll enter your consciousness. I may ask you about what I'm seeing in there. Tell me as much as you can, but if at any point it becomes uncomfortable for you—emotionally, I mean—just say so, and I'll pull back. Okay?"

"Oh, that sounds very intimate," he said. "I look forward to having someone as lovely as you exploring my psyche. Please, start at any time, and don't hold back."

I couldn't help but smile. Vani was right; Braz was a horrible flirt. But I got the feeling that he was also trying to put me at ease. I leaned forward so that I could look into his eyes. It was difficult at first. They appeared so tortured under the device he wore, but I reminded myself that he could feel nothing. His eyes were pools of deep brown. I stared into them and began.

"Ben tells me that you've been having trouble remembering the day before you went into a coma. Can you tell me the last thing you remember?"

"My last clear memory was making my morning coffee in the lab. I guess that would have been a week ago Wednesday. I was waiting for an e-mail from Dr. Ahmad in the oncology department.

We were expecting some results from one of his clinical trials that day. I was watching the coffee drip into the pot."

"Do you remember how you were feeling in that moment?"

"Oh yes," he said. "I was anticipating how delicious the coffee would taste. It was Ethiopian. I had bought it not long before from a specialty store in Adams Morgan."

As I looked into Braz's eyes, his longing for coffee drew me in and allowed me to submerge into his consciousness.

At first, I found myself floating through a sea of strange images that evoked a profound sense of sadness. "Dr. Belo—I mean Braz, sorry—what is it that I'm seeing? A stream running through a desert, hands untying knots... and two people—it looks like they're in some sort of, um, intimate embrace?"

"Ah, yes," he said with a sigh. "Don't worry, Amada, that's just Lewin Lima. He is a famous Brazilian-American poet—famous in Brazil, that is. Not very well known here before his death. He wrote poems of love and revolution, and his writing has been keeping me company these days. The images you see are from 'The Desolate Kiss.' For some reason, that poem in particular has been circling around in my head."

"Oh, I see." I could only imagine how desolate he must feel under the circumstances. I dived down further until I landed on something solid. When I looked up, I was standing on the patio of a penthouse apartment, high up with a view of a massive city. A movement caught my attention. There was a woman, young and beautiful, wearing a gauzy white dress. She laughed as she turned and ran through the patio door into the apartment. I looked back out over the city, only to have the woman catch my eye again, playing the same scene over. This vision kept repeating in an endless loop. I described it to Braz.

"That is my beloved wife, Pedra," he said tenderly, "and one of my favorite memories from our life in São Paulo. Right after that, I chased her inside, and we made love like the world was ending. She was my heart, my anchor in life. A large part of me died already, five years ago, when cancer took her from me."

Suddenly, the whole patio scene darkened as though a storm cloud was rolling in. "I'm so sorry," I said.

"Don't be, Amada. You cannot travel inside of me without finding Pedra. I talk to her every day. But perhaps we should move on."

"Of course." I tried to pass through the clouds of grief as I held in my mind what I was looking for: a memory so disturbing that Braz's brain had blocked it out.

All at once I found myself standing on the sidewalk outside of the Friendship Heights Metro Station. It was around midday, and people were bustling in every direction. A dark-haired woman in her mid-thirties swept up next to me, kissed me on the cheek, and asked, "Are we going for coffee?"

"Braz," I said, "now I'm in Friendship Heights. There is a woman here asking if we're going for coffee. She is small, petite, with long black hair."

"Ah, yes. That's Jennifer, my Jenny." Within the scene, the sunlight brightened. "She is my—well, you could say my paramour. We met soon after I arrived in the States. She is a graduate student in psychology and a fellow lover of poetry—especially Lewin Lima's. Our mutual love of his poems was the first thing we bonded over, in fact. I asked Skeet to contact her, to give her the official story about my illness. But he said she did not reply to his voicemail or e-mail." He sounded pained. "I am worried about her. I hope she is not in jeopardy because of her association with me."

"I'll check with Skeet. Maybe we can contact her another way."

"I would appreciate that, Amada." Relief was evident in his voice. "She is not my Pedra, but I still care for her. If anything happened, I would never forgive myself."

When I looked for Jennifer again, she was gone. I was surrounded by shops and restaurants but felt a strong pull toward one store in particular, a small newsstand. I walked inside and saw a man behind the counter. He greeted me and asked if he could help me with anything.

"Do you know a newsstand near the Friendship Heights Station?" I asked Braz.

"Yes, of course!" he said excitedly. "That's Ernesto's store. He's a friend of mine from university. We lost each other for years but found one another here of all places. I happened to walk into his shop one day searching for a Brazilian newspaper, and we were reunited."

"What a coincidence!"

"Yes. But I am wondering why you find yourself there."

"I don't know, but he's asking if he can help me. What should I say?"

There was a moment of silence, then Braz said, "Ask him for the usual—a pack of Derbys. I tried, but never could give up smoking. Ernesto always keeps my favorite brand."

A pack of Derbys, please. I directed the thought at Ernesto. He reached under the counter and handed me a cigarette pack, but it was all black with no label.

Ernesto's response slipped into my thoughts: *A black box. The key is inside.*

I'd never seen such an odd-looking pack of cigarettes before. "Braz, what does a Derby pack look like?"

"White, with a blue ribbon. Why do you ask?"

I described the pack Ernesto had given me and shared what he'd said.

"Ahhh," he said in a voice filled with wonder. "I believe I am remembering something now. I think you may have hit upon the core of the mystery—and I think I know exactly what we need to do to solve it."

With a *poof*, the whole newsstand scene disappeared. I felt something pulling at my consciousness, drawing it back up through the images from Lima's poem. Then, like water pouring into a glass, I flowed back into my own body.

"Braz," I asked in amazement, "did you just kick me out?"

He chuckled and said, "Why, yes! Did you think I would let you stay in there forever and discover all of my secrets?"

I laughed as much in delight as surprise. "That was so cool! No one has ever done that to me before. I didn't even know it was possible."

"You know what they say. When you lose some senses, the others become stronger. Truthfully, I didn't push you out on purpose. But I could feel you inside of me, and after a while, it became uncomfortable, like a splinter. I think my mind expelled you. I hope you are not offended."

"Of course not," I said. "It's your mind; you have every right to decide who gets to be in there."

"A very democratic attitude. Besides, we found out what we needed to know, didn't we?"

"Did we?"

"Yes, my dear, we did." Asa wore a self-satisfied smile. "All you have to do now is go to Ernesto's store and pick up a pack of Derbys."

I blinked. "I'm sorry, do what?"

"The black box—a symbol for all things secret, for information that is unknown. Back when we were university students in São Paulo, Ernesto and I were activists organizing protests against an oppressive regime. We used to send each other secret messages in packs of cigarettes. Obviously, whatever the secret is that my mind doesn't want me to remember is hidden in a box of Derbys at Ernesto's shop. I must have had enough wits about me to entrust it to him before whatever happened to me happened."

The poisoning, he meant. My heart went out to Braz. He was so courageous, but clearly it was too upsetting for him to say the actual words.

Braz continued, "You bring the pack here, and we'll see what's inside. It will no doubt hold the key to open up this locked memory of mine."

"You really think so?"

"Definitely. What else could it mean?"

The submergence had actually *worked*? Along with sheer amazement, I felt a hint of hope. "Okay, that shouldn't be too difficult. I'll talk to Ben. I'm sure he can convince Captain Abbott to send a couple of marines—"

"Oh no!" Braz shouted in alarm. "No, no, Amada. You cannot do it like this."

"What?" My nascent hope wavered. "Why not?"

His voice dropped low and intensified. "I don't know how much time I have left. You must listen to me very carefully. After one of our student protests, Ernesto was arrested and tortured by the secret police. He can smell a soldier or police a mile away," Braz explained, "and he can also smell a liar. Whatever secret is in that black box, it must be quite important if I hid it in that symbolic way and entrusted it to Ernesto. You will have to go on your own, I'm sorry to say, without these marines. He knows I would never send someone like that in his direction. Ernesto will trust you only if he can tell that you are a civilian, and that you are genuine. Otherwise he will not believe that you have truly come on my behalf."

My skin turned into gooseflesh. "But Braz, you don't understand. None of us are allowed to leave this floor without the captain's permission and a marine guard." I racked my brains for a solution. "He might let me go if I talked Ben into going with me."

Braz snorted. "I'm in a *coma*, and I can feel Ben's military pedigree every time he enters the room. One look at him would put Ernesto on high alert. Perhaps some other member of your group could accompany you?"

"Not an option," I explained. "Captain Abbott already told us that he won't let civilian staff members go anywhere without marines guarding us. Ben will back him up, and the other members of our group will back Ben up." Even as I spoke, I realized that there was a chance Kai might help me. But he was growing protective of me, too, so there was an equal chance he'd try to stop me. And if I only had one shot at getting the cigarettes, chances were something I couldn't afford take.

"Besides," I added, "Ben has a… a *thing* about me putting myself in risky situations." Not that I really blamed him. He had been completely torn up about my cardiac arrest incident. And having to rescue Elana and me from Don and his friends had only intensified Ben's over-protectiveness. He had even asked me outright not to put myself at risk for other people again. Although I'd told him I couldn't promise that, I *had* just promised him over coffee that while we were on our mission, I would talk to him before I tried to deal with any problems on my own. In this case, though, I knew exactly how the conversation would go, and it would *not* end in Ben sending me off to Ernesto's store with his blessings.

Asa held his hands out, palms up, and shrugged. "Where's the risk? A sexy young woman walking into a newsstand to buy cigarettes—why should that raise anyone's suspicions?"

I had to admit that he had a point—at least about the not-raising-suspicions part. It wasn't as though the CIA knew who I was or had any reason to be on the lookout for me. For goodness' sake, we'd arrived in an SUV with tinted windows and hadn't left the subbasement since. Still, I couldn't believe I was actually considering doing something behind Ben's back. The mere thought made the blood pound rapidly through my veins.

"You could be right, but even if I agreed with you, Captain Abbott has this place under tight control. They won't even let us leave the floor, let alone the building."

"No problem," Braz said confidently. "I am an escape artist from way back. I can tell you how to get around this Captain Abbott. It's quite simple."

Oh God—this is for real, I thought. *He can actually tell me how to do this*. I dropped my head into my hands. "If I sneak out of here and get caught...."

"You won't get caught, my dear. I can tell you how to slip in and out unnoticed." Braz's tone became grave. "But Amada, I can hear the anxiety in your voice. If you like, we can forget we made this black box discovery and speak of it to no one. I will simply go on to the next life, and whatever is locked in my brain will go along with me. However, if my physician is correct, should you choose to take this adventure, you should do it very soon."

I knew he was right. Braz's subconscious had signaled very

clearly that it wasn't going to take us any further into his memories without whatever information was hidden in the cigarette pack—and for all I knew, that information could be cryptic or coded in such a way that only Braz could make sense of it.

So I had to retrieve the pack before he died—and I had to do it without letting Ben or Captain Abbott know. Even if they approved the idea of my going to the newsstand, I knew they'd insist on sending some marines with me for protection—in which case, according to Braz, Ernesto wouldn't give me the time of day, let alone the cigarette pack.

I felt backed into a corner, but I knew it wasn't Braz's fault. After all, sneaking out was the only workable idea we had. It was also probably our only chance of finding out what we wanted to know: who poisoned him and why. Without that information, we couldn't deal with his killer—not to mention the mysterious dark armies Eve had seen in her vision.

My thoughts churned desperately. If I couldn't help solve the poisoning mystery, then why had Ben brought me in the first place? What would be the point, if I couldn't even make use of the information I got from Braz? What use was I as an empath if I couldn't contribute anything of substance? And what was the point of giving up my psychotherapy career and all of my clients if joining the MacGregor Group turned out to be a wasted effort?

If what Braz said was true, I could slip in and out of the building and no one would be the wiser. I'd get Ben what he needed before anyone even realized I had left. That settled it: I would go. I would do it for Ben—whether he liked it or not.

I steeled myself and straightened up in my chair. Taking a notepad and pencil from the table, I said, "Okay, Braz. Tell me how to sneak out of here."

CHAPTER NINE

"Thanks, Hector. Thanks, Kevin." As I shook their hands, I smiled the most charming smile I could muster. Like the other members of Yankee Company, they reminded me of big cats, moving with the controlled, confident ease of predators who were prepared at any moment to make a deadly strike. I was grateful once again that in the interest of keeping things casual and non-intimidating, the marines had asked us to call them by their first names. It was going to require enough courage for me to give the slip to two massive, intimidating men in uniform. I wasn't sure that I could do it at all, had I just addressed them as "Corporals."

Captain Abbott had approved my field trip to Braz's office after I convinced Ben and Skeet that I needed to confirm some things I'd learned during our empathic submergence session. I told them that it would help me to spend time in Braz's space going through his papers and "absorbing his pre-coma energy." And since Braz's office was in the same hospital building we inhabited, the captain decided that the risk was minimal. During that meeting, Ben had watched me like a hawk. I knew he suspected that something else was going on. He wanted to come with me to Braz's office, but Captain Abbott asked him to stay behind to work on something. I told him it was just as well because I would concentrate better if I were alone—with a marine guard standing outside, of course. In spite of his obvious reservations, Ben had acquiesced. While I was pleased that he had chosen to respect my judgment, it made me feel even guiltier than I did already about lying to him.

If things went as planned, though, no one would ever find out. Braz told me that there was an emergency exit door leading directly from his office to the stairwell. He had long ago disabled the door's alarm so that he could slip into the stairwell and have a cigarette without being detected. The plan was for me to get some privacy in the office, sneak out through the stairwell, catch a cab to Ernesto's store, run in and pick up the cigarettes, then take the cab back to NIH and return to Braz's office before anyone was the wiser. Then I would produce the cigarette pack and tell Ben that I found it in Braz's desk. Easy peasy.

Kevin and Hector had walked me over to Braz's office. Then, as promised, they'd waited outside while I went in and shut the door. I was so nervous that I hadn't been able to eat lunch. My stomach was wild with hunger and nerves. I glanced around the room. There were a few random piles of books and papers, but for the most part, it was fairly organized. I did notice that it was heavily populated with potted plants—mostly ferns—and they looked like they needed watering. I would have to remember to take care of that when I got back.

There was a framed photo on Braz's desk—a woman I recognized to be his wife Pedra in her later years. Thinking Braz might like to have her picture near him even though he couldn't see it, I slipped it into the messenger bag Ben had given me in case I needed to carry anything back.

I'd told Kevin and Hector that I would need at least an hour, maybe more, and that I didn't want to be disturbed. As an extra precaution, I turned the lock on the office door to slow down anyone who might try to enter.

Then it was time to try the emergency exit. *If the alarm goes off, I'm screwed*, I thought. Gingerly, I pushed on the bar handle, and the door gave way. Silence. *Thank you, Braz.*

I let out a great sigh, unaware that I'd been holding my breath. Then I closed the door carefully, using a sheet of notepaper to cover the latch so it wouldn't lock behind me. I skittered down the staircase, following Braz's directions to a second floor exit that was also without an alarm, then found the nearby elevator bay, took it one floor down, and walked out to the front of the building.

I squinted like a startled mole as I emerged into the bright, crisp autumn afternoon. As my eyes adjusted, I took in the enormity of the hospital. It looked more like the capital building in the middle of a city than the clinical center of a campus. But I didn't have time to stand around gawking like an impressed tourist. I made my way over to the taxi stand Braz had promised would be there and climbed into the backseat of the first car.

I had to clear my throat twice before I could get out the words, "Friendship Heights Metro Station."

"No problem."

Within minutes, we were whizzing down Rockville Pike as the driver carried on an impassioned conversation on his cell phone in a language I didn't understand. I rubbed my sternum in an effort to soothe my tightening chest and sent a silent plea out to the universe: *If you get me through this, I'll never do anything like this ever again, so help me God.*

When we reached the metro station, the driver pulled over so quickly that my body was slammed against the door. "Um, sir," I asked, "would you mind waiting for me? I just have to run in for some cigarettes. Then I'm returning to the same place."

"Sure," he said. "Five dollars extra."

"Of course. No problem." I climbed out, my heart pounding on the inside of my ribcage like a boxer punching a bag. *I can't believe I'm doing this,* I thought as I scanned the streetscape. There was Ernesto's newsstand in the middle of the block, right where I had expected it to be. A light sweat coated my skin as I crossed the street and walked up to the door. The store appeared to be completely empty.

Come on, Duncan, I told myself, *this is what you came for. Just get it over with.* I pushed the door open and a bell rang, announcing my presence. My nerves were drawn so tight that I yelped as a man stood up from where he had apparently been bent over behind the counter.

He smiled charitably. "Can I help you, miss?"

It was Ernesto. I recognized him from my visit inside of Braz's mind: tall and thin, with a sharp nose that looked as though it had been whittled to a point. I cleared my throat again and spoke the words I had practiced. "Hi, Ernesto. Braz sent me to pick up his special pack of Derbys."

Ernesto's expression changed instantly. He scowled. "What Braz?"

Thankfully, Braz had prepared me for his questions. "Dr. Braz Belo, your friend from university."

"Ah, that Braz." Ernesto rubbed his goatee. "What special pack?"

"The one he told you to keep safe and not to give to anyone." To my embarrassment, tears pressed themselves into the corners of my eyes. "If he could have come himself, he would have."

"I see." Ernesto coughed in an attempt to conceal his own emotions. "Are you his girlfriend?"

"No, just a friend."

"Then I have something to tell you." He leaned forward and said softly, "Braz's girlfriend was here on Sunday—the pretty one with the long black hair. She was asking if I had heard from him or knew anything about him. She said she had been unable to reach him. I told her the truth, that I didn't know anything. I thought she might ask for the pack of Derbys, but she did not."

I nodded, swallowing hard. "I'll tell him."

Ernesto disappeared behind the counter again, this time emerging with a cigarette box—white with a blue ribbon, exactly as Braz had described, but with the top of the cellophane wrapper torn off. He held the pack against his chest as he spoke. "Also, tell Braz that I think it's best if he doesn't come to visit for a while. Some strange creatures have been hanging around here lately, giving strange looks."

The bell on the door rang. Sounds from the street came in with two fit-looking young men in dark suits. They animatedly discussed some football results as they wandered over and began browsing the magazine selection.

I looked back at Ernesto. His body had gone as taut as a pulled bowstring. "There are two of the strange creatures now," he murmured. He subtly pointed at his ear, pretending to scratch it.

As casually as I could, I glanced over at them. Sure enough, they were both wearing identical, nearly invisible earpieces with wires that disappeared under their shirt collars.

The spinning of the earth slowed. I heard every deafening pulse of my blood and felt each ragged breath as my chest rose and fell. I turned back to Ernesto. With great effort, he tried to appear unconcerned, giving me a flirtatious wink. "You also should not come back soon. You are very memorable."

I tried to smile to show my gratitude for his warning, but I couldn't quite manage it. "Thank you," I whispered.

He handed me the cigarette pack. "Go. Tell my brother that I love him."

But I was paralyzed, unable to move. My body had ceased listening to my brain's panicked commands.

Ernesto became somber. He reached across the counter and squeezed my shoulder. "Go *now*."

Fortunately, his touch activated me. The world sped up again. I slipped the cigarette pack into my messenger bag and nearly tripped over my feet in my rush to reach the door.

Once outside, I saw that my cab wasn't where I had left it. I figured the driver must have had to circle the block. I started to walk down to the corner where I could meet him when he returned.

I had taken about a dozen steps when I heard the bell on Ernesto's shop door ring again. I tucked my head down and to the side, trying to be discreet. I caught a glimpse of the two men in suits leaving the shop. They turned and walked in my direction, still arguing jovially.

Coincidence…? But I was on a secret mission. My cab driver had apparently disappeared without taking any payment. Two strange men with earpieces were following me.

I glanced back again, trying to look as casual as possible. The men had stopped talking to each other. Both of their expressions were now hidden under black sunglasses. My heart fluttered and jumped like a moth caught on a glue strip.

In desperation, I thought of Ben, but I had no way of reaching him since there was no cell phone coverage in the subbasement. I couldn't call anyone else for help, either. I had left my cell phone in my room; I thought it might look suspicious if I took it with me, and I also didn't think I'd need it. *Well, that was dumb,* I thought. *And now the poisoners are after me.* Fear clutched at my throat. Although it was broad daylight and we were surrounded by people, I had seen enough spy movies. I knew that they had their ways. I'd feel a slight sting in my leg and would go down instantly like a shot deer. The autopsy report would read, "apparent heart attack." Well, there was no way I was giving in to *that* fate, and no way I was going down without a fight. *Not here, not now,* I thought. *Not when I've just found Ben.*

I began to shift into a run when suddenly, I found myself flanked by two men—but not the ones I was running from. Instead, Hector and Kevin were on either side of me, holding me by the elbows. I barely had time to wonder where they'd come from before they lifted me up off of the ground and deposited me into the open door of a van that was idling at the curb. They slid the door shut and climbed into the front seats.

"Buckle up," Hector shouted over his shoulder to me, then growled into his cell phone, "We got her."

I sensed a presence behind me and turned to see two of the other marines from Yankee Company sitting in the back of the van wearing camouflage uniforms. They were stone-faced, looking out the back window and poised for action.

Oh hell. A wave of guilt amplified my terror. "Kevin? Hector?" I leaned towards the front seat. "I'm so sorry...."

"Later!" Kevin said, then addressed the men in the back. "Are they gone?"

"Yes, sir," one of the marines replied. "As soon as they spotted you, they turned around and went the other way."

"Good," Kevin said. "Make sure they stay gone."

"Yes, sir!" The two marines in camo exploded out of the back doors and slammed them shut. Kevin threw the van into gear and we tore off at high speed.

I was tossed back against the seat. Trembles of adrenaline mixed with relief wracked my body. I tried to force myself to repeat the mantra, *You're safe now.* But it wasn't long before the tears I had been holding back rolled freely down my cheeks. I reached into the bag and held onto the cigarette pack, trying to reassure myself that the whole thing hadn't been in vain.

CHAPTER TEN

We drove into the hospital's underground garage. By the time we had spiraled down to our floor, I was completely disoriented. Kevin and Hector stayed on either side of me as we marched through the maze of passageways. We stopped at the door to the conference room. Hector opened it, and I walked inside. He closed the door firmly behind me.

Of all people, I wasn't expecting to see Skeet. He was alone in the room, leaning back in his chair and examining his hands. "Oh hi," he said warmly. "Come on in, have a seat."

I looked around the room to see if I had missed something, or someone. With caution, I sat down across the table from him and asked the obvious question. "Where's Ben?"

"Hmm, let's see." Skeet tapped the corner of his mouth with his index finger. "Judging from the shouting I heard as I walked by Captain Abbott's office, I'd say he's busy being drawn and quartered right now. 'You can't control your people, they're putting my marines in danger.' Something to that effect."

Skeet appeared to be pleased with his imitation of Captain Abbott, which unfortunately had been accurate enough to make me cringe on Ben's behalf. I folded my arms on the table and laid my head down.

"Yes, well." I heard Skeet clap his hands and rub them together. "There's nothing we can do about that right now. However, I have been tasked with finding out what you've been up to. Of course, I told them that you must have been doing something very important, and for excellent reasons."

I couldn't tell whether Skeet had really told them that or was just

97

trying to be encouraging. I lifted my head and placed the messenger bag on the table. Then I pulled out the cigarette pack and slid it across to him.

"What's this?" He looked from the pack to me and back again. Then he opened it, peered inside, and began emptying the cigarettes onto the table. We both heard a soft, sharp *tick* as a small piece of plastic fell out. Skeet picked it up and examined it. "A flash drive. Well done." He strode over and opened the door, handing the drive to Hector. "Please get this to Captain Abbott immediately. Tell him Cate brought it."

Thinking of Braz, I slipped one of the loose cigarettes into my bag while Skeet's back was turned.

"Yes, sir!" Hector took off down the hallway. Skeet closed the door and returned to his seat.

"Well, that ought to give them something new to talk about." He beamed at me. "Do you know what's on it?"

"No, but I know it's important." With every moment that passed, however, my trepidation over the inevitable confrontation with Ben grew. I started to chew on my lip.

"Then there's nothing for you to worry about," Skeet reassured. "You're back safe and sound, and you've brought back something worthwhile. I'm sure it will all smooth over in no time."

If that was what he thought, then Skeet was clearly out of touch with reality. I slumped against the back of my chair.

He chuckled. "You think I'm overly optimistic. Well, maybe I am. But look at it this way. No matter how much of a hard-ass Abbott is, you're rid of him after you leave this place. And as far as Ben is concerned—well, I've known quite a few marines, so I'm sure he can be somewhat... single-minded when it comes to certain things. Still, I'm sure he'll appreciate that you only did what you did in an effort to help our patient... right?"

"Of course," I said, annoyed that any other motivation might even be considered.

Skeet smiled and spread his hands out in front of him. "Well there you have it. Personally, I think you showed a lot of courage. I'm proud of you, Cate."

I squinted in confusion. Proud of me? That was a weird thing to say. But before I could reply, the door flew open. I shot to my feet.

Ben burst into the room like a runaway train. His face was completely devoid of emotion, as though it had been chiseled out of rock. In less than a second, he had his hands on my shoulders and was looking me up and down, examining. When his eyes finally met mine, his mask slipped for a moment, and I caught a glimpse of the agonized expression that lay beneath. "Are you all right?"

The intense pain in his voice made me freeze in place. "Yes," I managed to whisper. "I'm fine."

He checked me over again, as though to verify my claim. Eventually, he appeared satisfied that I was all in one piece. Putting his stony expression back into place, he turned to Skeet. "Captain Abbott would like to see you," he said, his voice as smooth and hard as a steel beam. "He would like you to be present while they examine the disk."

"The disk *Cate* brought back," Skeet said.

So Skeet *was* standing up for me. I felt myself soften a little towards him.

"Yes," Ben replied sternly, "at great risk to herself, four marines, and the entire mission."

"Well, it's a good thing she was so successful, then." Skeet winked at me. "I won't keep Captain Abbott waiting." He walked out, shutting the door behind him.

Ben looked at the wall just beyond me. His voice taut, he asked, "This was Braz's idea, wasn't it? He put you up to this?"

"What?" I looked up at him, eyes widening. With everything that was going on, Ben's first priority was to assign blame? Well, I wasn't going to throw Braz under the bus. "Nobody 'put me up to' anything!"

"His idea. Just as I thought." He gestured towards the door. "Let's go."

As controlled as it was, I could still sense the rigid edge of Ben's anger, cold and impossibly hard. I tried to think of something to say in Braz's defense and my own, but my adrenaline-soaked brain was struggling to find words.

Ben walked over to the door and opened it, then stood to one side. "Let's *go*, Cate."

Propelled by the sheer determination in his voice, I walked out of the conference room, careful to hold my chin up. As we headed back to my room, I braced myself for what I expected would be one hell of a dustup.

• • •

We passed a few marines in the hallway. It was clear that they were trying not to stare. Obviously word of my little adventure had already spread.

When we reached our room, there were two marines standing on either side of the door. *This does not bode well*, I thought. Ben exchanged nods with them, opened the door, and gestured for me to step inside.

I walked into the middle of the room and turned around, waiting to hear what he had to say. As it turned out, though, I was waiting in vain. Ben was still standing in the hallway addressing the marines, but in a voice loud enough for me to hear. "Take her to the mess hall for dinner then bring her back here. Per Captain Abbott, she is only to leave this room for meals or work activities, and then only with a two-marine guard."

"A what?" I walked back to the open door. "Ben, what's going on?"

He stepped just inside the doorway. Again his mask slipped, and I saw the combination of raw pain and anger striating his face, heard it in his voice. "Cate, I can't tell you how relieved...." He closed his eyes for a moment, as though he were grasping at the torn-apart pieces of himself and trying to pull them back together. When he spoke again, it was with forced calm. "Look, until I get back, just try to get some rest, and follow the marines' instructions, all right?" With an annoyed edge he couldn't hide, he added, "For once? And Vani will be over shortly."

"What?" Anger rushed through me, and I felt my insides trembling. "I already have a marine guard; I don't need a babysitter!"

His brow furrowed. "I just thought you might want some company after—"

"I don't want 'company.' I want to talk to *you*!"

"I know." He raked a hand violently through his hair. "And we will talk—later. But right now, I have to go and assist Captain Abbott with the investigation. If you don't want Vani, I won't send her. But if you change your mind, or need anything at all, just ask the marines." Then he turned on his heel and left the room.

I managed to wedge my foot in the door before he could close it. "But... what... that's not... Benjamin!" My arms flapped like broken wings at my sides.

He looked back at me through the opening in the door. "Yes?"

"It sounds like you're holding me prisoner!"

"Not me. Captain Abbott." But something in the set of Ben's jaw gave me the distinct impression that while putting me under some kind of guard might not have been his idea, he probably hadn't objected to it, either. He leaned in and looked at me through the crack in the door, eyebrow arched. "I'll be happy to tell him if there's a problem," he said, his voice a low rumble. "Do you have somewhere else to be?"

His question felt like an indictment. I took a step backwards— just far enough for Ben to shut the door. "Goddammit!" I flung the door open again to find the two marines standing with their backs to me, blocking my exit. I heard Ben's footsteps marching down the hall away from us. Despairing, I carefully shut the door.

I staggered backward until I collapsed onto the bottom bunk and covered my face with my hands. *This is not good,* I thought. Tears once again wet my cheeks. *This is really, really not good.* I said a silent prayer that whatever information was on that damn disk would be so impressive that the next time I saw Ben and Captain Abbott, they would both be on their knees, apologizing.

Chapter Eleven

It wasn't too long before one of the marines knocked on the door and told me it was time for dinner. My guards introduced themselves as Mike and Andre, and to my surprise, they had a sympathetic manner about them. It was nice to have someone speak kindly to me, even though it was obvious that they were determined to enforce Captain Abbott's orders regarding my prisoner status.

The mess hall looked a lot like my high school cafeteria. There was a buffet line at one end and the rest of the room was filled with long tables with attached benches. Although the mess hall was full, it fell nearly silent when we walked in. After Andre led me through the food line, I spotted Pete, Vani, and Eve sitting at a table near the back, waving me over. I was so glad to see them that I nearly dropped my tray. I sat next to Pete, and after they exchanged greetings, Andre and Mike sat a respectful distance away, presumably to give us some privacy.

Vani and Eve dropped their forks as soon as I arrived.

"What?" I asked defensively.

Eve spoke first. "Are you okay?"

"Yes, I'm fine."

"Because you look awful."

I smirked. I had put on the navy blue sweatshirt again to fight the chill. "It's this sweatshirt. Not really my color."

"Oh good," Vani deadpanned. "So your looking awful has nothing to do with the fact that you suffered a jolt of extreme terror followed by a crying jag."

"Maybe that too." There was no hiding anything from an aura reader.

Vani reached over and squeezed my hand. "We're just relieved that you're back in one piece."

Pete nodded slowly. "Yeah, and that you're so reliable."

I frowned in confusion. "Meaning what?"

"Reliably stupid!" He guffawed and slapped his knee. "It's good to know there are still things in life we can count on."

As I dropped my head into my hands, Pete reached over and tussled my hair. "I'm just kiddin', sis. Come on, eat somethin'."

The food looked decent, and the smell was tempting, but my stomach was still jittery. "No, thanks."

"Come on," Pete encouraged. "Give it a try. Here." He handed me a piece of cornbread. "This is really good. Lots of lard." He grinned as my eyes narrowed. "We can't have you passin' out on Mike and Andre, can we?"

"Seriously, Cate," Vani said, "Ben said you missed lunch. After a shock like you've had, you need some sustenance."

Ben was sharing a few too many details for my liking. "I appreciate everyone's concern," I snapped, "but if you must know, I'm not sure I could keep anything down right now. I hope that's not too graphic for you."

The three of them exchanged concerned looks. "If you're feeling sick, I can give you some acupuncture," Eve offered.

Guilt tugged at me. I knew they cared about me and were just trying to help. And though I hated to admit it, they were right. I felt weak; I knew I should at least try to eat something. "Okay, fine," I said with a sigh. I took a bite of cornbread. Chew, chew, swallow. I sipped some soda to wash it down, and my stomach rumbled—whether in objection or appreciation, I couldn't tell. "Happy now?"

"Happier," Vani said with a satisfied look, while Eve gave me an encouraging nod.

"Told you it was good," Pete said, taking his own bite of cornbread.

I just shook my head at them and tried not to smile. "Where are Kai and Asa?"

"After you got back," Pete said, "Ben decided to have a word with Dr. Belo—which as you know requires a team effort."

My whole body stiffened. "He *what*?" That scene began to play out in my mind, and I didn't like what I was seeing. I pressed my palms against the edge of table in preparation to stand, but Pete's enormous hand gripped my thigh and held me down on the bench. I was reminded that Pete had spent years handling large livestock.

"Whoa," he said quietly. "Yes, Ben's mad, and yes, he blames Braz for you takin' off like you did. But he and Braz get along all right, and besides, Ben's hardly gonna yell at a man in a coma. So just relax, sit here, and eat your dinner, because if you try to get up and run out that door, you won't get two feet before Andre and Mike over there have you on the ground in plastic handcuffs. And I could be wrong, but I think you've had enough excitement for one day."

Vani and Eve kept eating their meals as though nothing was happening, but they glanced anxiously between Pete and me. "The veggie burger is quite good," Vani offered.

I threw my hands up. "Okay, you win," I said. "You *all* win." Pete gave me an approving pat on the leg before removing his hand. Violently, I cut off a piece of veggie burger.

Vani and Eve finished first. They left me alone with Pete, saying they had some work to do. Pete finished his meal long before I did, but with all of the strange glances I was getting from the other marines, I was glad he stayed to keep me company.

"You know," Pete said as I started in on my broccoli, "I'm not sayin' it's necessarily a bad thing, but you're really messin' with Ben's head big time."

"*I'm* messing with *his* head?" I asked, incredulous. "Pete, in case you haven't noticed, he's letting Captain Abbott hold me prisoner! And he's barely said two words to me since I got back from—well, you know."

"So he's fit to be tied. Don't tell me you're surprised." Pete gestured towards the remaining marines in the room. "Look around you, sis. Think about where Ben comes from. Protectin' people is pretty much in his blood at this point. Especially the people closest to him. And after his dad died, he got even more intense about it. All the security measures he put in at the church and at his mother's house...." Pete tipped his hat back and rubbed his hairline. "Then here you come along, turn yourself into the center of his world, and start doin' stuff like givin' yourself a heart attack, fightin' drug dealers, and danglin' yourself out there as CIA bait and whatnot." He shrugged. "It's tearin' him up is all I'm sayin'."

Pete's words made my heart lurch in my chest. I hated the fact that I'd caused Ben more pain and worry. I was also sick with the thought that he might finally decide I was too much trouble and write me off. But regardless of what was coming, holding me prisoner and refusing to talk things out were not acceptable ways of dealing with the situation. "You know very well that Ben's not the easiest person to deal with either, Pete," I said, "and everything I've done, I've done for good reasons."

"I'm not arguin' with you there." Pete pushed his hat back down into place. "I'm just lettin' you know how things look from another angle."

"Okay, I get that." And I *did* understand what Pete was saying— but one part didn't make sense. "I thought Ben's dad died of some alcohol-related illness. Surely Ben doesn't believe he could've have protected his father from that. I don't understand what that's got to do with his obsession with security."

"I don't know all the details. I do know that Ben found his dad's body, and it wasn't a pretty scene. He felt responsible somehow, like there was somethin' more he should've done. But that's not the point I'm tryin' to make here."

I folded my arms across my chest. "I know the point you're trying to make, Pete."

But he pushed forward anyway. "I know Ben screws up from time to time, and you know I'm the first one to call him on it. But I've never seen Ben fall for anybody like he has done you. I like you, sis, and I like the two of you together. Try to make it to your one-month anniversary at least before you give him a heart attack, all right?"

Our one-month anniversary. If all went well, I'd be done with my ParaTrain internship by then. Finally free of the no-sex-during-training rule, Ben and I could have a *real* celebration. In spite of everything, Pete's words brought a hint of a smile to my face.

"Besides," he added, "Kai is real fond of you, so if somethin' bad happens between you and Ben, he's gonna blame me. He thinks I can control Ben for some reason. He'd make my life hell for a year at least. I'd prefer to avoid that if possible, so anythin' you can do to help me out there would be much appreciated."

The image of Kai berating Pete for not controlling Ben made me smile in earnest.

"Here he comes now." Sure enough, Kai was heading towards our table. "Tell him I'm gettin' his coffee, all right?"

Pete left the table seconds before Kai sat down next to me and grabbed my hands. "Oh my God, are you okay, baby? Really? For sure?"

"Yes, I'm fine, really."

"Thank God. You scared me half to death." Then he pinched me hard.

"Ow!" I exclaimed, rubbing my arm.

"I'd say 'Don't ever do anything like that again,' but I know you will," Kai said. "Next time, though, you'd better at least tell me about it first!"

"I actually did think about telling you, but I thought you might get worried and tell Ben."

"Well hell, girl, now that I know the alternative is you going off half-cocked all by yourself, I promise to keep any of your future crazy plans on the down low!"

"Okay," I said, "I'll tell you next time. I promise. Not that there's going to be a next time."

"There better not be." Kai gave his hair a sharp toss. "Pete went to get my coffee?"

"Yes."

He stretched his arms over his head. "I sure need it after that last session."

I bit on a fingernail and asked, "Is Braz okay?"

Kai waved his hand in the air like he was shooing away flies. "Yes, yes. He's fine. But Benjamin? Good lord, he's all out of sorts. Unnervingly stoic, as usual—he didn't let on to Braz, or anything—but still. It's going to take him a while to walk it off."

I looked down at the table. "I was trying to help."

"Oh, don't get me wrong," he said, patting me on the arm. "I think you *did* help, although I still can't believe you did what you did. I also think it's good for Ben to get his blood pumping every so often."

"Yeah, right." I wasn't at *all* certain about the benefits of getting Ben's blood pumping.

Pete returned, placing a cup of coffee in front of Kai. "Here ya go, darlin'."

"Thank you," Kai said sweetly.

"I'm sorry to interrupt, but I got to get Cate back to her room."

"Oh, that's too bad. At least I got to see that you were okay with my own two eyes. Bye, honey," Kai cooed, blowing me an air kiss. "See you later."

"Bye, Kai," I echoed. As Pete and I walked towards the door, I asked, "Why do we have to leave now?"

"Captain's orders—no dilly-dallying. He's kind of a hard ass."

"You don't say."

Pete chuckled. "And don't worry about Ben. He'll calm down eventually. Just remember what I told ya."

Andre and Mike were waiting by the door. As they walked me back to my room, it occurred to me that I should probably prepare myself for a very long night.

• • •

In my dream it was about two in the morning, judging from the darkness of our old living room and the low-budget infomercial on the television. The light from the set illuminated Mom's face with a flickering glow. She looked peaceful. When she saw me, Mom picked up the remote and turned the sound down.

"Can't sleep?" she asked, patting the couch next to her.

I rubbed the sand out of my eyes. "I must be sleeping if you're here." I sat on the couch and curled up against her. She took the corner of her fuzzy blue blanket and threw it over me.

"Good point." She wrapped her arm around me and rubbed my shoulder. "Don't worry, honey. This too shall pass."

"That's what I'm afraid of." I held up my right hand and looked at the ring Ben had given me. "What if he takes it back?"

"Never going to happen," she said with a confident shake of her head. "Geese mate for life."

I rubbed my eyes again. "Geese?"

"Yeah," she said. "You and Ben had a past life together."

"Really?" I didn't believe in past lives, but I didn't argue.

"You were geese," she said. "Canada geese to be exact."

I couldn't help it; I giggled. "Geese? You're kidding, right?"

"Why?" She frowned at me. "You thought you were the King and Queen of England or something?"

"No, but I figured we'd at least be human."

"All the patterns in nature are the same," she said. "It doesn't matter what species you are. Take you and Ben for example. Do you want to know what happened?"

"To the geese?" I asked with a dramatic eye roll.

She smirked. "No, to the King and Queen of England. Of course, to the geese."

I decided to humor her, since she was dead and we were in a dream. "Okay, sure."

"Like I said, Canada geese mate for life." She reached over and took my right hand, examining my ring. "You and Ben were mates, and you were migrating south one year. You were hungry. The whole flock was; you'd been flying for a long time. But you, my lovely daughter, spotted a really fabulous-looking field full of corn. You wanted to land there for a meal, but Ben objected. He thought there was something suspicious about the field; something didn't feel right. The other geese agreed with him and kept on flying. But not you. You convinced yourself that the field looked fine and all of the other geese were just being too careful. Besides, you'd never been wrong before. So you headed down for a snack. Ben followed you, trying to stop you and get you to return to the V formation. But before he got the chance, boom boom!"

I jumped as she shouted the last two words, holding her fingers in the shape of a gun. "Before you knew it, you were both somebody's Thanksgiving dinner."

"Oh, come on," I said, trying to sound cavalier even though the hair on the back of my neck was standing up. "You're making that up."

"Think what you like." She held up my adorned finger. We both stared, momentarily mesmerized by the two birds intertwined in gold.

"He cares about you deeply, Catie. I know you know a lot about a lot of things, but he knows better how to keep you both alive. You can give him that much, can't you?" she said with a wink.

"I'll think about it." I smiled and nestled up against her, unable to keep my eyes from closing once again.

• • •

Nessa was stationed outside of my bedroom door.

"Oh hi," I said, trying to act casual as I peeked outside.

"Hi," she said, in unison with the other marine who was standing guard.

I'd slept since returning to the room after dinner. The clock on the wall read 9:30 p.m. I was surprised that Ben hadn't come back to talk to me yet.

"Does either of you happen to know where Ben is?"

"He's with Captain Abbott," Nessa said. "They've been working with Dr. Belo and Dr. Gastrell to put together what's on that disk you brought back."

"Oh." I looked down and kicked at the ground. "So he might be a while."

"Yeah." After an awkward moment of silence, Nessa asked, "Hey, can I come in for a minute?"

I'd been wondering what Nessa and the other marines thought about my escapade. It was as good a time as any to find out. "Sure, come on in—although I'll warn you, there's nothing to do in here but stare at the four walls."

"I don't mind." She said something to the other marine and joined me in the room, closing the door behind her. She sat at the desk and I took the bed. "I just wanted to tell you that I think it was really brave, what you did today."

I gaped at her. "Really?"

"Yeah. I still don't know why you did it on your own, and in secret. I hope you don't mind my saying, but that was really dumb. Still, it took a lot of guts. And judging from how many man-hours they've been putting into that disk you brought back, it must contain pretty important information. The rest of the guys and I admire you for what you did, even if we don't agree with how you did it."

"Wow. Thanks." I tried to blink my eyes back into my head. "I thought everybody hated me for putting the marines who had to rescue me in unnecessary danger."

"Hah! Are you kidding?" She grinned. "We love danger! We live for that stuff. Do you have any idea how boring it can be, protecting people? Most of the time we're just sitting around or running drills. Now that we're keeping watch over that newsstand, at least we get to leave this godforsaken basement once in a while."

Oh no—poor Ernesto! "You're keeping watch over the newsstand? Since when?"

"Since they picked you up this afternoon. They'll be discreet, though, don't worry," Nessa reassured. "Captain Abbott just wanted to make sure those agents didn't come back and bother him. Hector said they smelled like CIA."

I hoped to God they'd figured out a more discreet method than wearing camo and carrying large guns in the middle of Friendship Heights. Still, after my run-in with the goons that afternoon, I was glad to hear that someone was looking out for Ernesto. "That was thoughtful of the captain."

Nessa shrugged. "It's all part of the mission. I don't mean to give you the wrong impression, though. Our job isn't always quiet. We've been in some hairy situations, even lost some marines overseas."

Trying to sound innocent, I asked, "Where were you stationed overseas?"

"Come on, you know I can't tell you that," she said with a smirk. "Your security clearance is limited to this project, and it's only top secret at that. No one's going to give you any information that isn't essential to this mission. Not even Ben."

"Well, it was worth a shot. I can't help being curious." Since I was far from certain that Ben was ever going to speak to me again about *anything*, her prediction seemed to be a safe one. "So how much do Kevin and Hector hate me now?"

"They were pretty mad at first, but mainly at themselves for letting you get away from them in the first place."

I cringed. "I feel really bad about that. They were so nice, and they trusted me."

"It's not that. They just embarrassed themselves, and now they're never going to hear the end of it." The way she smiled told me that she would personally see to it that they didn't. "But even they've been giving you props."

Not quite believing what I was hearing, I rubbed my face vigorously. "Thanks, Nessa. I appreciate your saying all of this. But you're right; it was a dumb move. I thought I'd be able to slip out and get back without anyone knowing, but clearly I was wrong. Those agents at the store were a complete surprise."

"They must have had the place bugged and under surveillance. Whatever conversation you had with the owner must have raised their suspicions."

"Oh, right," I said, wincing. "I didn't think of that."

"Why would you?" She shrugged. "Under normal circumstances, you'd never have to think about stuff like that. But it's a different world down here. That's why I was surprised at first that Ben decided to bring you, given how little experience you've had with all of this. But you ran your own covert operation today! I guess you showed everybody what a quick study you are."

With a powerful shot of humility, I realized that if Nessa had been asked to go out and save me that day, she would have, no questions asked. Not only was my boyfriend an honest-to-God hero, so was everyone around me. That realization left me speechless. I felt about as significant as a speck of dust by comparison.

"Maybe not as quick a study as Ben, though," she added. "He must know you pretty well, even after only a week."

"Why do you say that?"

"He must have suspected something to plant that GPS tracker on you."

I had a flashback to our argument about the surveillance cameras he'd put up around my house. "He did *what?*"

"In the messenger bag. Ben dropped the tracker in before you left. Then he got worried about you because you didn't eat lunch or something, so he asked Kevin to get you a sandwich. After they broke the door down and found out that you were gone, they locked onto your tracker."

I covered my eyes. So Ben hadn't bought my story, after all. I'd been wondering how they found me. "Of course."

"It's a good thing, too. If they hadn't reached you when they did, who knows what would have happened?"

I shuddered as I remembered the terror I'd felt while the agents were following me. "You have a point." Given how things had played out, I couldn't exactly argue with the wisdom of Ben's decision to LoJack me, even if it did have me buzzing like a hornet's nest on the inside. Nessa clearly thought Ben had been in the right, though, so to avoid an argument, I decided to change the subject—and to take advantage of the opportunity to learn more about Ben's past. "Hey, can I ask you something?"

"Sure."

"I know you and Ben served together for a long time. Did he ever say anything to you about his dad?"

Her face twisted into a puzzled frown. "His dad? What about him?"

"Well, Ben never talks about him at all. I don't know anything about him—not even exactly how he died, even though according to Pete, it was really sudden and had a big impact on him. But Ben's a total closed book about it."

"Oh, I get it." Nessa nodded slowly. "That's probably because they had a really rough relationship."

My heart dropped. "Rough how?"

"His dad was a heavy drinker. I guess he'd struggled off and on for years. But after Ben joined the Marines, his dad started abusing painkillers, too. Ben was always getting calls from his mom—bad stuff, like his dad was found unconscious and having to go to detox, or he got in trouble for writing himself too many prescriptions. His dad was a doctor; you'd think he would have taken responsibility and done what he had to do to get better. But Ben always blamed himself. He'd say he should never have left home, that it was his job to look out for his parents, that kind of thing. So when his dad died, I think the guilt was too much for him to handle. If I had to guess, I'd say that was why he left the Marines and never came back. It was too late to save his dad, but at least he could go home and take care of his mom."

As she spoke, my heart tried reached out to Ben's through our portal, but all I could sense was an emotional wall between us. "God, that's awful. I had no idea."

"Yeah, it was bad." There were a few moments of silence as we were both lost in our own reactions. Then she shrugged. "So that's the story," she said, signaling that she had nothing else to share.

That was fine with me. Armed with the background I'd learned from Pete and Nessa, I felt more confident that I could talk to Ben about his father without stepping on an emotional landmine. "Thanks for telling me."

"No problem. Thank *you* for bringing a little bit of life into this mission. Just don't try to give *me* the slip, okay? I'm not always this nice."

I held my hand up as though making a pledge. "Don't worry. I'm a committed homebody from now on."

CHAPTER TWELVE

As I spoke those last words, we heard three loud knocks. The moment I said, "Come in," the door swung open and Ben marched in.

I jumped, startled, but Nessa appeared unruffled. "She's all yours," she said to Ben before giving me a wave on her way out the door.

Ben inclined his head towards the door. "Keeping each other company?"

"Yes, actually." When I saw how deeply exhausted Ben looked, the rush of worry I felt pushed aside all of the other emotions churning inside of me. I got up to help him when he started to take off his suit jacket, and to my surprise, he let me. I hung it in the closet as he sank onto the desk chair.

I sat on the bed and faced him, but he didn't say anything. He just stared at the floor.

Eventually I couldn't stand the silence anymore. Wanting to say something positive and uncontroversial, I settled on, "The veggie burgers at dinner were pretty good."

Ben rested his elbow on the desk, rubbed his chin and examined me for a moment. Then he said simply, "Good."

Well, that was better than "Bad," or nothing. A small seed of optimism sprouted.

His eyebrows formed a sullen ridge. "I heard that you and Pete talked about my father."

"A little." Given his mood, I decided the less said about *that*, the better. "Did you get dinner?"

"Yeah, in Captain Abbott's office."

"Oh, right." I decided to risk another question. "Were you looking at the disk?"

He gave me a long, bone-weary look. "Yes. There will be a briefing on its contents first thing in the morning. Then we'll ask you to meet with Belo again afterwards to help clear up a few outstanding questions."

"Of course," I said softly. "I'll be happy to."

Ben rubbed his eyes and asked, "So I've been wondering, what exactly did Braz tell you that made you decide to risk your life for him?"

I bit my lip. The conversation was moving in the wrong direction. I closed my eyes, concentrating hard, and made one last attempt to reach into the portal between Ben and me, to find opening, some way in….

Apparently, he noticed. "If you're trying to read me through the portal, don't waste your energy. I'll tell you exactly how I feel." He came over and sat next to me on the mattress. Then he looked down and, with a labored sigh, slowly raked a hand through his hair. "You nearly killed me today, Cate."

As he spoke, Ben's expression transformed into the raw agony I'd seen when he'd found me in cardiac arrest—and that hadn't even been the *only* time I'd put that look on his face. Tears welled up in my eyes. "Ben, I'm—"

He looked up, locked his eyes onto mine, and pressed his finger gently against my lips. Then he spoke slowly and with extreme care, as though he had rehearsed what he was going to say and wanted to be certain that I absorbed every word. "I know that you're used to being accountable only to yourself. But we're together now, and part of what that means is that we're accountable to each other. Do you understand?"

I *thought* I did, but I wasn't sure how it related to what had happened that day—and it seemed gravely important to him that I grasp what he was saying. "I'm not sure exactly what you mean," I confessed.

"Okay." Ben exhaled slowly through pursed lips. "What I'm trying to say is that the decisions you make don't just affect *you* anymore. When two people are in a relationship, they need to consider one another before they take important actions. Does that make sense?"

My temples began to throb. "Yes, but...."

Ben took my hand, looking at me like a teacher who desperately needed his pupil to understand something. "Yes, but what?"

"But I *did* take you into consideration," I said. "I was thinking about you the whole time."

He looked at me as though I were speaking in tongues. "What are you talking about?"

Here we go, I thought. "That's the whole reason I'm here, right? To help you access whatever information Braz's brain has locked away about what happened to him. Well, while I was submerging into him, I found the cigarette box. He and I both could tell it was important; his subconscious refused to give us anything more without it. I decided to retrieve it so that I could finish what you brought me here to do." I said a silent prayer that he would understand my reasoning. "I didn't *know* that I would be putting myself in danger."

"You didn't *know*?" Ben stood up, pressing his head between his hands as though trying to prevent it from splitting in half. "You're sequestered in a secret subbasement. You're under the protection of a special Marine Corps unit. Captain Abbott told us outright that everyone working on this project could be in danger. None of those things clued you in?" His knuckles turned white as he gripped the back of the desk chair. "Cate, if this were the only time something like this had happened, I'd chalk it up to gullibility, poor judgment, and high impulsivity. But in the short time that I've known you, this is the third time you've nearly gotten yourself killed. You're averaging more than once a week, and trust me, that's above average!"

Frustration and fear rolled off of him in waves. I felt an intense pressure to explain, to defend myself. "I knew you wouldn't let me go without a marine guard, that you would think it was too risky."

"So you *did* know you were in danger."

"I didn't *know*. I thought it might be a possibility." Determined to say my piece, I plowed ahead. "Braz told me that Ernesto—his friend with the newsstand—was tortured by the secret police when they were in college, so there was no way he would trust the cigarette pack to anyone other than a civilian—and *only* to a civilian. He also said that Ernesto has a sixth sense. He can tell right away if someone is military or police, so he would have known if I had guards in tow, even if they were in plain clothes. Then he never would have given me Braz's cigarette pack. Ben, please believe me, I wanted to talk to you about what was going on. But I knew that if I did, you'd stop me, so I had no choice. If I was going to get the information, I had to do it by myself."

The waves of energy coming off of Ben slowed, along with his breathing. I thought he might be calming down, but then I realized that he was just forcing himself to control his emotions.

"You had no choice."

I nodded.

"There was no other way to get that cigarette pack."

I formed the suspicion that Ben was building to a point—a point that would not be in my favor. "Not that I could see."

"Not that you could see. That's exactly what I'm trying to explain." Ben sat in the desk chair and leaned towards me, elbows resting on his knees. "We could have gone in there, convinced Ernesto to let us look around, and found the pack of cigarettes in question. Derbys, right? They're a specialty brand; he couldn't have had more than half a dozen cartons. Where did he keep them? Behind the counter, like every other newsstand owner in the country? Or would we have had to search the store?"

The image of Ernesto being coerced in any way seared me to the core. "He would never have agreed to let you search the place. And Braz never would have told me about any of this if he'd thought there was even a *chance* that Ernesto would be traumatized again—which definitely would have happened if you had busted in there like a bunch of storm troopers!"

Ben shot to his feet, his body a live wire. "Someone out there has already poisoned one person. Who knows what their plans are? And Eve told you about her vision. What makes you think that how *any* of this is handled is up to Braz—or that I would prioritize sparing some stranger a bad afternoon over protecting your life?"

"But Braz is my client! I could never betray his confidence by using what he said to hurt someone he cares about."

"Cate, look around you! This is *not* a mental health clinic, and Braz is *not* your client. What do you think is going on here?"

What was he getting at? Blood pounded in my temples. "We're not at *war*, Ben!"

"Maybe not, but we *are* in an ongoing battle. If only you knew why Yankee Company was formed in the first place…." Ben's face twisted with regret. "That's why I was trying to keep you away from all of this to begin with. This isn't your world, Cate. It's too dark. You don't belong here. Neither do the others. It was a mistake to ask you to come."

Ben came back and sat on the bed next to me, his shoulders slumped in defeat. I realized that he wasn't nearly as angry with Braz or me as he was with himself. I laid a hand gently on his shoulder. "You're right. This isn't my world. I'm not sure I really understood to what extent that was true before today. But if you have to deal with this world, and there's some way I can help, this is where I want to be. *I'm* not sorry you brought me here."

He covered my hand with his, and my heart leapt. "Besides," I continued, "I'm a therapist. I can handle dark. As for Kai and Vani, they have enough life experience to make their own decisions. And Eve and Asa—are you kidding? They're so thrilled to be here they can hardly contain themselves. To them, it's like being in a real-life video game. They're all proud to contribute their gifts to such an important cause, and so am I."

Ben returned my hand to my lap and shifted so that he was leaning back against the bedpost. He lowered his head and sat in silence for several moments. Then he asked, "You wanted to know about my father?"

Startled by the abrupt change of subject, I could only nod.

"All right," he said, his voice edged with pain. "I'll tell you. My father used to go to seedy motels, pay for his room in advance, put the 'Do Not Disturb' sign on the door, and swallow pills with vodka until he was obliterated. Somehow, though, he always managed to call my mother and check in, morning and evening, to let her know that he was okay. One afternoon I arrived home on leave. My mother was frantic. My father hadn't come home the night before, he hadn't checked in, and he wasn't answering his cell. He'd been gone just short of twenty-four hours, so I talked her into staying home and calling in a missing person's report to the police when the time came. Meanwhile, I drove out Route 40 to check some of the dives I knew he frequented. Eventually I found the right place. They said he'd checked in the night before and paid for a couple of days. He didn't answer the phone or respond to knocks on the door, so for fifty bucks, they opened his room for me." Ben exhaled hard as he shoved a hand through his hair. "Finding my father's body in that motel room was one of the worst moments of my life, Cate. But it wasn't even close to the torture I went through today. For fifteen minutes, I didn't know whether you were alive or dead."

My heart liquefied and melted into my shoes. How indescribably horrible it must have been for Ben to find his father like that. I couldn't even imagine… and I had made him feel even *worse*? "Ben, I'm so sorry…." But I had no more words.

He looked up at me, his face a mask of self-reproach. "And you would have never been in danger if I hadn't brought you here."

Like bellows blowing life into banked coals, Ben's words sparked my indignation. I hated that he blamed himself for so many things that weren't his fault, for other people's choices—for mine. I raised my voice, desperate to pull him out of his spiral of guilt. "Don't you *dare* hold yourself responsible for things I do! I'm an adult; I take full responsibility for my own actions. You were right. I didn't think things through today, at least not completely. Everything that happened today was *my* doing, not yours."

And it *was* my doing, all of it. I flashed back to the moment in Ernesto's store when I'd been so scared I couldn't move. Ben's words slowly began to sink in: *You were in danger*. And he was right—I could have died. That thought pulled the air from my lungs and I began to tremble. Blackness crept in around the edges of my field of vision and stars began to form in the middle. "Ben...."

He slid over next to me. "Cate?"

As he wrapped his arm around my waist, I was able to gasp in a little air, then a little more. "Breathe, just breathe," he said, holding me against him. "It's okay. You're safe now."

We stayed like that for several moments. Finally, the portal between us opened, and his affection and concern flowed through, washing over me. Eventually my breathing normalized. I focused on the sensation of his arm, warm and firm, wrapped around me, and let my head fall against his shoulder.

"Are you all right now?"

"Yeah, I think so." Embarrassment sent flashes of heat across my cheeks. "I guess I'm not as brave as some people think."

With exquisite tenderness, Ben smoothed a few stray pieces of hair away from my face. "We both know that's not true."

But I didn't want to talk about me anymore. I wanted to shift the focus onto Ben, and to find some way to ease his pain. "I'm so sorry about your father," I whispered. "Do you want to talk about it?"

"Not now." He pulled the cuff of his shirt over his thumb and used it to dry the tears I hadn't realized had fallen on my cheeks. "Another time."

"Okay." I nodded, relieved that at least the subject was finally open.

He stroked my cheek. "I love how much you care about people, even people you don't know. And as much as it drives me crazy, I even love how courageously you act when you think it's going to help me or someone else. But today you were trying to steer around an iceberg when all you could see was the tip. That's why I asked you to talk to me before you rush in to solve things. I might see things that you don't—especially in a situation like this where you're out of your element. The opposite is also true: there are situations where you'll see things that I won't. That's one of the benefits of working together, as a team—we're stronger, smarter, more resilient."

I peered up at him. The idea of Ben and I forming agreements with one another felt both comforting and oddly confining. "I know what you're saying makes sense. I'm just not used to consulting with other people before I do things."

"I know. I'll tell you what," he said. "For now, just promise to talk to me before you do anything that could get you *killed*. Can you agree to that?"

I had to work hard to suppress a smirk. "Yes."

"Good." Softly, his finger traced the contour of my cheek. "I feel better knowing that we *both* have your safety at the top of our priority lists."

"Hang on a second." I frowned and pulled away from him just enough so that I could look at him face-on. "What about *your* safety? Isn't that *also* at the top of your priority list? Because it's certainly at the top of mine."

He gave me a heartbreaking half smile. "Oh no. That's way down on my list."

I leaned back beside him, eyes narrowed. "That's not fair!"

"It's entirely fair."

"How can that *possibly* be fair?"

"I'm a marine, professionally trained to protect other people, remember? Putting my own safety further down on the list is part of the deal."

"You're a *ex*-marine." I poked him in the chest.

"Yeah, about that," he said, grabbing my poking finger and pulling my hand flat against his chest. "You've used the term 'ex-marine' before. I should probably tell you, there's no such thing as an ex-marine. Some people even consider the term offensive."

If he'd thought that was going to derail our conversation, he had another thing coming. However, I certainly didn't want to offend anyone. "I remember. 'Once a marine, always a marine.' What term should I use, then?"

"Marine veteran is fine. Or former marine."

"Okay, got it. Thank you." The temptation to start caressing his chest was too strong, so I pulled my hand back. "The point is, you're a marine *veteran*, which means you don't answer to them anymore.

As the woman in your life, I say your safety should be at the top of your own priority list."

His eyebrows arched into sharp points, forming an *m*. "That didn't take long."

"What didn't?"

"You getting comfortable with the idea of being the woman in my life." The corners of his mouth twitched upwards. He slid his arm around me and began to rub circles into the middle of my back.

His nearness was making my voice hoarse. "Don't try to change the subject. How many people are above you on your list?"

"Well, let's see…." He ran his thumb along his jaw. "You're number one, of course. Then comes my mother. Then Eve, Vani, Asa, Kai, any patients we're treating, anyone in the vicinity who is in immediate danger of losing life or limb… then me." He grinned. "Pete's not on the list. He can take care of himself."

"That's not funny!" I slid away from him. "There are way too many people on that list!"

He shrugged. "That's just how it is."

"Oh, so I don't get to have any input into *your* decisions? You just get to have input in to *mine*?"

"Of course you get to have input into my decisions," he said, "a *lot* of input. Just not on this."

As I sat there steaming, my mother's words from my dream about the geese came back to me: "You can give him that much, can't you?" I didn't like it, but they were both right. It did kind of make sense to defer to Ben in his area of expertise, at least. I realized that I just didn't like the idea of deferring to anyone on anything. Maybe I had my own control issues to work on—not that I would ever admit that to Ben.

I'd heard people say that relationships required compromise; was this the kind of thing they meant? I folded my arms across my chest. "Okay, look. I'll give you this one—for now. But I reserve the right to revisit this subject in the future, anytime I choose."

An affectionate smile spread from his lips to his eyes, which flashed gold. "That's very generous of you."

I tried hard not to smile back. "I know."

Ben rubbed his forehead, and all at once I saw the accumulated fatigue of the day writ large across his face. "You should get some sleep," I said.

"You're right," he impishly replied. "See? I listen to your input."

"Hah!" I picked up my pillow and tried to hit him in the chest with it, but he grabbed it just prior to impact. Then he used it to slowly push me down until I was lying back on the mattress, my resistance drained by the desire simmering in his eyes. We just stayed like that for several moments, lying there with the pillow between us, held hostage by a magnetic pull.

Finally, with a heavy sigh, Ben got up off the bed. "You should get some sleep, too." Leaning over to help me situate the pillow behind my head, he asked, "Do you need anything before I go?"

"Hmm." I bit my lip. My whole body swirled with heat. I wished fervently that he would lie down next to me and stay the night, but I knew he'd never agree to that. "How about a goodnight kiss?"

Ben immediately obliged, and despite our virtuous intentions, we forced sleep to wait for us a little while longer.

Chapter Thirteen

ParaTrain Internship, Day Three

"Miss Duncan," Captain Abbott bellowed. "It has come to my attention that you were not pleased about being put under guard after you returned from your little field trip yesterday."

Not knowing how to respond, I looked pleadingly at Ben and Skeet, the only other occupants of the conference room. They remained silent.

"Ben tells me that he thinks it's safe to remove your guard now," the captain continued, "but for some reason, that idea makes me uncomfortable. You don't want me to be uncomfortable, do you, Miss Duncan?"

"No," I said, and it was true. At that moment, that was the last thing I wanted. But his glare told me that my answer was insufficient. "Sir?" I ventured.

"Good," he barked, "because I'm keeping the guard on. And rest assured, for the remainder of our time together, if you put so much as *one toe* out of line, it won't be them you're dealing with, but me. And believe me when I tell you that I will make dealing with them look like having an ice cream cone at Disneyland. Is that understood?"

I swallowed hard and nodded.

"Let's get started then." Captain Abbott pulled himself up to his full height and stared off at some point in the distance. "Thanks to Miss Duncan's admittedly brave, but goddamned foolish stunt yesterday—"

Ben gave me a subtle wink, as though to indicate that the captain's words were intended as a compliment.

"—We now have a good idea of what's been going on here. The marines who assisted Miss Duncan pegged the men at the newsstand as CIA. Well, it turns out they were right. The information on the flash drive is somewhat jumbled and incomplete, and some of the files were encrypted. Nonetheless, we were able to gather enough evidence to prove that Dr. Belo was being spied on by some ambitious son of a bitch at the agency. He calls himself Anglerfish, and he runs a small, independent cell that includes three other agents. So far they've managed to keep their little project a secret, even from their own bosses. No doubt Anglerfish wants to make a name for himself and doesn't want anyone else stealing the credit for his ideas, should they succeed. But we'll see to it that his ideas do *not* succeed." Captain Abbott pulled out a chair and sat down. "Skeet, would you like to fill Miss Duncan in?"

"Certainly," Skeet said. His boyish face had become drawn. "You know what Braz was working on—looking at how damage to the pineal gland affects morality, conscience, the sensation of having a soul. Well, it appears that the CIA has a problem, and Anglerfish thought Braz's research might help them solve it."

"What problem?" I asked.

"It would seem that CIA field agents suffer from such irritants as consciences, ethics, and senses of morality," Skeet explained in a grim tone. "These things sometimes interfere with their willingness to perform certain unsavory tasks, particularly when it comes to things like torture and murder."

I grimaced.

"My thoughts exactly," Skeet said. "Apparently, Anglerfish was interested in finding out whether Braz and the oncology department would stumble across a cure for the common conscience via damaging the pineal gland. According to the information on the disk, their idea was to find a way to diminish a person's moral sense without destroying it altogether. After all, someone with no sense of ethics at all might not see any point in remaining loyal to their agency or country."

"Oh my God," I moaned. "That is so incredibly sick!"

Ben added, "It looks like in a real sense, they were trying to create those dark armies Eve saw in her vision."

"Because that's what the world needs, armies of government agents with no hearts, no souls." I shuddered. "So, what—they were spying on Braz somehow, waiting to get the results of his research? I mean, I guess that wouldn't be that hard to do if they had good enough hackers."

"And they do," Ben said. "But that doesn't explain how the CIA's data ended up on a flash drive in a box of his cigarettes at the newsstand."

"Which brings us to you, Miss Duncan." Captain Abbott tapped his finger on the table. "Ben spoke to Dr. Belo last night and told him what was on the disk, but he was still unable to recall the origin of the information or how he got it in the first place. The information on the disk is enough to launch an investigation, but we've scoured the contents, and it's clear that Anglerfish's group was very careful. All of the documents have been scrubbed of any identifying data, and the participants are all referred to only by their code names. We tried to get a positive ID on the two agents you encountered at the newsstand, but they seemed to know the location of every camera in a four-block radius, including inside the newsstand. They managed to get in and out without showing their faces, and their vehicle had fake tags. We think their code names are Lancet and Daggertooth, because the fourth member of the cell, Blackdragon, is female, judging from the pronouns used in their internal communications."

I wanted to kick myself for not being more observant while I was in Ernesto's store. "I'm so sorry I didn't get a better look at those agents. I just caught a glimpse, really, and there wasn't anything particularly distinguishing about them...."

"It's not your fault," Skeet said. "You were focused on other things, and besides, they make an art of not standing out. But if you can get a description or some kind of identifying information for at least one of these agents from Dr. Belo, it could be the break we need in our investigation."

I certainly shared his urgency in wanting to identify whoever had poisoned Braz. "I understand. I'll do my best. But if you don't mind, there are a few things I need before I talk to Dr. Belo again."

Ben said, "You name it."

"Well, first of all, Braz said that he was worried about his girlfriend, Jennifer. Skeet, he said you tried calling and e-mailing her but didn't get any response. He's worried that these CIA agents may have harmed her because she's close to him. His friend at the newsstand said she came in there on Sunday, but is there anything else you can do to make sure she's still okay?"

Skeet nodded. "I can check with the university and find out if she's been going to her classes. Braz said she was studying psychology at Georgetown. If that doesn't work, we can get her home address and check there."

"Thank you. I know that would mean a lot to him. And I know this sounds strange, but is there any way you can find me a copy of a poem? It's called 'The Desolate Kiss,' by Lewin Lima. I think it might be important."

"Of course."

"Thank you." I turned back to Ben. "The last thing is about Braz's office. The plants need watering."

All three men looked at me like I was a small dog dancing on its hind legs and balancing a ball on its nose.

"I mean it!" A sudden bolt of despair drove tears into my eyes. "It's not the plants' fault that any of this is happening! Don't you think there's enough dying going on around here?"

Skeet interjected. "Don't worry. We have a tradition here that when someone leaves, the others adopt whatever plants they leave behind. I'll see to it that all of Braz's plants go to good homes."

"Thank you," I said, blinking the tears back. "Oh, and Captain Abbott?"

He turned, looking surprised that I dared to address him directly. "Yes?"

"Thank you for guarding the newsstand. I'm sure Braz would appreciate that you're keeping his friend safe."

Captain Abbott looked at me like I was some sort of strange species he had never seen before. "That's none of your concern, Miss Duncan. I would advise you to stay focused on your part of the mission."

"Oh, I will. Sir," I called after him as he and Skeet stood and headed out the door.

Ben took my hands in his. "Don't mind Abbott. He's used to people cowering in front of him, not spontaneously expressing gratitude." The lines in his forehead deepened. "Are you sure you're ready for this?"

I took a breath and released it slowly. It was time for me to earn my keep—not to mention maybe make up for some of the problems I'd caused the day before. "I want to be of some use here—without screwing things up, that is."

He put his hands on my shoulders and massaged gently. "Cate, you don't owe anything to Braz or me or anyone else. You've already played a crucial role here. If you don't feel up to this, just say the word."

A pool of affection formed in my heart. Knowing that I was more important to Ben than the mission made me more determined than ever to help him, to prove myself at least somewhat worthy of the feelings he had for me. Besides, I wanted to do what I could to bring Braz some justice, or at least a bit of closure, before he passed on.

"No, I want to do this," I said. "Really, I'm fine. As soon as Skeet gets me the poem, I'm ready to roll."

• • •

By the time we reached Braz's room, Kai was putting the finishing touches on Asa's trance. My body automatically tensed up when I entered the hospital room. Ben must have felt my reaction. He slid his hand under my hair at the back of my neck and began gently massaging.

He and Kai looked around a little awkwardly for a moment

128

until I realized that they were waiting for me to tell them whether to stay or go. "Look, guys," I said, "this is kind of nerve-wracking as it is. I think I would be more comfortable if you left Asa and me to work on our own."

"Okay," Ben said, sounding uncertain. "You sure you're going to be all right? You've got everything you need?"

I rose up on my toes and kissed him on the cheek, then patted the messenger bag. "I've got everything, and I'll be fine. Go on. I'll let you know when we're done."

"I'll be right outside." Ben and Kai walked out and shut the door behind them.

I pulled a chair up to face Braz and Asa. Braz looked paler and somewhat jaundiced, and that awful contraption was holding his eyes open again. Asa sat with his hands on his knees, but instead of the peaceful, meditative expression I was expecting him to wear, his features were hard with worry. I gathered that Asa's consciousness had already taken a backseat, and he was channeling Braz.

"Hi," I said softly.

"Amada," he said gravely. "No one else will give me a straight answer, so you must tell me the truth. Did my little plan put you in danger?"

I reached out to put my hand on Braz's arm, but then remembered he had no sense of touch. "There's nothing to worry about," I said. "I'm fine."

"The answer is yes, then," he practically moaned. "I am so sorry, my sweet girl. I had no idea...."

"Of course you didn't. It's not your fault, Braz. You didn't remember anything about the CIA being involved."

"No. Skeet told me they suspected the CIA, but I thought that was too preposterous to be true. Oh! But to think I put you in any real danger, my dear, it torments me. You're sure you're all right?"

"I'm sure," I said, trying to sound as soothing as possible. "Really. And Ben was looking out for me, so I was never in any real danger."

"Thank God." Asa's expression eased a little.

129

I steered the conversation back to more positive news. "Ernesto said to tell you that Jennifer came looking for you on Sunday. She was worried about you."

"Ah, so she is unharmed," he said with profound relief.

"Ernesto also said, 'Tell my brother that I love him.'"

Asa nodded and smiled. "Of course. We will be brothers always, even after death. It is like that with the people who share your ideals in life, especially in youth. Your souls are bonded forever." His nose twitched. "Amada, did you do something wonderful?"

"What do you mean?"

"I smell a Derby. Did you bring a dying man a Derby?"

Smiling to myself, I said, "Yes, but I'm not going to light it and hold it up to your ventilator. I just thought you might like to smell one."

"Ooooh." Asa groaned with pleasure. "Yes, please, my dear. I love you more than life!"

I pulled the cigarette out of the messenger bag and held it near Braz's nose. There were a few moans of ecstasy, followed by the plea, "Oh, take it away, I can't stand anymore. It's too wonderful!"

I put the cigarette away again and sat back down. Asa grinned broadly. "That was such a wonderful gift. You are truly a compassionate woman, Amada. I hope that Benjamin knows what he has in you."

But I was less and less certain exactly what Ben *did* have in me. I decided to change the subject. "I'm glad you enjoyed it. I also brought a picture of Pedra, the one from your desk. I hope you don't mind, I had to take it out of the frame."

"That's so lovely. Thank you. Please put her under my pillow. I want her close to me."

I gently slid Pedra's picture under his pillow. "There you go."

"Thank you. But I can hear in your voice, there is something on your mind, something you're not saying."

"You're right; there is. It's something else I have to tell you about Jennifer."

Asa's expression became grim. "What is it?"

I tried to find a way to put the facts delicately. "We're not sure what's happened to her since Sunday."

"Meaning? Please, I want to know everything."

"Well, you know that Skeet left her voice and e-mail messages and she never returned them. He tried again with no luck, so he contacted the psychology department at Georgetown. They said she hasn't been to classes since last week. Then he sent someone over to her apartment. Her roommates said they hadn't seen or heard from her for about a week, but they just assumed she was with you."

Scowling, Asa rubbed his chin.

"What is it, Braz?"

"That's a bit concerning; it would not be like her to miss a class. As for her roommates not having seen her, Jenny has a key to my place. She came and went as she liked. I hope she hasn't been staying there—not with those goons snooping around. Will you…?"

"Of course," I said quickly, "I'll have Skeet check into it."

"Thank you." Worry lined Asa's face. "I'm sorry. I don't think I'll be of much help to you today. I've been flogging my brain, but I can't remember any more than I've already told you. You can try to submerge into me again, but I strongly suspect that my brain will not let you back in—not after the way it kicked you out last time."

The last thing I wanted was to cause Braz any further discomfort—emotional, mental, or otherwise. Then, all at once, I felt like a cartoon character with a light bulb over her head. Why hadn't I thought of it before? "There might be one more thing we can try," I said. "It's not intrusive at all. It's a Reiki technique called the Talking Symbol. Would you allow me? You don't have to do anything…." I stopped and silently reproached myself as I realized what I had been about to say.

"Don't do anything, just lie here?" After finishing my thought, Asa broke into hearty laughter. "Oh, Amada, thank you. I needed a laugh after all of that heavy conversation."

Braz's reaction was so unexpected that I couldn't help smiling as well. "No problem."

"Yes, please, go ahead and try whatever it is you were going to try. I do believe we are at that point where, as they say, we have nothing to lose. Are we not?"

I was amazed by his lightheartedness under the circumstances. "Okay, let's give it a shot. I'll try to communicate directly with your subconscious. If I get anything interesting, I'll tell you afterwards. But first I have to figure out how to put my hands on your head."

"Just climb on top of me. Don't mind the tubes and machines."

"Very funny. You know that's exactly the moment when someone would walk in."

"Better yet!" Asa grinned. "You are still a free woman who can do what she pleases."

"That's what you think," I muttered.

"Meaning?"

"Nothing; never mind." I was glad that no one had told Braz about my prisoner status. "Please just behave yourself and don't say anything for a couple of minutes, okay?"

"Ah, Amada, you are a harsh taskmaster," he murmured. "Okay, go ahead."

I lowered the rail on the side of his bed and sat on the mattress next to Braz's shoulder. I closed my eyes and tried to remember the procedure Asa had taught me the previous week during our Reiki training session. Pete had volunteered to let me practice on him. Using the Talking Symbol technique, I'd been able to have a conversation with the subconscious portion of Pete's mind—a conversation that only I remembered afterwards.

I touched the clasp of the chain that held my pendant and hesitated. Kai had made the necklace to shield me from other people's energy and ordered me to never take it off. Not unless I had to remove it to perform certain rituals, that was—Reiki rituals being among them.

I pushed my uncertainty aside and told myself it would be fine. After all, during my training, Asa had given me no reason to believe that using the Talking Symbol technique would be risky or dangerous in any way. *Trust your own clinical judgment for once*, I told myself. *You have to take the training wheels off sometime.* Besides, with

Braz's condition deteriorating, I knew it might be my last chance to find out what we needed to know. I unfastened the pendant and put it on the bedside table.

Taking a deep cleansing breath, I mentally summoned the Reiki healing energy Asa had said would always be with me, waiting to be called upon. Next, I drew the appropriate Reiki symbol in the air near the top of Braz's pillow, followed by another over his forehead. Then, with a bit of twisting and reaching, I was able to slide my hands beneath the frame of the tear-dropping device and place them on either side of Braz's head. It wasn't identical to the hand placement Asa had taught me, but I hoped it was close enough. I felt a catch in my throat as I noticed that someone had been meticulously caring for Braz, washing his hair and keeping his face shaved.

Then I closed my eyes and tried to direct my thoughts at Braz. *Braz, this is Cate. Is there anything that I can help you heal today?*

But all I heard was music—some instrument I didn't recognize that was both haunting and soothing at the same time. I repeated the question. Still nothing but music.

Music spoke to the subconscious; I hoped that meant that I was in the right neighborhood, at least. Then I realized that to a lesser extent, poetry also spoke the language of the subconscious. I decided to use the Lima poem Braz had been thinking about so much recently. Maybe it would create some kind of opening.

I took my hands off of his head just long enough to retrieve the poem from my bag. Skeet had found it online and printed it out for me. I laid the paper on the bed where I could see it. The first two stanzas described the images that I had encountered while submerging into Braz: the stream in the desert, the hands untying knots, the lovers' embrace. I directed another thought at Braz, the next line in the poem: *We were forged together, a double helix, as inseparable as the building blocks of life....*

The music stopped, and there was silence. I wondered if I had broken some kind of spell and ruined everything. I wished Asa were "awake" to guide me. But then, as though from a great distance, I heard Braz's voice in my head, continuing the poem like a call-

and-response: *Tumbling and roaring through the city, then sleeping in the dream we made.*

I felt a jolt of excitement and continued the thought: *So bitter it is to dream.*

Braz's voice echoed: *Better to be blank and empty, sleepwalking through each day, than to know the foul taste of dreams torn away by the same lovers who gave them life.* A searing pain flowed from him into me.

Who tore your dreams away? I thought at him. *For whom is the "The Desolate Kiss?"*

For Jenny.

I gasped. I had expected him to say Pedra. I'd assumed the poem referred to the dream of their life together being torn away when she died. I hadn't heard of him speak of any sadness Jennifer had caused him. *Why for Jenny?*

Because she is the one who betrayed me, his thoughts rang out. *She has killed me.*

My hands flew from Braz's head to cover my mouth. Jennifer had poisoned him? Could Jennifer be CIA? Perhaps she was the poisonous female my mother had warned about in my dream days before. "Oh Braz…."

"What is it, Amada? Did it work? Did you find something?"

There was a dull ache in my chest. I knew that Braz would have no memory of the exchange I'd had with his subconscious mind, just as Pete hadn't after my session with him. Jenny's betrayal had been so traumatic for Braz that his brain had blocked it out completely. I wrestled with whether to tell him.

As though we'd switched roles and Braz was reading *my* thoughts, he said, "My dear, whatever you have seen, please bring it out. All my life I have sought truth, and I do not want to hide from it in my last hours. Please."

I had to respect his courage and his wishes. I looked into his eyes and held his hand, even though I knew he couldn't see or feel me. "You said the 'The Desolate Kiss' is in your head for Jennifer."

"Really? Not for Pedra?" So he was surprised as well. "I thought

I was thinking of that poem so much lately because I have been so desolate without my wife, and we are soon to be reunited."

"That's what I thought, too," I said carefully, "so I went a little deeper, and Braz—I don't know how to tell you this."

"Go on, my dear. Say it out."

I squeezed his hand. "You said that Jennifer betrayed you, that she killed you."

"Oh," he said on a long exhale. "Oh no, Amada."

"What is it?"

"I am remembering something."

Every molecule of air in the room stilled. "What is it?"

Tears began to stream down Asa's cheeks. "I don't know if I can speak it," he said, his voice rough with emotion. "It's unthinkable."

Doubt felt like a weight on my chest. Maybe I shouldn't have told him after all. I stepped over to Asa and dried his tears. "I'm here, Braz. You can tell me as much or as little as you like."

"All right, Amada, I will try." There was a long pause, followed by a labored sigh. Then he again began to speak. "Jenny was over at my place one afternoon last week. I think Tuesday."

I sat back down next to the bed, pulled out the notebook and pen Ben had given me, and began to take notes.

His speech was halting at first, but gained strength and momentum as he told the story. "We had a beautiful session of lovemaking. I was usually the first one to fall asleep afterwards, but this time, she drifted off. I was fully awake, so I went to the kitchen and started a pot of coffee. I tried to get online to check the news in Brazil, but my damned computer was doing some kind of update, and it was taking forever. I didn't think Jenny would mind if I used hers. It was sitting open on the coffee table. It was password protected, but it only took me a few tries to guess hers. It was a variation on Lewin Lima's name."

He paused and smiled wistfully. "Not a very strong password—at least not for someone who knows her as well as I do. Then again, maybe the better part of her secretly wanted me to find out what was she was up to. Of course I wasn't intending to be nosy;

I only wanted to look at the news. But when the screen came up, I recognized my own words—private notes I had written on my research, which she must have found and scanned in at some point. You know when you get that feeling in the pit of your stomach? That awful feeling?"

"Yes," I whispered.

"Well, I had that feeling. So I looked around more. I couldn't open all of the files, but I saw enough to know that she had stolen a great deal from me, and that she was working with other people, some government agency. I found their e-mails. It was quite juvenile, in truth. They had each taken a code name. Jenny was Blackdragon, of all things, and there were others—Lancet, Daggertooth, and one who seemed to be the boss, Anglerfish. I read enough to put together that they wanted to use my research for some nefarious purpose, something about trying to find a way to damage the conscience. Although I was in shock, I had the presence of mind to copy everything I could onto the flash drive I kept on my keychain. Then I heard Jenny stirring in the bedroom. As I slipped the drive into my pocket, all of the pieces started to come together in my mind. That was when she walked up behind me."

My breath caught in my throat. "What happened then?"

"We argued, of course. At first she tried to sound innocent, asked what I was doing on her computer. Maybe she thought I hadn't seen much. But I told her I had seen everything. I poured us two cups of coffee, sat her down, and I let her have it, as you say here in the States."

Cold tendrils of fear crept up my arms. Having just found out that his girlfriend was a secret agent spying on him for the government, Braz had let her have it? And I thought *I'd* done some risky things. "What did you say to her?"

"I told her that I knew her heart, and that she had no business working for these goons." The fire and indignation in his voice gave me a taste of what it must have been like in the room during their confrontation. "I told her that she didn't have to live like that, so contrary to who she really was. I told her that Skeet could find her work at NIMH, that she could do psychology research there. Or if she was too afraid of whoever she was working for, we could go back to Brazil and start a new life."

I marveled at his generosity, his insistence on believing in and nurturing her best self in spite of what she'd done. I began to see why Skeet—and most everyone else, it seemed—had become so attached to Braz.

"She tried to push me away, of course," he said in a softer voice. "She told me that I was a naïve, silly old man. Did she think a beautiful younger woman like her would sleep with me without an ulterior motive? Cheap shots like that. But I know her well enough to know that she is not cold. She is not evil like the e-mails I was reading. And there was a true connection between us—maybe not love, but a spiritual kinship. I kept insisting that she leave those criminals, maybe turn them in if she could safely do so."

There was another long pause. Then, in a raw voice, he recited the last stanza of the poem: "This beaten dog's pure and hopeless hope is kept alive by my subversive heart: somewhere in your mansion of black rooms there is one devoted to me, and to regret. Like a mystic, I sicken and die with this faith."

Hot tears stung my eyes. I wanted to give Braz my comfort, my condolences. Instead, I waited for him to continue.

"I think that's what got to her," he reflected. "It was the fact that I knew her heart, and that no matter what she said, I would never believe she was really one of them. So she had to prove it to me somehow, prove it to herself. That was when she pulled out the pen."

"The pen?"

"Yes. She was so angry but crying at the same time. She said, 'I'll show you who I really am.' Then she came at me and pressed the point of the pen into my neck—not very hard, just behind my ear. She moved so fast, I didn't even have a moment to defend myself. That was the poison, I guess. I felt a slight sting, but I assumed it was a regular pen and that she was making a clumsy attempt at a dramatic, symbolic gesture—going for my jugular, so to speak.

With everything we had between us, all that we had shared and felt for one another…. In retrospect, I suppose I was a naïve fool, but it never even entered my mind that she would actually try to harm me. As soon as she pulled away, the look of regret on her face told me that I had been right; she hadn't really wanted to hurt me. She quickly gathered her things and ran out of the apartment. I was yelling at her the whole time to come back, to give up all of that nonsense and come with me to Rio."

Asa shrugged. "I figured she would be back by dinner. I thought that surely she would think about things and change her mind. I opened a bottle of wine, sat down, and waited. But she didn't come back. As I finished a second bottle, I started to think back to my younger years, remembering my days as a political activist with Ernesto and others. I remembered how we tried to elude the security forces and intelligence agencies, and our trick of hiding information in Derby packs. As I thought about Jenny's activities and those of her fishy colleagues, some old, self-protective instinct awakened in me. It told me to hide the flash drive with Ernesto, just to be on the safe side." He chuckled. "Ernesto must have thought I was going mad when I wandered into his store, drunk, asking him to hold the pack for me. But, God bless him, he simply took it from me without asking any questions. I told him that either I or one of my friends would come back for it." With a guffaw, he said, "You know, when I first started to feel sick, I blamed it on a bad bottle of wine. Thank God I'd gone to Ernesto's before I became too ill."

We sat in silence for some time, as I imagined how Braz must have sat, waiting for Jennifer to return. He had shown so much courage—on his behalf, but mostly on hers—and now he was losing his life for it.

As though he knew where my thoughts had gone, he said, "Don't worry about me. I have no regrets. I have worked enough and loved enough to make my life worthwhile. I am not sad to be going soon. I know that Pedra is waiting for me, and truthfully, ever since she died, I have been longing for the moment we would see each other again."

I could understand something of how he felt. There had been many moments when I'd longed to be with my mother again—so much so that, at times, dying in order to make it happen didn't seem like such a bad trade off. But that was before I met Ben.

"Amada, Abbott's men are going to go after her, aren't they?"

I didn't have the courage to lie to him. "Yes, they will."

"Then do something for me," he said. "She has been taken down the wrong path, but she has a good heart. Please ask Skeet to invite her to help them make a case against the others. If they give her the opportunity to do the right thing, I know she'll take it. Tell them it was my dying wish, if necessary. Tell *her*."

"I will," I said, determined to honor his memory by honoring his belief in her, even if she had trampled all over it. "But Braz, aren't you even a little angry at her? She tried to kill you!"

"No need to be delicate, my dear. She *has* killed me. Hah! Not many people get an opportunity to say that, do they?" When he spoke again, though, his voice rumbled. "Of course I am furious with her! She didn't believe in herself, and so now here I am, stuck on all of these machines. I hope that if my death does anything, it cures Jenny of her ridiculous belief that she belongs among those monsters."

Unbelievable. Braz was dying because of her, but he was still fighting for her. "You know," I said softly, "I think I'm starting to fall for you, too, Braz."

"Of course you are," he said, instantly in better cheer. "Don't worry, I promise not to tell Ben."

I laughed. How was I laughing? What about the situation could be remotely funny? And yet we both laughed, and it felt perfectly natural.

As much as I would have preferred to linger there as long as I could, Braz's mention of Ben reminded me of the contingent of people waiting for me to tell them what I'd learned. "Is there anything else you can remember that you want to share or that you think would be useful to us?"

"Hmm." He rubbed his chin again. "I don't think so. I'm

sure Skeet and your marines will do a better job of figuring out the information on the disk than I could. And you have done quite enough for me already. I'm so sorry that my stupid, brash plan put you into danger."

"It's okay. I'm just glad it all worked out." I thought about telling Braz that Skeet was going to find good homes for his plants, but that felt too much like the sort of thing you would tell someone just before saying good-bye, and I wasn't ready for that.

"Only one request, Amada, if I may."

"Sure, Braz. Anything."

Asa shifted around uneasily, illustrating Braz's discomfort. "These machines—all of this. If you have everything you need from me, I would like to be released so that I may join Pedra as soon as possible."

A cold rock settled in the middle of my chest. My thoughts flashed back to being in the hospital room with my mother as she slowly drifted away from me. "Braz, I can't...."

"No, no, my dear. You misunderstand. I would never put this responsibility on your shoulders. I only want you to relay that message to my physician. That is all I'm asking."

"Oh, okay," I said with a catch in my throat. "I'll tell him."

"I will miss you, Amada, and we only just met." As he continued, his tone took on a new urgency. "You are a rare and precious thing. You must take great care of yourself, because you are not of this world. This world is brutal, painful. Your soul is of the next world, on loan to this one to bring light and healing. Promise to protect yourself, and let those who love you protect you. Otherwise the ugly things will weigh you down, and the temptation will become too great for you to cut your ties to this life and fly into the next one before your time."

Again, I thought of my mother. Her spirit had spoken to me through Kai during my initiation ritual the previous week. Braz's words echoed her description of what had led up to her suicide. My mother had also warned me that if I didn't take care of myself, I might meet the same fate she had. But I had no intention of letting that happen. "I promise. I'll miss you too, Braz."

"Go now," he said. "Tell them what I told you, what I remembered. And tell my doctor the favor I have asked. This absurd, wonderful journey is almost at an end."

I leaned over and hugged Braz as gently as I could, saying, "I'm hugging you right now."

"I cannot feel your touch," he said, "but I feel your heart. Thank you."

"Thank you, too." I caught sight of my pendant on the table and fastened it around my neck.

When I stepped into the hallway, Kai and Ben were pacing like two expectant fathers outside of an old-fashioned birthing suite. "I'm done," I said to Kai. He gave me a quick squeeze and then went into the room to un-trance Asa.

As I turned to Ben and saw the concern on his face, all of the emotions from my conversation with Braz rose to the surface. My eyes again filled with tears. Before I even said anything, Ben's arms were around me. "Everything's going to be okay," he murmured, stroking my hair.

And maybe for the first time, in my heart, I believed him.

CHAPTER FOURTEEN

Ben and I went to the conference room. We reviewed my notes, and I filled him in on everything Braz had told me. As we were wrapping up, Hector joined us to get my description of Jennifer. It turned out that he had been a police sketch artist before joining the Marines. At first, Hector didn't look at me directly and spoke only when necessary. But the tension between us subsided as I described the vision of Jennifer I'd seen when I submerged into Braz, and Hector began to draw. The marines already had her ID photo from Georgetown and some images from security cameras at Ernesto's store and Braz's apartment building, but Captain Abbott wanted to make sure all of our information matched up before they went on the hunt.

Ben left us to our work, taking my notes and promising to share everything I'd told him with the captain. By the time Hector and I were finished, he had drawn what I considered to be a nearly photographic likeness of Jennifer. My genuine admiration for his work further defrosted relations between us. Much to my relief, when I made my awkward apology for having deceived Kevin and him, he accepted it good-naturedly.

Hector and I delivered the sketch to Captain Abbott's office. "That's her," the captain confirmed after comparing the drawing to the other images they'd gathered. "Let's get cracking." Hector and a few other marines who had gathered in the office started to pack various printouts and electronic devices into green duffle bags. I wondered where Ben was.

Unsure of the right method to get an officer-in-charge's attention, I raised my hand. "Um, Captain Abbott?"

His head snapped around as though he'd forgotten I was there. "Yes?"

"Did Ben tell you what Braz said?" I asked. "His dying wish about Jennifer?"

Captain Abbott looked at me as though it were a burden to have to explain things to a civilian. "As perplexed as I am that Dr. Belo isn't eager to have Jennifer executed immediately, be assured that we fully share his desire to persuade her to cooperate with us in nailing those other three bastards. It would be much faster, cleaner, and more cost-effective than any of the alternatives."

I guess everyone has their priorities, I thought, chagrined. Somehow I found the courage to press my point home. "But I think…. I mean, also, he kind of wants you to be *nice* to her." The look on Captain Abbott's face prompted me to clarify. "Not to hurt her, at least. And to reward her cooperation."

Although it was hard to tell because he was always so prickly, I thought I saw him bristle. "I appreciate your concern, but you are out of your depth here, Miss Duncan, and so is Dr. Belo." Captain Abbott leaned out of the office door and addressed my ever-present guards. "Please take Miss Duncan back to her room."

Apparently my guards' shift had changed again. Nessa and Kevin appeared in the doorway. I scowled at Captain Abbott, but he had already forgotten about me and was going over some papers with Hector.

As we walked, Kevin and Nessa chatted amicably, using so many acronyms and Marine Corps slang words that I couldn't understand what they were saying. It brought home to me once again that I was an outsider in their world. It was almost a relief to get back to the room, where my isolation was absolute.

I didn't know where any of the members of our group had gone. No doubt they were all busy doing useful things. But a small feeling of pride crept in as I realized that I, too, had done something to help this time—and without creating chaos in the process. Since there seemed to be no immediate need for my services, I decided to reward myself with a long, hot bath. Who knew when I would get another opportunity?

I left my clothes in a pile on the bed and ran only the hot water at first, filling the bathroom with steam. I poured in a few drops of shampoo to create a bubble bath. When the tub was almost full, I added a few shots of cold water. Then I lowered myself in, invigorated by the sensation of searing heat on my skin.

My hair floated around me like a dark brown cloud. I closed my eyes and imagined that I was in a luxurious hotel suite somewhere else in the world—or better yet, in my own house. I tried to picture the familiar objects in my bathroom, letting my mind's eye wander into my bedroom, my kitchen….

The anxiety of the past few days began to melt into the water. I dunked my head under and surfaced feeling baptized, cleansed. The whole subbasement nightmare would soon be behind me. Ben and I would get back to a normal life, and after I finished my training, we could even start to have a normal relationship.

"Mmm," I purred as I thought about all of the "normal" things I wanted to do with Ben. I closed my eyes and splashed more steaming hot water over my face and the tops of my breasts. Then I made the mistake of opening my eyes and looking down at my body, distorted and wavy under the water's surface. I was pale and soft with outsized curves, and not a sign of muscle definition anywhere. It was a decidedly civilian body, untroubled by hard effort or self-discipline. Kevin had been right; I *was* soft.

I'd been both surprised and encouraged by the understandings Ben and I had reached in our conversation following my escape. But he'd still had to stop himself before telling me why Yankee Company was formed. How many other things was Ben going to have to keep from me forever?

The question of why Ben wanted to be with me once again reared its ugly head. Wouldn't it make more sense for him to choose to be with another marine, or at least someone with a similar security clearance? Then he could be himself without reservation. Was I just a novelty to him? I hoped *that* wasn't it, because novelty always wore off. Or was it really the fact that I was an empath? Of course he might be fascinated by someone who sat squarely in the crosshairs of his field of interest and his life's work. But I didn't want that to be the main reason he cared for me.

Who cares if your gifts attract him? I reasoned with myself. *They're part of who you are, and Ben himself said they would never go away.* Would I rather that he was repulsed by them? And wasn't it better for me to be with someone who could understand me on a paranormal level? Still, when I considered the possibility, something sharp pricked my heart.

The bath was growing tepid. I climbed out of the tub and wrapped myself in a towel. *I'll bet Pedra never wondered for a moment why Braz loved her,* I thought. Even though I knew it wasn't fair to him, I felt a flash of anger at Ben.

Poor Braz was probably lying alone in his room, waiting to die. As I put on some fresh clothes, my stomach growled repeatedly. I would go spend some time with Braz—right after I asked my guard to take me to the mess hall for lunch.

I wondered if it were possible for my life to get any more bizarre.

• • •

Much to my delight, lunch was mac and cheese, one of my favorite comfort foods. Eve and Asa were in the mess hall as well, so we were finally able to catch up a bit. While I had spent a lot of time with Asa recently, most of it had been while talking to Braz. Asa confirmed that he didn't remember any of the conversations that took place while he was in the trance. Much to my relief, he also reassured me that he didn't have any headaches afterwards.

"That reminds me," I said, "I've been meaning to ask you a stupid question."

"No such thing. Go for it."

I was pretty sure that there was such a thing as a stupid question, and I was about to ask one. "Why do you shave your head? Does it help with telepathy or something?"

Asa looked around to make sure no one else was within earshot. Then he said, "I've been shaving it since I was twenty. I had early-onset male pattern baldness, so I figured, *zhoop zhoop!*" He mimed shaving his shiny brown dome with an electric razor. "Instant badass!" He grinned. "But don't tell anybody. I always tell people that being bald is a Reiki thing, that it keeps my crown chakra open."

Eve giggled at that, but then expressed disappointment that Asa wasn't having any more headaches. Apparently she enjoyed having an excuse to stick needles into him. It was some consolation to her, though, that she was learning so much from working on Braz. Never had Eve had the opportunity to work with medical personnel in the same room and on the same patient. She said it was fascinating to collaborate with them and discover how their different methods of healing could complement one another.

Still, we all commiserated about our cabin fever. Stuck down in that subbasement, we were even losing track of what day it was. They both expressed envy that I had escaped for a little while, even though it had caused all kinds of trouble. Eve said that she and Asa were planning a way for us to celebrate once my guard was removed. Knowing that they were thinking about ways to lift my spirits improved my mood considerably.

Asa asked if I wanted him to come visit Braz with me, but I told him that I didn't need to bother our patient with any further interrogations. I just wanted to sit with him; it didn't seem right to me that he should be alone. Eve and Asa agreed, so we decided to visit in shifts so that someone would always be by Braz's side.

When my guards delivered me to Braz's room, I was surprised to find that he wasn't alone after all. Skeet had taken up residence in Asa's chair and was sitting quietly. I knocked on the open door. Startled, Skeet looked up at me.

"I'm sorry to disturb you," I whispered. "I just came to sit with Braz, but I can leave you two alone."

"No need," Skeet said, also keeping his voice soft. "Come on in. I'm sure Braz would appreciate having your company. I certainly would."

I sat in my usual chair next to Braz's bed. "He looks paler."

"He does. I think he's nearing the end." Skeet cleared his throat. "Ben told me what you said, that he wants to be taken off life support. I let his physician know."

"Thank you." I fussed around Braz a bit, tucking in his blankets and smoothing his hair away from his face.

"You like him too, huh?" Skeet asked. "It's hard not to."

"Yeah. He's one of a kind, for sure."

We sat with our own thoughts for a few moments before Skeet spoke again. "Is everything okay between you and Ben?"

At first, I wondered what he was talking about. But then I remembered that he had witnessed the tension between us after the marines had hauled me back to base. It felt too awkward to discuss Ben with a man who was a virtual stranger, though. "Everything's fine."

"Glad to hear it." That was followed by an uncomfortable silence, which Skeet mercifully broke. "You know, the MacGregor Group is very highly regarded at NIMH. Dr. MacGregor does a lot of excellent research on the use of paranormal gifts for healing purposes. I always read her papers with great interest." He leaned towards me, his eyes alight. "Have you talked to her yet about the competing theories about the origins of paranormal gifts? I understand that she's investigating Bronze Age history. Very exciting stuff."

My eyes widened. A prominent NIMH research scientist was interested in the Bronze Age origins debate? "She mentioned it briefly."

"Well, believe me, it's nothing less than fascinating. If I were you, I would ask her to fill you in at the first opportunity."

I smiled to hide my bewilderment. "Thanks, I will."

There was another long silence before Skeet continued, "Is research something that interests you?"

"Yes, actually."

Skeet pursed his lips, looking thoughtful. "In that case, if you're ever interested, I'd welcome your participation in research studies here."

Something inside of me became very still, like a gazelle scenting a lion on the open plains. "You mean as a researcher, or a subject?"

Skeet chuckled. "Well, unless you're looking to change jobs and come to work for me, it would have to be as a subject."

"Oh, of course," I said, feeling like an idiot. "Well, I'm not interested in switching jobs."

"You let me know if you change your mind about that," he said with a conspiratorial wink. "In the meanwhile, though, as a subject, there would be no risk or cost to you of any kind, and no sacrifice but your time. And it would be rewarding—and not just monetarily, although we always compensate our participants generously. You'd have the satisfaction of knowing that you were contributing to science."

I glanced over at Braz, wondering if he was awake and listening to Skeet's pitch. "What kind of research do you do?"

Skeet began to sound like a smooth salesman reading out of a brochure. "Our focus at NIMH is twofold: optimizing the mental health of sensitives, and investigating ways in which paranormal gifts can be used to treat ailments in non-sensitives. We have a wide variety of projects going on at any given time. I oversee the studies involving empaths, which is my personal area of interest—"

Some inner impulse pushed me to interrupt. "Why?"

His mouth half-open, Skeet looked at me as though trying to decide whether I was being rude. Eventually his expression relaxed. "I'm glad you asked," he said warmly. "As a researcher, I've always been fascinated by the question of what motivates people. Through a long and unconventional journey, this interest led me to my work with people with your gift. The ability to actually experience what it's like to be another person gives you a depth of knowledge about others that can't be gained in any other way. Telepaths can read thoughts, but so much of our true selves exist outside of the realm of thought. To a skilled reader, auras provide a good deal of information, but in limited categories. Even the spirits with whom the mediums communicate only share information in bits and pieces. And precognition can tell us some things about the future, but usually those visions only capture a single, potential point in time, and they're often cloaked in the mysteries of metaphor."

As he continued, Skeet slid forward to the edge of his seat, his whole body charged with energy. "Only empaths have the ability to truly know what it's like to be someone else—in your case, on the emotional plane, where the roots of our motivations live. It's a unique gift, Cate, made all the more powerful by your clinical training as a therapist. You have the potential to heal many people whom healing might otherwise elude. And that's just one of the many possible uses for your abilities."

Ben had been teaching me about being an empath, but so far his emphasis had been on protecting me from the costs. It was strange to hear someone speak about my gift in such grandiose terms, and the way he weighed the various paranormal gifts with such cool pragmatism made me a bit uncomfortable. I glanced over at Braz again. Based on their friendship alone, I decided to give Skeet the benefit of the doubt.

"That sounds fascinating," I said truthfully. "But since I've only been with the MacGregors for a week, I know relatively little about all of this. What kind of studies do you do with empaths?"

"We started years ago with basic research, trying to discover what exactly empaths do, and learning more about how your gifts work. Although we've learned a lot, those studies are ongoing. But we've also started to branch out a bit, to explore the possibilities and limits. Currently we're experimenting with reversing the polarity, in a sense."

"Meaning…?"

"It's about directing energy outward instead of only absorbing or receiving it," he said, eyes shining with excitement. "Because you have multiple gifts, you would be eligible to participate in either of our two current studies. The first is looking into whether empaths can project emotions into other people."

Intuitively, that idea struck me as coercive. I couldn't help grimacing. "Why would anyone want to do *that*?"

"There are any number of potential applications, including helping people with impaired emotional intelligence to develop greater empathy," Skeet said. "But if you aren't interested in that study, we have another one on psychic portals. I understand that opening portals is something you can do. We're trying to find out whether it's possible for empaths to open portals to people with whom they've never had contact."

I had only opened portals to people with whom I had relationships of mutual trust. If the first study seemed coercive, the second sounded horribly intrusive. "I don't understand," I said carefully. "What would be the purpose of that kind of research?"

Skeet tilted his head and looked thoughtfully towards the ceiling. "Again, at this point, we're operating from a standpoint of scientific curiosity, trying to put together as broad a knowledge base as possible. But if portals can be opened remotely, then we might have the potential to gain crucial information about people who are stranded, in shock, or—as in Braz's case—unable to communicate due to some injury. We could help soldiers in the field, for example."

"Oh," I said softly, chastising myself having such a knee-jerk negative reaction. I supposed there could be ethical questions, but Skeet's ideas about how the research could be applied seemed altruistic, not to mention quite creative.

He must have noticed my initial expression of distaste, however. Smiling to himself, Skeet took off his glasses and rubbed the bridge of his nose. "Rest assured that these are all double-blind studies with fully informed participants. If you were to become involved, you'd see that everything we do is above board and in the service of moving mental health care forward. We have to answer to the American taxpayers, after all."

"Of course; I apologize," I said, offering a conciliatory smile. "But isn't it sort of kept quiet that NIMH has a paranormal division?"

The corners of Skeet's mouth curled tightly upwards. "I meant that we're accountable to the government agencies that fund our work. But yes, you're right; the existence of the paranormal division is something we like to keep quiet. We work in obscurity not because we want to, but because our stakeholders feel that most voters would not as open-minded as you are, and might see our work as a *waste of money.*" He spoke the last words as though they tasted disgusting.

"Oh, I see." I figured he was probably right about that last part; most people probably would object if they knew a portion of their hard-earned paychecks was going towards the study of parapsychology. "So who *are* your stakeholders?"

Skeet visibly tensed for the merest second before he sat back in his chair and crossed one ankle over the opposite knee, trying to appear casual. "Unfortunately, I can't divulge specifics, but I can tell you that there are several—most of them government, some private. A broad funding base is what allows us to pay our participants so well."

"I'm sure that's appreciated." So Skeet had both government and private funding for research that could be used for good—but could also be used to coerce and intrude on people. I wondered if he had any safeguards in place to ensure that the latter didn't occur. "I'm embarrassed to say that I'm not very familiar with the life cycle of a research project. How much say do your stakeholders have in what research is done or how the results are applied?"

"You *do* have a keen interest in research, don't you?" But I sensed in that moment that he wished my interest wasn't quite so keen. "In your role, you wouldn't have to worry about any of those details," he said in a charming, self-deprecating manner that I was sure had hooked many a research subject. "However, as a respected member of the MacGregor Group and someone with a desire to learn, were you to join our studies, I would certainly be happy to try to shed some more light—perhaps over lunch?"

"That's very kind of you." I was tempted to open up my empathic senses and reach into Skeet a little bit, to find out what his true motivations were. But some instinct warned me off, making me feel that it would be unwise. One glance at Braz reminded me that it was neither the time nor the place to indulge my curiosity.

I decided instead to shift the subject to a question that had been rattling around in my mind ever since our briefing that first day. "I've been wondering, how did you and Braz meet?"

Skeet's face fell for a second—I assumed because his sales pitch hadn't succeeded in securing the "yes" he was looking for—but he recovered quickly. "It was at a conference in Brussels many years ago. We've corresponded ever since—at first, just about our mutual research interests, but over time we became friends. As you know, he came here to work with the National Cancer Institute, but because we're friends and his primary field is mental health, I offered to facilitate his stay here." Skeet looked down, removed his glasses, and began cleaning them with the edge of his lab coat. "I'm sure he regrets coming, now."

I reached out and took Braz's hand. I wondered whether he was sorry that he wouldn't be able to complete his work.

As though he'd read my mind, Skeet said, "I've spoken to his colleagues at the NCI, and we're all determined to ensure that his research will be finished and published." As he spoke, his gaze again fell on Braz, and I saw that his eyes had misted over.

I tried to think of something comforting to say. "I'm sure that would mean a lot—"

But I was interrupted by a knock at the door. Ben came in first, followed by Kai and Asa. Then a man wearing a doctor's white coat and carrying a clipboard entered. He was tall and broad, the silvery-white of his short cropped hair and beard contrasting with the deep brown of his skin. His eyes went immediately to Braz. I stood up so that we could switch places.

"Oh hi, Matt," Skeet said. "Cate, this is Dr. Matt Washington, Braz's physician."

I shook his hand and noticed that while his eyes were kind, the doctor's expression was stony. "Cate," he asked, "you're the one who Braz told that he wants to be taken off life support, correct?"

I nodded.

"I don't have any objection," Dr. Washington said. "Even the machines can't keep him going for much longer. Fortunately, he signed an advanced directive, so we can accommodate him."

"Wait a minute," I whispered in alarm, "you're going to do this *now*?"

Dr. Washington nodded as Kai and Asa went to their usual spots to begin the trance. "If that's what he wants. We'll ask him."

Ben positioned himself behind me and slipped his arms around my waist. "Are you okay?" he whispered softly into my ear.

I swallowed hard. "I just… I wasn't expecting it so soon," I whispered back, letting my head fall back against his chest. As Ben's arms tightened around me, I breathed in his scent and closed my eyes, willing myself to maintain my composure.

After several minutes, Kai asked Asa, "To whom am I speaking?"

"I will miss you, my Greek goddess," Asa said, his voice deep and with a hint of mirth. Asa's mind had stepped aside, and Braz was once again among us.

"I'll miss you too, although I have no idea why," Kai teased. "As you requested, the gang's all here."

"Hi, Braz," Dr. Washington said, taking the chair next to the bed. "You know Kai and Asa are here, but so is Skeet, along with Ben and Cate. Is that all right?"

"Of course. All of the people I would love to be with me right now."

Dr. Washington cleared his throat. "Cate tells me that you want to be taken off life support."

"Yes, Matt. As you said, we both know I don't have long anyway. The closer I get to death, the more impatient I become to see my Pedra. She's here, isn't she, Kai?"

Kai looked at a spot near the headboard to Braz's left. "Yes, her spirit has joined us."

"Good. I thought I saw her in my mind's eye. At least now I know I'm only dying, not going crazy!" Asa's laugh was robust, and the sound brought a few weak smiles to the room. Then his tone grew serious. "Amada—Cate—did you tell the captain what I wanted, my dying wish?"

"I did."

"And what did he say?"

I noticed that Braz hadn't mentioned Jennifer by name, perhaps because Pedra's spirit was in the room. I tried to be equally circumspect. "He said their goal is the same as yours."

"I am glad to hear that. Well, then, we have done all we can do. Benjamin, have you any more questions for me before I catch my train?"

"No, you've answered plenty," Ben said. "Thank you for all of your help. I'm sorry we couldn't do more for you. We'll do our best from here."

"Very well, but I have another dying wish. Please take good care of my friend Cate. She is very precious, but she needs someone to keep her tethered to the earth, or she may fly away."

Keep me *tethered?* I wanted to object, but I wasn't sure if it was appropriate to start an argument with a man who was about to die.

Ben moved his hands to my shoulders as though to keep me from levitating. "Don't worry, Braz. There will be no flying away on my watch."

"Good. All of you, thank you for everything you've done," he continued. "This is not something I asked for, to be sure, but the whole experience has been full of miracles. You have my love and gratitude, and I promise to watch over you from the other side—after Pedra and I have had sufficient time to catch up, that is." It was disconcerting to see such a salacious wink channeled through Asa.

"Thank *you,* Braz," Skeet said, "for all you've contributed, and for your friendship. I'll personally see to it that your research project gets completed."

"That is very generous of you. I appreciate it, my friend. But Pedra is looking at her watch. Matt, I think it's time for me to go."

I looked over at Kai, who nodded. Apparently Pedra actually *was* looking at her watch, although why one could possibly need a watch in the afterlife, I had no idea.

"Very well, then," Dr. Washington said. "Braz, given how medically compromised you are, it's likely that you will pass on as soon as I take you off life support. I just need you to tell me when you're ready."

There were a few moments of silence. Then Asa sighed heavily, wearing an expression of profound contentment. "I am ready."

"Understood." The room became quiet except for the soft beep of the heart monitor. Kai proceeded to bring Asa out of his trance, murmuring in his ear and using his fingers to tap various places on Asa's body: forehead, sternum, wrists. Then Dr. Washington walked around to the various machines, turning knobs and flipping switches.

I kept remembering my mother's last moments of life. It felt wrong to me that no one was touching Braz, comforting him. I slipped out of Ben's embrace and walked over to the side of the bed. I took Braz's hand, even though I knew he couldn't feel it. "Godspeed," I whispered as the beeps grew further and further apart.

The air was so thick with emotion that my throat began to close up. Finally, the heart monitor fell into one long, continuous beep, and we knew that Braz was gone.

At the same moment, like a hand puppet from which the hand had just been removed, I collapsed. Ben caught me under the arms as, of their own accord, my eyes closed.

I heard a flurry of activity and alarmed voices.

"Did she faint?"

"Is she all right?"

"Cate, wake up."

I tried to open my eyes, to speak, but my body wouldn't obey my commands. Instead, it remained completely limp. I felt Ben slide his arms under my knees and shoulders. He lifted me up and held me against his chest, and all at once, I realized that having Ben close to me was all I wanted, all I needed. I breathed him in, felt his body against mine—and fell under a heavy curtain of sleep.

CHAPTER FIFTEEN

Ow! Something sharp pricked my fingertip, but I didn't flinch. I found that I couldn't pull my hand away, even when the next jabs came. *Ow, ow!* I thought the words, but couldn't say them. *Goddammit, what is going on?*

"Still no response." It was Dr. Washington's voice, speaking over the sound of the Tibetan singing bowls. "We won't know for certain what's going on until Asa is ready."

"Any minute now," I heard Kai say.

How embarrassing. I had fainted—and at such a sacred moment as Braz's death. A hot flush warmed my face, but for some reason, I couldn't open my eyes. Or speak. Or move.

I wondered if I was experiencing sleep paralysis. I had gone through that once before, after a long, sleepless week of final exams in college. It happened as I was waking up one morning, and it was a bizarre feeling: I was conscious and aware but completely unable to move. It had probably only lasted seconds or minutes, but it felt like hours. *Wake up wake up wake up!* I ordered myself, concentrating hard on moving. Still nothing.

So it was a particularly stubborn sleep paralysis—but I couldn't have slept through that sharp poking thing. *I must be awake. Open,* I told my eyelids. *Something—anything—move!* But it was as though my body was staging a rebellion against my brain.

Suddenly, I had the sensation of no longer being alone in my own skull. Another consciousness was crowding in next to mine.

"Until Asa's ready," Dr. Washington had said, and there was the ringing of the Tibetan singing bowls. Had Kai put Asa into my head with me? I tried again—this time desperately—to force some part of my body to move. Absolutely nothing happened.

I heard Kai's voice. "To whom am I speaking?"

Was he talking to me? He couldn't be talking to me.

Asa spoke my thoughts: "Is he talking to me? He can't be talking to me."

"Yes, I'm talking to you," Kai said sharply, "but who is 'me?' Cate or Asa?"

"Um, it's Cate, I think?" Asa captured my tone of disbelief.

"Thank you," I heard Ben whisper. Then I felt him, smelled him. He was lifting my torso into his arms and pressing me against him. I longed to put my arms around him, but my limbs were behaving like recalcitrant children.

"Ben, try not to move her too much," Dr. Washington said. "We don't know what's going on yet."

"Wait a minute," I said through Asa, "what do you mean, you don't know what's going on? I fainted, and now I'm having sleep paralysis, right? Why did you put Asa in my head?"

Ben gently laid me back down on the bed. I felt his weight depress the mattress as he sat down next to me. "Cate, you've been unconscious for almost four hours. They ran a bunch of tests on you upstairs in the hospital. You were out the whole time."

Something sharp poked my finger again. "Ow!" I yelped.

"She's definitely awake now," Dr. Washington confirmed.

"Was that really necessary?" I asked, glad that Asa's voice captured my irritation.

"Sorry, but yes," Dr. Washington said.

"This doesn't make any sense, though! If I'm awake, why can't I move?"

"That's what we're trying to figure out," Ben said.

"You mean you don't *know?*" I pictured Braz lying in a coma, colonized by tubes. My heart ricocheted around in my chest.

"We're not one hundred percent certain," Ben said, and I could tell he was making an effort to sound calm. "But at least we've determined that there's nothing physically wrong with you."

"Then why do you keep stabbing me in the fingers?"

"We might not have to, now that I can talk to you," Dr. Washington said. "Do you mind if I do another exam? I promise to be gentle."

"Okay, I guess." It was strange hearing my thoughts spoken in Asa's voice, although his pitch was a little higher than usual. But as weird as it was for me, I knew it must have been even more so for Ben and the others.

Dr. Washington proceeded to do a full physical exam, asking me if I could feel this and that, testing my range of motion, reflexes, making sure I wasn't in any pain. Then he said, "Cate, I'm going to shine a light in your eyes to test your pupil reactivity. Let me know if you can see anything." He lifted my eyelid.

"Ow, yes," I said in response to the painfully bright light.

"Good," the doctor said. "Pupils are normal. Can you see me?"

It took me a minute to focus, but I could finally make out his face. "Yes, I see you."

"Good." He let my eyelid close. "Listen, Cate, if you'd like, we can use the same machine we used on Braz to keep your eyes open so you can see what's going on."

I felt my body shudder. "Please, no! That thing creeped me out."

"All right," Dr. Washington said. "Still, the fact that you can see and focus your vision is a good sign."

"A good sign of what?" I asked.

"That this paralysis must have an emotional or paranormal cause—possibly a combination of the two—but not a physical one," Ben said. "Vani thinks she has it figured out, in fact."

"Vani? Is she here?"

"Yes, I'm here," Vani said. A small, cool hand slipped into mine. "Cate, your aura is completely covered over by that surfeit of negative emotional energy you carry around. I know you manage to keep it locked away most of the time, but it's as though something broke the lock and let it all out, triggering a massive toxic surge. Now it's surrounding you like a giant bubble. I've tried to clear it, but there's so much of it that whenever I begin to make a hole, the bubble just closes in around it."

I desperately hoped she was wrong. I'd had one too many horrible encounters with toxic surges. The idea of tangling with another one did not appeal to me in the least. "But toxic surges are painful, and I'm not in any pain," I pointed out. "And they've never paralyzed me before."

"We know this isn't your usual presentation." Ben again sat down on the bed next to me and stroked my hair. "It's certainly a relief that you're not in any pain, but we think the paralysis is related to the surge. It may be a severe episode of cataplexy."

"Wait a minute," I said, "I remember that word. Your mother used it to describe what happened to me after... you know."

Ben's hand disappeared. "You mean, after the time you blatantly disregarded my instructions, used an off-limits Reiki technique, and gave yourself a heart attack?"

I couldn't believe Ben had the nerve to speak so sternly to me, especially while I was lying in a hospital bed. I hoped Asa was glaring at him. "Are you going to tell me what it is or not?"

"Cataplexy," Ben said coolly, "is what we call it when someone suffers a brief loss of muscle strength—in your case, when you experience an extreme excess of negative emotions. But it rarely involves every muscle in the body, and it never lasts this long. As usual, your case falls outside the norm."

"Of course, the fact that your cataplexy is amplified by a toxic surge could explain the abnormality perfectly," Vani said.

Something small and cold pressed against my chest, and fingers took hold of my wrist. "Her heart rate and breathing are speeding up," Dr. Washington said, "probably due to anxiety. I'd like to put this in her IV."

"Good idea," Ben said.

"I have an IV?" I asked, my throat tightening.

"Only fluids. I'm adding some Ativan and Benadryl," Dr. Washington said. "It will help keep you calm."

"Why should I be calm?" I cried out. "I have no reason to

be calm! I can't move, and I can't open my eyes, and I can't speak except through Asa, who apparently expresses every single one of my thoughts whether I want him to or not! I don't want to be calm if what I should be doing is freaking out. Do *not* put anything in my IV!"

"It's already done," Dr. Washington said. "I'm sorry, Cate, but since you're technically unconscious and you never assigned a health care proxy, as your doctor, I'm responsible for making the medical decisions I deem to be in your best interest."

My positive first impression of Dr. Washington was quickly souring. "I am *not* unconscious!"

"I'll believe you when you can tell me that yourself," he replied. "Let's make that medication a standing order," he murmured to someone.

"Don't you dare!"

But Dr. Washington ignored my objection. "I'll keep you up to date on any new test results. Let me know if there are any changes."

"Braz got a lot more respect when he was unconscious! Isn't anyone listening to me?"

"Of course we are, Cate," Ben said gently. "Just hang on a second. Matt, we'll keep you informed. In the meantime, at least we have the paranormal theory to work with."

"It's not a *theory*," Vani said pointedly. "It's Cate's weirdly strong reaction to Braz's death, made worse by toxic emotional energy. It's plain as day—to me, that is."

I tried very, very hard not to think, *If a toxic surge is to blame, it's too bad Sid's not here.* After all, Sid's body had served as my healing poultice ever since the toxic surges had begun.

Apparently I didn't try hard enough, however. "If a toxic surge is to blame, it's too bad Sid's not here," I heard Asa say, followed quickly by, "Goddammit, Asa!"

"Don't blame *Asa*," Kai said. "He's just the messenger."

"Actually, I already thought of Sid," Vani said. There was a pause, and I could picture the sour look Ben must have been giving her. "They wouldn't have to have sex, Ben," she said, confirming my suspicion. "But he *is* an effective catalyst, and their energies are obviously compatible. If we could get him here, there's a ritual we could try that might allow him to absorb all of her excess toxic energy. The only touching involved would be pressing their palms together. I've never performed the ritual before, but I saw it done once. I'd have to call London for the details."

"Do that," Ben said brusquely. "We'll talk about it when we reconvene in the conference room. Right now, I'd like to be alone with Cate—and Asa, of course—if that's all right with you, Dr. Washington."

"Of course," the doctor said. "But don't stay too long. She'll be getting drowsy soon and she needs her rest."

I heard everyone shuffling around and the door closing. The next thing I knew, Ben's lips were on mine, giving me a brief, gentle kiss that sent sparks zipping through me.

"Did you feel that?"

"Yes," I said breathlessly.

"Oh." He drew back. "Uh, I'm sorry. As much as I'd love to kiss you again, it's just a little bit too bizarre for me to hear Asa responding."

"Yeah, I know. But I'm still glad you did it." Tears burned my eyes and dripped down my temples. "I can't believe you let Dr. Washington medicate me!"

"He's an excellent doctor, Cate—among the best—and he's doing what he thinks is best for you." Ben dried the sides of my face. Then he stroked my cheeks, my hair. "Please don't cry. We're going to fix this."

But that wasn't my foremost concern at the moment. "I didn't mean what I said about Sid," I blurted out. "I don't even know why that thought came into my head."

"Maybe because you're scared, and Sid has always been able to help you in the past." His tone softened. "Now that I'm over my initial surprise, I can see that it's actually not a bad idea. In fact, if you don't get better in the next half hour, I'm going to have Vani give him a call."

I tried to imagine Sid's reaction, getting a call from the new guy I'm dating asking him to come to a top-secret subbasement and pull me out of a coma. I expected that he would come, but..... "He wouldn't be in any danger, would he? I mean, with the CIA guys around? I'd never forgive myself if anything happened to him because of me. And I'd also never forgive myself if having Sid involved made you feel bad in any way." Having my every thought verbalized was getting old quick. "Will Asa *ever* shut up?"

"I certainly hope not," Ben said, sounding a little too pleased. "I'm enjoying having unfettered access to your thoughts. I didn't realize how much you were holding inside. It's nice to hear the entire internal monologue for a change."

"Well, *I'm* not enjoying it. And I don't want you to know everything I think because then you'll know how messed up I am inside, and then you won't want to be with me anymore. Not that you're going to want me anyway if I'm paralyzed. Oh my God, Ben, what if I'm paralyzed for life?" I asked at a near-hysterical pitch.

"Shhh," Ben said. I felt his hands cradling my cheeks. "You're getting yourself all worked up over nothing. First of all, crazy, paralyzed, whatever—you're my girl. That ship has sailed. Secondly, I told you we're going to fix this, and we are."

Ben's reassurances were no match for the chaotic swirl of anxiety building inside of me, which seemed determined to spew every fear I had out into the open. "But what if we can't fix it? What if Sid can't even help? What if I never move again? Or we do fix it, and I can move, but I've lost my gift, and I'm not an empath anymore? Then you *definitely* won't want me—although maybe that's for the best. God knows you'll probably get tired of me soon, anyway. I hate that I can't stop thinking, goddammit!"

But I could already feel the Ativan kicking in. My racing thoughts began to slow. It was as though my body were calming itself down in spite of my brain's efforts to bring on a panic attack.

"Whoa, settle down," Ben said. "Let's put these fears of yours to rest one at a time, all right?" Ben straightened up, and I could picture him ticking off my problems on his fingers as he spoke.

"What if you can never move again? First of all, that's not going to happen. Physically, you're fine. The problems are overwhelming emotions and negative energy. Those are things we know how to manage, and if by some chance we can't fix them, we know people who can. I promise you. We will deal with this."

The urge was strong to bite my lip. "You say that, but I hear an undercurrent of fear in your voice. Now, see, that's the kind of thing I would normally think but not say."

"Then I wish you would speak up more often," Ben said. "What you're hearing in my voice isn't fear that you won't get better. I *know* that you will. What you're hearing is concern, anger and frustration, because I can't stand seeing you like this, and I'm wracking my brain trying to figure out what went wrong so I can prevent it from happening again. You're also hearing impatience because I want to take you in my arms and kiss you until your eyes cross, but I really don't want to hear Asa's voice calling out my name in passion."

I heard a strong note of conviction in his voice. "Okay, I believe you."

"Good. Now on to the next thing. What's this about me not wanting you anymore if you've lost your gifts?"

Tears started to flow again. "I'm afraid to tell you because I'm afraid it's true."

I felt Ben dabbing my cheeks with a tissue. "You never have to be afraid to tell me anything, Cate. Whatever it is, we'll work through it together, I promise."

"Well, I don't want to talk about it anymore."

"Then why did you bring it up?"

"I didn't bring it up on purpose!"

"Fair enough," he said gently, "but now that it's out there, we'll have to talk about it sometime."

I didn't know if it was Ben's reasoning or the drugs wearing me down, but I couldn't stop myself from thinking, "Okay, look. There's a part of me that is worried that the only reason you're interested in me is because of my gifts. Well, not the only reason, but the main reason you chose *me*, as opposed to all of the other women on the planet."

There was a long pause, followed by a baffled, "What?"

"I'm not saying it wouldn't be understandable if it were true. It's your professional area of interest and being in a relationship with an empath would certainly give you a unique vantage point. Plus it's the only really interesting thing about me, so it would certainly explain a lot." Helplessness screamed through me as Asa continued to reveal my darkest fears. "I just wonder what would happen if I weren't an empath? Would you still want to be with me?"

I felt Ben's hands on my cheeks again. Then his thumb gently lifted my left eyelid. As I focused my vision, my heart leapt at the sight of him.

"Now listen to me carefully," he murmured. "I care about you because of *who* you are, not *what* you are. I adore your heart, your soul, your mind, your quirks, your indescribable sexiness, your creativity, your compassion, your sense of humor, your hard-headedness…."

"You adore my hard-headedness?"

"Yes."

"You don't act like it."

"That's because I don't like it when it puts you in danger." He released my eyelid, and everything went dark again. "But we'll talk about that later. The point I'm making right now is that I want to be with you in spite of your gifts, not because of them. Honestly, part of me would be relieved if you lost your gifts. I know being an empath is an integral part of who you are. But the more I learn how much harm it has caused you, and continues to cause you, the better I understand that it isn't always a gift. If you weren't an empath, it would be fine with me. And I would want you just as much as I do now. More, actually, because every time it seems that I couldn't possibly want you more, I do."

My cheeks began to heat up. "Really?"

"Mm-hmm," he murmured, "and I'm looking forward to showing you just how much I want you, empath or no empath—once you're able to move, that is."

The blush spread across my entire face. "Just FYI, it would be okay with me if you wanted to show me now—as long as Asa isn't in the room."

"Which brings me to that third thing you said." Ben sounded intensely focused, like a detective searching for clues. "What was it? Something about you worrying that I'll get *tired* of you?"

"It's definitely not fair for you to know everything I'm thinking when I don't know everything you're thinking."

"I'm *telling* you everything I'm thinking—everything that's not above your security clearance, that is, but that hasn't become an issue yet in this particular conversation."

I *so* wanted to glare at him. "You're hilarious."

"So tell me what put that crazy thought into your head."

"Kevin and Hector. They said they would never have imagined you with someone like me."

His tone grew serious. "Was this part of that conversation you overheard?"

"Yes, and I kind of get what they meant. Like you said, you'll always be a marine, and I'll always be a civilian. There's a gulf there—things you can never tell me, things I'll never be able to fully understand. At some point, I imagine that's going to get tiresome for you."

"Now, that's a concern I can understand," he said softly, "because I've wondered the same thing, but from the opposite perspective—whether dating a former marine would become a burden for you."

"Wait—what?" I hoped Asa looked sufficiently baffled on my behalf. "Why would it be a burden on me?"

"Because it's hard when the person you're closest to has to keep secrets. It's not an ideal situation in a relationship. It's something that has to be carefully considered and accepted, something you have to consciously reconcile yourself to. I was planning on having this conversation with you later, but since it's come up—"

"I don't care about that! So you have to keep things secret. Big deal. Yes, my curiosity will get the better of me from time to time, but I certainly understand it. That's not even an issue. I'm a therapist, remember? There are things I have to keep confidential, too."

"Of course. And I'm glad to hear that you're so at ease with the situation. But that leaves me even more confused as to why you'd think dating a civilian would be an issue for me."

"Well, because if you want to talk about secret military stuff, who will you talk to?"

"Pete," he said, as though the answer were blindingly obvious.

"Oh." I paused to absorb that information. "So I'll have to share you with Pete."

"Yes," Ben said, "something you can commiserate about with Kai. Similarly, I'll have to share you with Simone, your mother's family, and anyone else with whom you might share confidential information, or common history and interests that you don't share with me."

"Oh," I said again. That actually made some sense. My blush deepened as I remembered how little experience I actually had with relationships. "That won't bother you?"

"Not at all. You have friends, family, and colleagues; I can't replace them, nor would I want to. And the same is true in reverse. I don't expect you to be everyone to me—just the most important person in my life."

My heart skittered. "The most important...?"

"Yes. Believe me, that will be more than enough."

I wondered if Asa was biting his nails as much as I longed to. "And it won't bother you that I'm soft and have poor self-discipline and don't follow orders—basically that I'm the opposite of all of those Marine Corps-type things?"

"Why would I mind? Those are some of your most charming qualities." With a touch of sensuality, he added, "Especially the 'soft' part."

I suddenly felt feverish. "Really?"

"Mm-hmm."

I remembered with a combination of arousal and chagrin how easily he'd pinned me during our play wrestling match the week before. "You know, even though I'm soft, I *would* like to win at wrestling sometime."

"Of course. Just tell me ahead of time."

"And you'll let me win?" Asa couldn't hide my surprise in his voice.

"Naturally, if you wanted me to."

As I relished the image of Ben pinned beneath me, he added, "For a while, anyway."

Then I pictured myself pinned beneath *him*. Suddenly, I felt like I was broiling under a hot sun. "Um, Ben?"

"Yes?"

"Can I have some water? My mouth just went dry."

"Oh, I'm sorry." His voice grew tight with concern. "I'd give you some, but I want to get Dr. Washington's approval before feeding you anything. I'll find him." He took my hand. "Is there anything else before I go?"

"You're sure you won't be... upset if Sid comes?"

"The last thing you should be worried about right now is what might upset me."

"Well I'm going to worry about it anyway, so you might as well answer the question."

There was another pause, and I hated that I couldn't see his face. "What upsets me is that I can't snap my fingers and make you well. If it turns out that Sid is the best solution we have, he'll get nothing but gratitude from me."

I hoped Asa was narrowing his eyes at Ben. "That doesn't really answer my question."

"Maybe not," Ben said sternly, "but you need to stop worrying about other people and focus on getting well. Speaking of which, I'll go find Dr. Washington and see about that water for you. Kai will be coming in to take Asa out of his trance. I'll be back soon. Try and rest in the meantime, okay?"

Hit by a sudden blast of frustration, I asked, "How did Braz do it?"

"Do what?"

"Have all of his thoughts broadcasted without sounding like an idiot."

Ben's kiss sizzled on my forehead. "You do not sound like an idiot. And as much as I hate you being in this condition, I am thoroughly enjoying hearing Cate unplugged. So to speak." I heard him walk over and open the door. "Kai? We're done for now."

As Kai came in and started his work with Asa, the Benadryl hit me. I managed one last "Goodnight!" before Asa's mind and mine were decoupled and the curtain of sleep draped over me once more.

CHAPTER SIXTEEN

ParaTrain Internship, Day Four

I heard voices coming from far away.

"What do you mean, he's being held by the FBI? For what?"

"On suspicion of terrorism. They said they got a tip from someone at the CIA."

I must be dreaming, I thought. *I have to stop watching so many spy movies.*

"Bastards. Anglerfish, right?"

"We think so. It's because we've got Jennifer. We expect him to contact us about making some kind of deal."

"Can't we just explain the situation to the FBI? How did they even know about Sid?"

Sid? What about Sid? It sounded like Ben and Skeet speaking in hushed tones, trying not to be overheard. *I hope I wake up soon,* I thought. *This dream is getting freaky.*

"They must have photographed Cate at the newsstand and done a background check on her, found out who she's close to. We told the FBI that Sid is known to us and is not a threat, but the FBI isn't going to release him just on our say-so. They'll at least have to do an investigation, and who knows how long that will take."

With dread, I began to suspect that I *was* awake, after all. My heart pounded in my ears.

"Are you getting any useful information out of Jennifer?"

"Yeah, she's cooperating bit by bit. She's clearly in pieces over what she did to Braz, although she hasn't confessed yet. She did say that they were under orders to eliminate anyone who found out about their operation. Braz was right about her. If we can guarantee her safety, she wants out of the CIA. We can't keep her safe, though, until we catch the other three."

I tried to open my eyes, to speak, to move. *Oh yeah*, I remembered in slow-motion horror, *I'm paralyzed*. Fingers of panic tightened around my throat. Had something happened to Sid?

"Something's wrong," I heard Skeet say.

"She must be awake," Ben said. I felt a hand on my forehead. "Cate, it's Ben. It's okay. I'm here. Pete, could you put that in her IV?"

No, not again! I didn't want to be drugged. I didn't want my senses dulled. I wanted to know what the hell was going on! Nonetheless, I heard the *clomp* of Pete's cowboy boots next to my head as he carried out Ben's instructions. Pete murmured, "I wonder how much she heard."

"We better get Kai and Asa in here." Ben stroked my hair. "Cate, we'll be able to talk to you in a few minutes, okay? In the meantime, everything is fine. Try to relax."

Relax? Was he insane? I fought to move like a caged tiger, but my body was completely uncooperative.

"Cate, Ben's right, you should try to relax," Skeet said. "It's not good for you to let yourself get worked up like this."

Not let myself get worked up? Who the hell did he think he was? A stream of vile obscenities tore through my mind, and I was glad for the moment that Asa wasn't in my head yet. I heard the door open. Multiple pairs of footsteps entered. Then Kai said, "We'll get set up."

I knew no one would hear me, but I mentally cried out, "What happened to Sid?"

"Ow, my head!" Asa moaned. "Geez, Cate, hang on, will you? She wants to know what happened to Sid. She's thinking *very loudly*."

Inwardly, I winced. I didn't mean to give Asa a headache. As far as I knew, up until then, he'd had to focus on a specific person in order to read their thoughts; I hadn't believed he would actually "hear" me.

Pete chuckled. "Eavesdroppin' again, sis?"

"Ow, Cate! Stop, please," Asa begged. "She says, 'Very funny.' She's pointing out that you were talking in *her* room, and she had no way of letting you know that she was awake, so it doesn't count as eavesdropping."

"Cate, what are you trying to do to the poor boy?" Kai sounded as alarmed as I felt. "Try to control yourself!"

I hadn't even purposely directed that last thought that at Asa; he had just picked it up somehow. Guilt made my skin flush even hotter. I tried to quiet my mind.

Ben's voice was firm. "Cate, please. Try to wait until Asa can get into his trance. Everyone, stop talking and let them concentrate."

I heard Ben murmur something in a low tone. Then Skeet said, "Right. I'll leave you to it." I heard the door open and close and felt a sense of relief that Skeet was gone. I didn't want him there when Asa was channeling me, just in case I had any less than diplomatic thoughts about Skeet or his research.

I focused all of my efforts on trying to quiet my mind as bodies arranged themselves around the room. Then, blessedly, I heard the sound of the Tibetan singing bowls.

Time seemed to drag. I had to resort to mentally chanting "om." Finally, I felt Asa's consciousness nestle in beside mine again. I sent him an apologetic feeling, hoping that he would receive it. Then Kai said the magic words: "To whom am I speaking?"

"It's me, Cate!" Relief flooded me as I heard Asa speak my thoughts again. "And I wasn't eavesdropping! I thought I was dreaming part of the time, but did you say that something happened to Sid?"

"Sid is fine," Ben said with a bit of an edge, and I realized that he might not be thrilled that I was showing so much concern for my ex-lover. "He's in FBI custody, but we've seen to it that he'll get the VIP treatment while he's there. Apparently our CIA friends are playing dirty. They figured out that he's of value to us, and we have Jennifer in our custody. We're expecting them to try to make some kind of deal."

"But Sid has nothing to do with this!" I cried out. "Did you say they were holding him on suspicion of terrorism? He's the furthest thing from a terrorist, for God's sake!"

"We know that," Ben said, his voice growing harder. "We told the FBI that he's a friend of ours, that the anonymous tip they got about him is bogus, and that he's being used as a pawn. They have to investigate the tip, but of course they won't find anything. Meanwhile, at least Sid is safe while he's with them. We put a guard on his family, as well—secretly, of course. We also contacted his parents and told them that Sid is doing a top secret job for us so that they wouldn't worry."

"That was thoughtful of you, but they're going to worry anyway," I muttered. "Ben, if any of them get hurt or in trouble because of me—"

"That's not going to happen," Ben insisted.

"But if they're going after people close to me, what about Simone—"

"We've already got eyes on everyone at the clinic and on your mother's cousin, Ardis, and her family," he said more softly. "Now, please try to calm down."

Once again, I didn't seem to have much of a choice. The Ativan was blanketing me like a blizzard quieting a city. "Please stop drugging me! I don't like feeling calm when I know I shouldn't."

Ben laid his hand on my forehead again. "I know. I'm sorry. Like I told you, doctor's orders. We can't allow you to get so agitated when your body is in this state, especially since we still don't know what caused the toxic surge. It's not safe."

I started to feel like that made sense, and everything was going to be okay. Intellectually, though, I knew the feeling was chemically induced. "But if Sid can't come, then how will we—"

"Shhh," Ben said, stroking my hair. "Don't worry. Vani and Kai have been working on some alternatives. But it would help if we had some sense of what went wrong in the first place. In fact, maybe you can settle a debate for us. Vani thinks there must have been a portal opened between you and Braz. That's the only reason she can think of that you'd have such a strong reaction to his death."

"But I know that's not possible," Kai cut in, "because I made your pendant myself, and I know it works. There's no way you could have accidentally opened a portal while wearing it."

"Um…." I wondered if Asa was squirming in his seat. "There was one time when I took the pendant off while I was working with Braz."

"You did *what?*" Kai exclaimed. "Can she feel pain? Because I want to smack her!"

"No beating up the patient," Ben said, but he sounded like he was chewing on nails.

"I *had* to," I explained. "In our last session, I had to use the Reiki Talking Symbol technique to overcome his amnesia about Jennifer, and I had to take off the pendant to do Reiki. Then I got wrapped up in what I was doing, and I forgot to put it back on until the end of the session. I didn't even think about whether I might be opening a portal."

Frustration radiated from Ben. "And it didn't occur to you to tell anyone about this?"

"Why would it?" I shot back. "I was only using the Talking Symbol technique. *That's* not dangerous."

"And you know that, because you know everything there is to know?" Ben stood, and I heard him pacing around the room.

Kai explained in his schoolteacher voice, "Even with the Talking Symbol, if you're not careful, it's possible to open a portal between you and your subject. And if you're with someone at the moment of their death and you have a portal open to them, it can throw a serious wrench into your aura's natural energetic defenses."

"Well, nobody told me that!" I snapped, but my voice was trembling. "You can't blame me for something I didn't know. Besides, I was with my mom when she died. I definitely had a portal opened to her, but nothing like this happened."

"No," Kai said, "you just went crazy afterwards."

"I did *not* go crazy."

"That's a matter of opinion."

"Enough," Ben broke in. "Cate, I apologize. I shouldn't have lost my temper, but you caught me off guard. Why would you use a technique you didn't fully understand?"

"I had to make a spur of the moment decision, and I thought I *did* understand it," I said, fighting back tears. "And the Reiki worked, by the way, which may be the only reason you have your precious Jennifer in custody, singing like a canary. So in case 'Thank you, Cate,' was what you *meant* to say, you're welcome!"

"All right, calm down. At least now we know what the problem is." I wished more than ever that I could see Ben's face. "Kai, would you mind sharing this new information with Vani so she can plan the ritual?"

"Okay, big guy," Kai said. Then he *clip-clipped* out of the room.

After several long moments, I felt compelled to break the tense silence. "Is Kai wearing those stiletto boots again?"

"Yes, he is," Ben said. "Good to know that your hearing is unaffected."

"I can hear you running your hand through your hair right now."

The tension in his voice lessened. "Supersonic hearing, then."

With the mood a little lighter, I tried to keep my mind quiet, but a confession stubbornly emerged. "I *did* hesitate a little before I took off the pendant. But given the pressing need and what I knew about the Talking Symbol, I really thought it would be okay."

"I understand. And you're right; nobody warned you that this could happen," he said, his voice softening. "We've put a lot of responsibility on your shoulders here, and you've accomplished more than anyone even hoped was possible. I'm sorry I haven't said it before, but you have every right to be proud of your work, and I'm incredibly proud of you, as is the rest of the group."

A sudden, deep blush made it feel as though my cheeks might burst into flame.

He continued, "You're expert in many areas, Cate, but when it comes to the paranormal, at this point in your training, you know just enough to be dangerous. Any time you have a question or feel that hesitation about removing the pendant, you should consult with Kai, Vani, or me." Ben again sat next to me on the bed and laid the back of his hand against my burning cheek. "I know that asking for help doesn't come naturally to you, but had you done so in this instance, you probably wouldn't be lying paralyzed in a hospital bed right now."

"Okay, fine, good grief! You might be right. Partially. About asking for help. But I'm not dangerous!"

Ben removed his hand from my cheek, and I heard him flicking his fingernail against what sounded like a plastic tube.

"I am getting enough Ativan!" I snapped.

"Good," he said. "We'll discuss those other issues later. Right now we need to focus on the problem at hand, which is how to get you back to normal so I can kiss you properly."

My body chose that moment to swallow. "You seem kind of fixated on kissing me."

"I am. Incidentally, they're keeping Sid in a five-star hotel room, not in a cell somewhere, if that's what you were afraid of. He's fine."

"I'm glad to hear that," I said, somewhat relieved. "Thank you. But still, this has got to be a nightmare for him. I mean, he's Iranian-American. He's dealt with suspicion his whole life, and now this."

"Don't you have a portal open to him?" Ben asked, keeping his tone neutral. "You can check in on him if you need to reassure yourself."

"That's true," I said, followed by, "Mary had a little lamb whose fleece was white as snow."

"What?"

"And everywhere that Mary went, the lamb was sure to go."

Kai *clip-clipped* back into the room. "Vani has been duly told about the impulsive pendant removal incident."

"Thanks, Kai," Ben said, distracted. "Cate? Are you okay?"

"What's wrong with her?"

"She just started quoting nursery rhymes out of nowhere."

"That's because I'm trying not to think about certain things!" I explained. "Lalalala!"

"Ah," Ben said crisply. "Sid, you mean. All right. We'll leave you alone to portal-check him."

"No," I pleaded, "don't leave like *that*."

Kai scolded, "Benjamin, you had better not be acting like a jealous teenager. Say something nice to the girl before we leave."

There was a pause during which I imagined Ben was glaring at Kai. Finally, Ben spoke softly. "Cate, I want you to do whatever's needed to put your mind at ease."

"Very good," Kai said. "Now come help Vani and me work on this ritual. I'll bring Asa out of the trance. He can sit with Cate for a while. I'll give him something to block out her thoughts."

"I'll miss you," I thought helplessly. Asa's voice sounded as pathetic as I felt.

"I'll be back soon." Ben's lips grazed my forehead. "Then we'll fix this. Okay?"

"Okay."

"Now that we're all okay, can I please release Asa?" Kai asked. "Much more exposure to Cate's unfiltered thoughts, and I'm afraid we're going to fry his brain permanently."

"Thanks a lot, Kai," I said. "Bye, guys."

"Bye," they said in unison. And I was once again rendered mute.

• • •

Once Asa had been un-tranced and filled in on what was happening, he sat quietly in the chair next to my bed and read a book. He opened my eyelid to show me the hemp bracelet Kai had given him. There was piece of black obsidian covered with white veins woven into the hemp—to protect Asa from *me*, of all people. I pushed down a wave of remorse, closed my eyes, and tried to focus on my heart, the center of my unmovable chest. I felt around until I found the portal that led me to Sid.

There he was, awake and blessedly full of life. He didn't feel hurt or scared, as I had feared—more like angry and loaded for bear. I had never seen Sid lose his temper, but as big as he was, I imagined he could be quite intimidating. I also sensed his caring for me, along with his love and concern for his family. That was understandable;

if the FBI was holding him on suspicion of terrorism, it was reasonable to think that his family might fall under the same cloud. But his worry was measured, not intense. It seemed he had figured out that more was going on than met the eye, and he was waiting with stoic patience to find out what it was.

Thank God he's got a healthy attitude about all of this, I thought. I felt terrible. It was all my fault; there was absolutely no reason for Sid to be involved. I felt a flash of vitriol towards the rogue CIA agents, and hoped that before it was all over, Captain Abbott would make them wish they were never born—and maybe let Sid watch.

Except for Jennifer, of course. As much as I hated her for what she had done to Braz, she seemed to have finally joined the good guys, just as he'd predicted she would. I still couldn't bring myself to sympathize with her, but if Braz was the one she had wronged the most and *he* could forgive her, the least I could do was give her a chance.

Not that any of it was in my hands. I didn't even know if I would ever meet her. I certainly had no desire to. All I wanted was to get un-paralyzed, free Sid, and go home with Ben. Was that so much to ask?

While I was checking on people I cared about, I longed to be able to connect to my psychotherapy clients through the portals I had opened to them. But as part of my training the week before, Vani had closed off all of those portals—temporarily, she'd said. She and Ben had told me that I had far too many portals open to other people, and that those openings were allowing in too much negative emotion, overwhelming me and draining me of energy.

In the couple of months between my mother's funeral and starting the training program, I'd become a virtual recluse, unable to work or leave the house. I hadn't realized how dependent I'd become on those psychic connections to my clients to soften the pain of my isolation. But when Vani closed the portals, I was devastated. It forced me to face the fact that, though I may have been helping my clients, I'd also been using my empath gifts in a manner that was hurting me.

So I couldn't check on my clients anymore—but Vani hadn't closed my portals to Simone and my mother's cousin, Ardis. I connected to both of them; they felt peaceful, content. As I sent good thoughts their way, the Benadryl portion of my IV drug cocktail finally hit my bloodstream, pulling me under.

CHAPTER SEVENTEEN

Mom, Braz, Pedra, and I were sitting at the four corners of a quilting frame, stitching away. It wasn't clear where we were; everything outside of our quilting circle was a white fog. Even the quilt was all white.

"This is the one," Braz said, pointing at me. It was a thrill to finally hear his voice. It was rich and melodic, just as I'd imagined. "She's the one who helped me."

"Very pleased to meet you," Pedra said, her eyes full of gratitude.

Then, Braz and Pedra exchanged a look of love so intense that it embarrassed me. I turned to my mother. "Do you have a thimble? I keep getting my fingers pricked."

She tucked a lock of hair behind her ear. "And they're going to *keep* pricking your fingers until you get out of this ridiculous fix you've gotten yourself into."

"Who is? And what fix?"

Although she sat several feet away, it sounded as though my mother were speaking directly into my ear. "Catie," she said gently, "when are you going to learn?"

"Learn wha—ow! Dammit!" I looked down and saw a drop of blood on my fingertip.

"We can't let her stay like this for much longer." My mother's lips formed the words, but she sounded like Vani, complete with English accent. "According to our colleagues in London, the longer she's in this state, the less chance there is...."

"We know," Braz said, sounding like a very grim Ben.

Pedra's lips moved, her voice replaced by Kai's. "The less chance there is she'll come out of it. Well, that's just unacceptable."

179

Mom, Braz, and Pedra waved to me as they were swept upwards into the sky. Once they were gone, my vision went black. I felt myself lying down, perfectly still and unable to move.

Oh hell. I was awake.

"So we can't wait until we get Sid back," Ben said gruffly, "and I don't know any other catalysts we can trust."

"What about Eli?" Kai asked.

"He's canoeing through Canada at the moment. No cell phone."

"Then we have to do this, and do it now," Vani said matter-of-factly. "There's no point in waiting. We do have a double kheir, so there's every reason to be hopeful."

"Every reason? One member of your kheir is paralyzed, and the other will be in a trance," Ben muttered.

"Must you be so negative?" Kai snapped. "Cate may be paralyzed, but she's fully alert. More than that, in fact, if she's broadcasting her thoughts to Asa when he's not even in a trance."

"I'd love to know how she's doing that," Vani mused.

"My best guess is that the first time we shoved Asa into her brain, Cate automatically opened a portal to him," Kai said. "Maybe because Asa's a telepath, the portal came out all screwy, and she can push thoughts into his brain now. At any rate, Ben, Asa will be in a trance, but it's his *energy* that's important. Besides, if plan A doesn't work, plan B is bound to."

I heard the door open. "Hey!" Eve called, apparently able to remain upbeat under any circumstance. "We brought the herb paste."

"And the rat!" Asa said with some glee.

The *rat?*

"Oh, no," Asa moaned, "she's awake—and she doesn't like rats!"

"Leave the room, Asa, leave the room," Kai said. "We can't have you getting a migraine. *We'll* talk to her."

I smelled Kai's perfume as he approached the bed and sat down next to me. "Now look here, you have got to stop shouting at that boy's brain. Try to control yourself."

I hadn't been shouting at him, just thinking at normal volume! But there was no one to hear my defense.

"None of us like rats," Kai continued, "but we have a two-part ritual planned. Hopefully we won't need part two, but if we do, it requires an animal sacrifice. Fortunately, NIH is rotten with rats—clean white lab rats. It's not like we picked one out of the gutter. This one is really cute, actually. If we don't have to kill him, I already decided I'm keeping him as a pet and naming him Little Braz. So relax."

An animal sacrifice? A rat? What part of that was supposed to make me relax? And what the hell was a double kheir?

Ben took Kai's place on the bed next to me. "This is it. We're going to fix everything. All we need is for you to do your best to follow Kai and Vani's instructions."

"That's right, honey," Kai said. "And don't worry. Ben's so sure this is going to work that he even had the nurse remove your IV and catheter while you were knocked out."

"I didn't want you to feel… encumbered when you woke up," Ben murmured. "We'll bring Asa back here in a minute so that you can talk to us. Eve's here, too, and she's going to be doing acupuncture on you throughout the ritual to keep your chi flowing optimally. But you know how light a touch she has; you won't feel a thing. Right, Eve?"

"I promise," Eve said.

So this was it. And everyone was there to help—except for Pete, who I guessed was probably off doing something more Marine Corps-y. The need to cure me must have been urgent if they couldn't wait until the FBI released Sid. A fearful tear crept out of the corner of my eye.

"Cate, please don't," Ben said, drying my temple. "We can't give you any Ativan because it might interfere with the ritual, so you're really going to have to concentrate on not letting your anxiety run away with you, okay?" He ran his fingers down my arm and squeezed my hand. "Everything's going to be fine. And when we're done, I can kiss you without Asa in the room."

I couldn't believe he was talking about kissing me. Then,

helplessly, I began to think about kissing him back. As Ben stroked my arm, my anxiety ebbed.

Kai spoke next. "Okay, Cate, try to keep that noisy brain of yours quiet for a few minutes. I'm bringing Asa back in. Ben, keep touching her arm. That seems to help."

Ben obeyed, and I tried to clear my mind. I heard Asa take his seat as Kai started up the singing bowls. Eve's movements were as quiet as whispers, but I could hear her unzipping her kit and getting her needles ready.

Vani spoke soothingly. "Cate, I'm going to tell you what's going on and what to do. All you need to do is follow instructions. We're going to do a high-powered cleansing ritual to end the toxic surge. Once that's done, you should be able to move again. Kai, how is Asa coming along?"

"Almost there," Kai said as he added more tones to the singing bowls' music.

"Cate, Eve is going to spread an herbal paste on the top of your head," Vani said. "It's to cleanse your crown chakra. It may feel cool and sticky, but don't worry, it washes out."

As promised, I felt Eve's nimble fingers rubbing circles of something cold and thick into my scalp. It reeked of foul-smelling herbs. *Ew*, I thought as I sensed Asa's consciousness sliding in next to mine.

"Ew," Asa exclaimed on my behalf with distinct displeasure.

"Cate, I presume?" Kai asked.

"Yes. Sorry, I didn't mean for that to come out loud."

"It's okay," Eve chirped. "It does stink, but it kind of grows on you."

"God, I hope not," I couldn't help thinking, which made Eve laugh.

"Cate, do you have any questions before we get started?" I felt Vani's delicate hand on my shoulder.

I had nothing but questions, but time was apparently of the essence. "I'll narrow it down to one. What's a double kheir?"

"Ah, well," Vani said, then whispered to someone, "May I tell her?"

"Yes, you may tell me!"

"You might as well," Ben said, but he sounded less than pleased about the idea.

"Okay!" Vani injected cheer into her voice. "Cate, do you remember our class from last week, Parapsychology 101?"

The class where she and Kai had taught me about the Bronze Age connection to paranormal gifts and the scientific versus spiritual theories about their origins. "How could I forget?"

"Wonderful!" Vani sounded genuinely pleased. "Let's do a quick review. Do you remember the five Bronze Age groups or tribes which originally received the paranormal gifts?"

"Um… is that relevant?" I hadn't been expecting a test, especially while I was in a coma.

"Very," Vani said.

Ben leaned close to me and murmured, "Remember, possibly hokum, but the jury's still out and we're keeping an open mind."

I hoped Asa was smiling on my behalf. "Right. Well, my tribe is Caledonia, or modern-day Scotland."

"Very good! Go on," Vani encouraged.

I tried to think back. "Okay, Vani, your tribe is the Indus Valley. Asa's is Egypt, Eve's is China, and Kai's is… don't tell me…." I gave my short-term memory a hard squeeze. "Mesopotamia?"

"Very good!" Kai sounded proud. "How about the five types of gifts? Do you remember those?"

I winced. They'd taught me the five categories of paranormal abilities, but they were harder to remember. "Ah, I think it was telepathy, precognition, mediumship… I'm sorry, Vani, I can't remember what you called empaths and aura readers."

"No problem," she reassured. "Empaths fall under psychokinesis, and aura readers under clairvoyance. Which brings us to the double kheir. As humanity progressed into the Iron Age and beyond, paranormally gifted individuals from all of the tribes began to mix and mingle, compare notes, and try new things together. One of the things they discovered was the phenomenon of the kheir. The word 'kheir' comes from an ancient Roman word for hand, the idea being that five fingers—or four fingers and a thumb, if you like—can accomplish great things. Picture the five Bronze Age tribes on one hand, and the five categories of abilities on the other. Got it?"

"Yes."

"Now that *you've* joined us," she continued, "all five tribes and all five categories of gifts are now represented in our group, and therefore in this room. That means that in paranormal terms, we have two complete hands—a double kheir. The information we have is patchy, gathered piecemeal from archaeology sites and historical records around the world. But we do know that the double kheir is a rare configuration that could potentially make us much more adept at using our gifts than we would be otherwise, so our chances of making this ritual work are greater."

"A double kheir." A rare configuration... much more adept.... My stomach dropped. In a small voice, I said, "So, Ben, you didn't just recruit me so you could have a full set of gifts and tribes. There was more to it, a whole other level of significance that you didn't tell me about."

"What is she talking about?" I heard Kai whisper. "Are the drugs making her paranoid?"

I felt Ben's hand softly stroking my cheek. "No, she's not paranoid." He leaned down, placed his mouth close to my ear, and spoke with soft intensity. "We were going to tell you, but we've had a lot of information to cover. Not to mention that you've kept us a little busy."

"It's true," Kai added. "We had planned a lesson on this for you this week. I even had a PowerPoint presentation with images of parchment just recently rescued from the peat bogs of Ireland, and there was a terrific soundtrack...." He sighed in frustration. "Coming down here has thrown us completely off schedule."

"Like I said," Vani added, "we don't even know much yet about what the double kheir means, or what it can do. We know more since terracotta tablets that reference the kheir were discovered in

China a few years ago. They're purported to have the most complete information found to date, but they're being kept tightly under wraps and haven't been fully examined yet. Only a few people have seen them. Fortunately for us, Dr. MacGregor is on the team from the Smithsonian that's helping to translate and interpret them."

Terracotta tablets. China. A memory rose to the surface of my mind. "Is this related to the discovery of the terracotta warrior army?"

"Yes," Eve said excitedly. "The new kheir tablets were found in a recently excavated underground chamber of the tomb of the first Chinese Emperor."

"Oh, wow." My annoyance was replaced by feelings of awe at being connected even tangentially to such an incredible piece of history. "Well, in that case, I certainly share Dr. MacGregor's fascination."

"You're welcome to discuss it with her later," Ben said gruffly, "but right now, let's focus on getting you healthy."

I flashed back to my conversation with Ben on our trip down to NIH. "Okay, but—Kai? I still don't know if I believe in all of that Bronze Age stuff—no offense to anyone. Is that going to be a problem?"

"Don't worry, baby." I felt Kai briskly pat my hand. "You already have some knowledge of how to use your gifts. The double kheir should give you access to even more knowledge—and that should happen whether you believe in it or not. After all, you didn't even know a double kheir *existed* last week, but we're pretty sure it was the reason why your initiation ritual was so off the hook."

My initiation ritual—the one in which my mother's spirit had come through more clearly than anyone had expected. Also, the strong influx of energy from the Other Side—which apparently was always cold—had turned me into a human popsicle. My mouth went dry again. "Ben?" I asked, tentatively reaching out for reassurance from the only other skeptic in the room.

I felt his hand on my forehead. "Look at it this way. If the double kheir is a real thing, then the fact that we have one here might help. If it isn't real, it's not like we've lost anything. Either way, you have nothing to worry about."

"That's right, don't worry about a thing," Kai soothed. "Are we ready to roll?"

I hoped Asa's body language wasn't betraying how nervous I was. I felt a blush creeping up my neck. "Sure, why not?"

"It'll be fine, Cate, trust me," Vani said. "Kai, go ahead and call the spirits."

"Will do," Kai said. I pictured him resplendent and surging with energy, as he'd appeared onstage the day of my initiation ritual. I wondered if he was wearing the same ceremonial robes and headpiece. His resonant voice filled the small room. "I ask the gods and goddesses, spirit guides, and guardian angels, spirits from beyond the veil, and all those who wish to support Cate Duncan in this cleansing ritual to be in attendance with us—oh, they're already here! Greetings, spirits, I feel your presence. If any of you wishes to speak, please go ahead. We're doing this quick and dirty." There was a pause. Then Kai said, "Cate, I hope you understand this, because I haven't the vaguest idea what it means, but the spirits are telling me that your quilting circle is here."

Gratitude suffused me. "It's Mom, Braz, and Pedra. They came to me in a dream earlier, and we were all… quilting."

"Ah. Okay then." I wished that I could see Kai's expression. "Well, welcome to Cate's mother, Rhona, Pedra, and Braz. Thank you for being here to support Cate. You know how stubborn she is, so any help you can provide would be much appreciated. Back to you, Vani."

"All right. Let's get started." Vani slipped into a smooth-as-silk voice that I knew was supposed to inspire confidence. I did my best to suspend my worry that the ritual wouldn't work and I would be paralyzed for life—not to mention my reactions to the disgusting herb smell, the presence of a rat in the room, and the fact that we might have to *kill* the rat in the room. Instead, I tried to allow myself to be lulled into a state of relaxation.

"Cate, here's what I need you to do," Vani said. "Picture in your mind's eye the black bubble of toxic energy that is currently surrounding you. Then picture it growing larger and thinner, like a balloon that is filling with air. Eventually, it will grow so thin that it will disappear. Does that make sense to you?"

"Yes," I said.

"Ben, you need to step away from her," Vani said, making my heart sink. "No one can be touching her while this is going on or you risk getting contaminated by the toxicity."

"Ben—" I whispered.

"It's okay," he reassured, giving my forehead a kiss before getting up off of the bed. "I'll be standing right here the whole time."

"Start anytime you like, Cate," Vani said as Kai began chanting softly in a language I hadn't heard before.

"Okay," I said tentatively. "Here I go."

"You'll do great," Vani said. "Just visualize."

I had never been very good at visualizing, but I tried to picture myself inside of one of those rubber punch balls I used to play with as a kid. It felt suffocating. I began to gasp for air.

"Cate, you're fine," Vani said. "There is plenty of air inside the bubble. You've been in there for a while, remember? You're not going to run out of oxygen."

I let her words sink in, and my breathing began to return to normal. "Let's get this over with," I mumbled. With new urgency, I imagined someone pumping the ball with air, and pictured it growing larger and thinner….

"That's a good start, Cate," Vani said over Kai's chanting. "Keep doing what you're doing, but see if you can put some more muscle behind it."

More muscle—into visualization? I had no idea how to do that. My confidence dipped. The pressure of the air inside of the bubble intensified around me, squeezing.

"I think this might work better if the rest of us form a circle around Cate," Vani said, her voice tense. "Kai? Eve? Let's hold hands. And keep Asa between you." I heard them shifting around. "Keep visualizing," she urged.

"Ben," I blurted out. "I want Ben in the circle." I didn't know why, but it felt important to me that he be a part of the ritual.

"You heard the lady. Let him in," Kai said, and I heard more movement.

"I'm here," Ben said softly.

Gradually, the air in the room began to vibrate. At first, I just felt it against my skin. Then, ever so slowly, the vibrations worked their way into my body. It felt as though every cell inside of me and every molecule in the room were aligning to the same rhythm, pulsing in unison.

"Can anyone else feel that?" I whispered.

"Yes, we all feel it," Vani said. "It must be the energy of the double kheir. See if you can tap into it and use it."

Again, I had no idea how to do that. But somewhere beyond the edges of the ball, I thought I could see Mom, Braz and Pedra sitting at the quilting frame, urging me on. As I tried to relax and focus inward, a quiet sense of knowing bloomed inside of me, like a long-forgotten algebra equation popping into my head just when I needed it. All at once, I knew exactly how to harness the rhythm of the vibrations in the air. I wondered if the double kheir was actually working—unlocking more knowledge about how to use my gifts. In any case, my self-doubt was dislodged by certainty as I willed the pulsating energy to press against inside surface of the ball and push it out further—and as I willed it, the energy obeyed.

But as the surface of the black ball stretched further out, the pressure of the air around me grew, intensifying until it became painful. Eventually, it reached a point where I couldn't stand it anymore. "Please, someone help—"

Then, with a sudden popping sensation, the pressure disappeared, and the ball along with it.

"And we're done!" Vani announced triumphantly.

The vibrations died down as Kai's chanting faded into silence.

"Whoa, that was cool," Eve said, awestruck.

"Told you," Kai said.

"Is it gone?" I asked, disbelieving. "I mean, really gone?"

There was a moment of silence, and I worried that I might have disappeared along with the ball. Finally, Vani spoke. "Yes—sorry, I was just double-checking. Yes, it's gone! Great job, everyone. The ritual worked like a charm. The toxic surge has disappeared, along with all of your built-up negative energy. Cate, as long as you do regular cleansing meditations it shouldn't accumulate like that again—and that means no more toxic surges."

I went on a quick internal hunt to try to find some remnants of the toxic energy, but came up empty-handed. "Oh, Vani, thank you so much! Everybody, thank you. I can't believe it." There was another silence that lasted a few seconds too long. "What's wrong? Why is everybody so quiet?"

"Nothing's wrong," Kai said tentatively. "It's just that we were hoping that once the toxic surge was over, you'd be talking to us on your own, not through Asa."

"Oh, well let me try." I sent a feeling of gratitude to Asa's consciousness and channeled my efforts into speaking. I tried desperately to push air from my lungs through my vocal cords and out from between my lips—but nothing happened.

"I'm sorry, Ben," Vani said softly. "I think we might have to move on to plan B."

"Hang on a minute," Eve said excitedly. "I think I saw her eyelid move!"

My heart jumped. "Really?"

"Yes! Wait, here. Let me adjust a few needles. Okay. Try now."

Open, my mind ordered my eyelids. They obeyed—then closed immediately. "Ow! Can someone please turn the lights off or down or something?"

"Yes, yes!" Vani chirped. "Okay, try again."

Cautiously, I opened my eyes again. Someone had turned off the bright overhead fluorescents, leaving only the warm light of the bedside lamp. It was still a little bright, but my vision adjusted quickly.

"Look," Eve said, her grinning face filling my line of sight, "she can open her eyes! Hi, Cate!"

"Hi, Eve!" But my eyes filled with tears as I realized that I still couldn't speak or move any other part of my body.

"Oh, don't cry," Eve said, her face contorting with worry. "This is a good thing! Ben?"

But he was already there, sitting on the bed with his hands on my shoulders, staring down at me with his caring, worried, handsome, squared-off, I-dare-anything-to-go-wrong face. "Hi," he said simply.

"Hi." My tears kept flowing, but this time they were tears of joy at being able to look at Ben for a prolonged period under my own power. "Does this mean we have to kill the rat?"

Ben, Vani and Kai exchanged a heavy glance. Then Ben turned back to me, placed his hand on my cheek and said, "Maybe."

"Oh no." More tears fell. After all, they had already named the rat Little Braz. "But if my eyelids are working now, maybe if we wait a few minutes everything else will start working. Maybe it's only a matter of time. If Eve moves some more needles around…."

Ben looked over at Eve. Then he shook his head. "No, I'm sorry, Cate. I'm very pleased that you can open your eyes, but Dr. Washington warned us not to get too excited if this happened. He said that even in coma patients with locked-in syndrome, frequently their eyes are still able to move. We could wait and see if more of your muscles regain function. But according to Vani's colleagues, your full recovery is best assured by doing the second part of the ritual as soon as possible."

Chapter Eighteen

My heart felt like it was falling down a flight of stairs. "So you're saying it's now or never?"

"Don't worry about never. We're going to take care of this now," Ben said, his voice hard with determination. "It'll be over before you know it. Vani, go ahead."

She made an admirable attempt at sounding confident. "Cate, this ritual is a bit different from the last one. It requires the participation of someone with whom you share a close bond. Fortunately...." She smiled tentatively and pointed at Ben. "The ritual will allow Ben to empathically submerge into you, even though he's not an empath. He'll enter your consciousness through the portal between you. Then he'll track down whatever emotion caused the state of paralysis in the first place and resolve it somehow. After that, you should be un-paralyzed."

"Resolve it *somehow*?" I asked as the pitch of Asa's voice rose. "But what if he can't?"

"I will," Ben insisted. "We'll do it together. Tell your anxiety to take five, and just focus on Vani's instructions."

"Okay, I'll try," I whimpered. My skin turned to gooseflesh. "Ben, I'm cold."

In a flash, Ben was covering me with another blanket and rubbing my arms. "Better?" he whispered.

"Yeah," I whispered back, my heart pulled helplessly towards his. "Thanks."

"Okay, first," Vani said, "everyone needs to turn to face the wall and close their eyes. Except for Ben, of course."

"What—why?" I asked.

Ben gave me an impatient "stop asking questions" look—then began removing his sweatshirt.

"Because the ritual requires you two to undress and lie together in a very specific position," Vani explained as she rotated Asa's chair to face away from us. "And don't worry about the rat. We only have to kill it if Ben gets paralyzed, too. In that case, Kai is very adept at animal sacrifice. The rat won't feel a thing."

"Wait a minute!" I objected as everyone but Ben turned their backs. "Why aren't you guys telling me everything? No one said anything about there being a chance *Ben* could end up paralyzed. We are not doing this!"

"It's not up to you," Ben said.

A tornado of panic and outrage swirled through me. "I'm the one you're doing the ritual *for*, for God's sake! Forget it, there is no—God, you undress fast," I said, shocked to suddenly find Ben in his boxers and socks. To my horror, I began to salivate.

He arched an eyebrow at me. "Now might be a good time to think of some of those nursery rhymes, because I'm about to take off the rest of my clothes. And you're next."

"But we can't do this!" I cried out. "It's going to be like the geese all over again!"

Ben stopped in mid-sock removal. "The *what*?"

"My mother told me in a dream that we were geese in a past life, and I got you shot!"

Ben shook his head and continued to remove his sock. "I don't believe in past lives."

Kai looked toward the ceiling. "Oh, please, Benjamin, don't be an ignoramus."

Ben put his bare foot on the floor and looked into my eyes, his focus intense. "Cate, look around you. Don't you think you have enough things to worry about in *this* life without being concerned with what happened in *other* ones?"

I barely had the courage to whisper, "But if anything happens to you—"

"Listen to me." Ben rested his hand on my knee. "Nothing

is going to happen to me. We are going to get this done, and it's happening right now. So come on. Nursery rhymes. Let's go." Ben started removing his other sock.

"Oh for the love of all that's holy!" I tried and failed to close my eyes, unable to tear them away from Ben. Something tickled my chin. "Please don't let that be drool," I whispered before out of sheer mortification, I forced my mind back to nursery rhymes. "Mary had a little lamb whose fleece was white as snow. And everywhere that Mary went the lamb was sure to aieee!" Asa gave a brilliant rendition of the squeal I would have made.

Ben had begun to pull his boxers off, but stopped at Asa's sound of alarm. "The lamb was sure to what?" Ben prompted as he tugged down on the waistband.

There was no way that I was going to allow my first glimpse of Ben in his full glory to take place in a room full of other people while I lay there paralyzed. I closed my eyes as quickly as I could— but not before catching a glimpse of an image on Ben's hip: a vicious-looking black dog with sharp teeth bared. "Good grief," I exclaimed, "what is *that*?"

"Oh honey, *please*," Kai said.

"She's talking about my tattoo," Ben said sternly as I slowly died of embarrassment. "That's Tank."

"Oh, the dog Yankee Company used to work with. A Rottweiler, right?" I squeaked out, grateful for the distraction. "Pete told me he was the reason they nicknamed you Rottie."

"That's right."

"He also said you and Tank really bonded, but I didn't realize to what extent."

"Pete talks too much," Ben grunted.

Kai chimed in, "That's the first time I've ever heard *that* complaint."

He had a point; Pete wasn't exactly known for being verbose. "What happened to Tank?" I asked.

"The mission ended," Ben said. "He got transferred, we got transferred."

"Oh. I'm sorry." Clearly Ben didn't want to discuss Tank anymore, but I'd forgotten where I was in the nursery rhyme. I shifted over to "one Mississippi, two Mississippi," strangling out number after number as my evidently inked, naked boyfriend proceeded to take off my hospital gown and climb into bed next to me. As terrified as I was of what might happen during the ritual—or worse, afterwards, if it *didn't* work—all of my nerve endings zinged to life as Ben turned me onto my side and slid his body in front of mine, facing me.

"Twenty-four Mississippi…" I opened my eyes and locked them onto his. "Twenty-five Mississippi…"

"Stay calm," Ben murmured. "Your breathing and pulse are too rapid, and your eyes are turning grey again. I need you to focus."

I was trying, but every point of heat where Ben's skin touched mine felt like detonators set to explode. "That's easy for you to say!"

Eve giggled.

Ben proceeded to twine our legs together like a knot. Then he slid one of my arms under his head and the other around his waist. He pulled one of the blankets up over us and put his arms in the same position around me. Then he looked into my eyes, and I could see that he was painstakingly suppressing whatever emotions he might be feeling as though in preparation for battle. "Okay, Vani, we're ready."

The Mississippis were weakening. If I didn't think of something else fast, I knew Asa was going to start saying things that I wouldn't want anyone but Ben to hear. "Vani, I swear to God, if you don't give me something to think about right now, I'm going to start having Asa sing *Top Hits from the Eighties!*"

"Oh good heavens. All right, listen," Vani said. "Cate, you need to open your consciousness up to allow Ben in. He's been training for this, so don't worry. Once he's inside, he'll know what to do. For now, just keep thinking the word, 'open.' Use the portal between you. Visualize the flow reversing so that *he* can enter *your* consciousness, instead of the other way around. Okay?"

I kept my eyes locked on Ben's as panic surged through me.

I had never let anyone enter my consciousness before. What if Ben didn't like what he saw in there? What if he found it repulsive or disturbing?

"Stop it," he murmured.

"Are you in my head already?" I asked in amazement.

"No, I just know you, and I know that look in your eyes. Stop worrying." He stared through me like a laser. "Now let me in."

"I'm trying! Open, open, open."

I soaked up the caring and resolve in Ben's gaze. Losing myself in my chant, I visualized the portal between us opening wide and the flow reversing. "Okay, I think it's starting to—*oh!*"

A wall of Ben slammed into me, invading me full-force. I felt him charging around inside of me. It wasn't painful exactly, but I felt like the china shop into which the proverbial bull had just been released. Or possibly a marine.

"What are you *doing* in there?" I demanded.

"Establishing a perimeter," Ben said. "Then I'll locate this paralyzing emotion of yours, fix it, and you'll be back in fighting form. Okay?"

"Establishing a perimeter?"

"Give me a heads-up if you feel me coming into contact with something particularly painful," Ben said. "That'll probably be pay dirt. Speaking of which, what's this thing?"

"Ow!" I cried out as Ben gave something inside of me a hard poke.

"What is that?"

"I don't know—ow!" I cried again as Ben poked again. "Stop that!"

"You don't know? Well, take a look at it and tell me."

"Okay, all right! Just hang on a minute." I closed my eyes and turned my attention inward to the now-bruised point Ben had poked. At once, I was transported to the inner landscape of my own consciousness. I was standing in a room with four white walls but no ceiling, only sky above. A replica of Ben stood nearby, wearing full camo and glowering with his arms crossed.

The painful object Ben had found lay on the ground. It was smallish, about the size of a bed pillow, but dark red and almost rubbery in consistency. I picked it up and examined it. "I can see it, and I can touch it," I said, still speaking through Asa. "I'm just not sure what it is."

"Why don't you try asking it?" Vani suggested. "It's an aspect of you. You should be able to communicate with it."

"Okay." I focused on the rubbery, pillow-like object and asked, "What are you?"

But it didn't answer. It seemed wounded, reluctant.

"I can *make* it talk," Camo Ben muttered.

"Good grief, wait a minute!" I sighed in exasperation. Then I spoke to the pillow again. "I'm sorry about him. He didn't mean to hurt you. All I want to know is, what are you?"

An awareness crept into me like a morning fog: *I am Despair.*

Despair? I held the question in my heart. *Despair about what?*

A realization rang through me like a bell: *Despair that no matter how much you care about others or how strongly you're bonded, eventually you always lose the people closest to you.*

"Oh." I whispered.

"What is it?" Camo Ben asked.

"It's Despair—the knowledge that eventually we always lose the people we love." A cold wind howled through me. "I lost Mom. Braz lost Pedra. We all lost Braz... and one day...." I barely choked out the words. "I'll lose you."

"Is *that* what this is about?" Camo Ben laid his hands on the rubbery pillow-like object. "You listen to me, Despair. Cate's with me, now, and I'm going to see to it that she's happy. The only reason I'd ever leave would be if she asked me to—and then I'd immediately do whatever it took to fix the problem and change her mind." Then he looked at me. "You saw that Braz and Pedra are still together, even after death?"

"Yes...."

"That's because bonds like theirs—like ours—never end. They

transcend every obstacle, even death." He addressed Despair. "Do you hear me?"

The rubbery object softened slightly. The ritual appeared to be working; Ben was making it work through the sheer power of his caring and determination. I held my breath.

But then Despair whispered to me again. I gasped as its words shot a pillar of pain through my core: *It's true. Some bonds never end. But yours do, Cate. You're just someone who people leave.*

"Cate, you just went pale," Camo Ben said. "What's going on?"

"Despair says it's not about whether bonds can transcend death," I whispered. "It's about *me*. I'm just not the kind of person people stay with—and you won't stay, either."

Camo Ben's expression hardened with determination. "Sorry, Cate, but Despair doesn't get to make my decisions for me."

"I know you think that whether you stay is under your control," I cried out, "but history is against you. My parents—the people who are supposed to love you unconditionally—both left of their own accord. I have only two friends left, and as needy as I've been, they might leave anytime. When it comes to *me*, no one stays, nothing lasts. Patterns don't occur without a reason, Ben. I've tried to figure out what the reason is, and the only explanation that makes sense is that something is fundamentally wrong with me. One day you'll figure that out, and you'll end up leaving, too." I swallowed hard as the pillar of pain transformed into a dull, throbbing ache.

Camo Ben leaned down and picked up Despair. "What you just said makes no sense. Your mother's spirit told you herself that her suicide was about ending her suffering, not about leaving you. You've said you don't know anything about your father, so it's hardly fair to jump to conclusions about the reasons for his actions. And when you say you only have two friends—who appear to be very loyal, by the way—I assume that you're not counting all of your new friends at the MacGregor group."

"But—"

Camo Ben held his hand up. "Hang on, I'm not done yet. Even if you did lose touch with some friends because of your dedication to your work, that doesn't mean you didn't have positive relationships. All of your clients, for example. Dr. Nelson. Your colleagues." He tossed Despair from one hand to the other. I saw that it was growing lighter—more and more like a real pillow—and the red color was fading to white. Camo Ben continued, "I don't know why you believe what Despair has told you about yourself; we'll have to look at that later. But right now, I can tell you this for certain: Despair is wrong about you, Cate. Dead wrong. And I'll make it my mission to prove that to you, day after day after day." As he spoke, Despair completed its transformation into an actual pillow—small, white, and filled with feathers.

A nascent hope stirred inside of me, but a lifetime of experience to the contrary was not so easily dealt with. "You say that now, but you barely know me."

"I know you well enough." With triumph in his eyes, Camo Ben looked all around my inner landscape. "And empathically submerging into you has been highly educational." Then he threw the Despair pillow at me, hitting me square in the chest.

"Oh, you've been *snooping*?" I had to suppress a smile; I should have known that Ben would use submerging as an opportunity to investigate me from the inside. I grabbed the pillow and threw it back at him. As he caught it, feathers floated into the air.

"You say snooping; I say gathering information," he corrected as he caught the pillow and placed it gently on the ground. "It's only fair. After all, you've submerged into me before. But as much as I'd like to stay in here and continue my reconnaissance, it would appear that the ritual was successful. The painful emotion has been disarmed."

"You're done?" Vani asked.

"I think so," Ben said. "What do you think, Cate?"

I shot Camo Ben a disapproving glare to let him know exactly what I thought of his "reconnaissance." Then I took a careful look around to be sure we hadn't missed anything. "Well, Despair certainly seems to have been rendered harmless. I can't see anything else right now."

"If despair presented itself, then that must have been what was causing the paralysis," Vani said. "Okay, Ben and Cate, time to reverse the flow and get Ben out of there."

Finally I knew what Braz meant about how uncomfortable it felt having someone else inside of your consciousness. I ran up to Camo Ben and shoved him. "Okay, you, enough spying. Get out!"

He grinned. "I'm going, I'm going. Where's the door?"

Judging from my own past experiences of submergence, I pointed upwards. He jumped up and flew into the air with one arm extended, Superman-style. I tried not to laugh, instead closing my eyes and focusing on reversing the flow of the portal. Before I knew it, Ben had left my consciousness. I quickly opened my eyes again to make sure he was still there in real life—and he was, lying on the bed next to me, beaming, his eyes locked onto mine.

Ben began to carefully disentangle our limbs.

"Do I hear movement? Oh good," Kai said. "We don't have to kill Little Braz now."

Ben's chuckle made the bed vibrate. "I'm glad to hear that *our* health was your main concern."

Still with her back to us, Vani gave us a thumbs-up sign. "Everything feels good aura-wise, Cate. Whatever the energetic source of your paralysis was, it's been rendered benign."

Ben propped himself up on his elbow. "Okay, then, you heard Vani. Move something."

I marshaled all of my effort and channeled it into my body. "Move!"

I blinked.

Ben blinked back. "Okay, good, but now move something other than your eyelids."

I tried again, gathering my energy and strength like a weather god calling up a storm. I ordered my body to move.

But nothing happened.

"It's not working," I said, and I became aware that my voice was still coming from Asa's mouth. Tension grabbed at my sternum like fists clenching a rope. "Ben, it's not working! I can't move! What's wrong?"

"It's all right," he soothed, leaning over and stroking my hair. "Calm down."

"Calm down?" Tears sprang into my eyes. "Vani, what happened? Why can't I move?"

"I don't know." A catch in her voice told me that she, too, was close to tears. "I'm sorry, I was so sure it would work."

"I was inside of her, Vani. It worked." Ben swung his legs over the side of the bed, keeping me covered with the blanket as he pulled on his boxers. Discreetly averting his eyes as much as possible, he slid my arms back into my hospital gown and arranged it around me, tying it closed in the back. Then he abruptly shifted back into manager mode. "Cate and I need a little bit of time alone to wrap things up."

"What are you going to do?" Vani asked, dismayed. "We can help."

"Trust me," he said—and it sounded like an order.

Meanwhile, I lay on my side, helpless to wipe away the river of tears soaking the pillowcase.

"Asa too?" Kai asked.

"Yes, everyone," Ben said. His tone that implied that he expected immediate compliance.

"No, not Asa," I pleaded. "How will I talk?"

"Don't worry," Ben said, "we'll be able to communicate. Blink once for yes, twice for no. Okay?"

"Okay, I guess, but...."

"Try to quiet your mind again, Cate," Kai said. "I want to take Asa out of his trance. Are you decent? Can we turn around?"

"Yes, I'm decent." I dreaded being mute again, but it seemed the die had been cast. Ben was the only one left with an idea. My whole body flushed, and my throat tightened as a panic attack threatened to take hold. I tried to push it back by mentally repeating "om" as I listened to the movement all around me. I felt tiny tickling sensations as Eve removed her needles. Out of the corner of my eye, I saw Kai standing in front of Asa, chanting and moving his hands around. It sounded like Vani was gathering things and putting them into some kind of bag. Then—in no time at all, it seemed—everyone was leaving the room. "Good luck, Cate," Eve said softly as the door clicked shut.

CHAPTER NINETEEN

Mute again. My tears continued to fall. What did Ben have planned? As he so often pointed out, he wasn't the energy-healing expert; the others were. Why had he sent them all away?

I looked down to see Ben at the foot of the bed, putting his shirt on. Then he walked around and began shifting me back into the middle of the mattress. "I think I know what's going on here," he said. "We've ruled out any physical problems and taken care of the paranormal ones. That leaves us one piece left to consider."

I tried to absorb some of his confidence. Ben carefully kept me covered with the blanket as he rolled me onto my back and straightened out my limbs. He must have intuited—wisely—that exposing my naked body wouldn't help calm me down.

"Look," he said, sitting down next to me. "We know two things for sure. We know the mind-body connection exists, and we know that it's particularly strong in you. In your first aura reading, Vani observed that you primarily experience your emotions in the physical realm. Do you remember?"

Once for "yes," I reminded myself, and blinked once.

"Good. So what if there's an emotional part of you that wants to keep you paralyzed? A strong, stubborn part of you that's deep in your subconscious, outside of your awareness. I wonder what will happen if we bring that shadow part of you out into the light and take a look at it."

What on *earth*? I widened my eyes, since that was the only thing I could do to communicate my incredulity.

"I know it sounds unlikely," Ben said, "but think about it. Your grief over your mother's loss paralyzed you before, in a sense; it left you homebound, unable to work. What if losing Braz triggered that again, and this paralysis the physical manifestation of that grief? What do you think?"

If that were the case, Ben was right—I wasn't conscious of it. But *sub*consciously…. Maybe he was onto something. It was possible, anyway. Unfortunately, however, his insight didn't help me move. Other than blinking twice, I remained as still as a stone.

Ben squinted at me, apparently watching for any new signs of movement. Seeing none, he continued, "All right, how about this? Maybe the past several days have been too much for you. If so, that's my fault. I shouldn't have expected so much. Maybe this subconscious part of you agrees, and this is its way of demanding a good long rest."

There could be some truth in that, as well. I *had* been feeling overwhelmed. But there was no way my subconscious would choose paralysis over, say, a pint of ice cream as a coping mechanism. I blinked twice to deliver that message.

Ben nodded. "Okay, not that." He began to massage my hand and fingers. At first, it was merely soothing, but the heat from his touch built steadily, traveling up my arm and spreading slowly throughout my body. "Here's another thought. Changes have been coming at you very quickly lately. Maybe there's a part of you that's anxious about starting your new life—with the MacGregor Group, with me—and is reluctant to leave your old life behind. Paralysis would certainly be an effective way to put on the brakes." He released my right hand and began to massage the left one.

As my internal temperature rose, a light sweat coated my skin. I forced myself to focus. That explanation sounded reasonable as well, but when I tried it on for size, still no dice. I couldn't un-paralyze myself. Ben's strategy wasn't working. After all, both my breathing and my heart rate were speeding up in response to his touch. I wanted nothing more than to reach up, pull his head down to mine, and draw him into a deep, eternal kiss. But all I could do was blink the tears out of my eyes.

"Please don't." Ben softly stroked my tears away. "Don't give up. I have other ideas, but before we try anything else, Cate, there's something I need to say to you." He held both of my hands in his. "Thank you for allowing me to submerge into you. That was very brave of you, and I consider it an honor. I've seen all of you now, even the parts you try to hide—and I know you were afraid of that, of what I might think."

He was right about that. I blinked once, hard.

Ben smiled gently and squeezed my hands. "Well, for me, submerging into you was like looking at the ocean for the first time, or visiting a place that feels more like home than any place you've ever been. And what I feel for you—it's in a completely different dimension than anything I've ever felt before. There's a power, a clarity…. I'm not even sure exactly how to describe it, except to say that it feels like for the first time, I know what really matters."

Ben looked down at his hands and cleared his throat. My chest tightened in anticipation. When his eyes again met mine, his voice was rough with emotion. "What I want to say is that however you feel about me, and whatever happens from here, I want you to know that I'm in love with you, Cate."

As he spoke those last words, a tide of emotion was unleashed through the portal. I felt his love swirling and crashing inside of me, filling me up until my whole being seemed to float on top of it. My heart began to tremble and swell.

"And because I'm in love with you, I paid sharp attention when Vani said that it's dangerous for you to stay like this for too long. Since my psychological tactics aren't working fast enough, we may have to try a more direct approach." He lifted up my right hand and kissed me on the palm.

Between the emotional bombshell he'd just dropped and the sensation of his lips on my skin, I nearly fainted. Not being able to move was maddening, and not being able to respond to Ben's touch was driving me to a breaking point.

He leaned down and kissed me on the cheek, then slowly kissed his way up to my temple and across my forehead, leaving a burning trail along my skin. He ended by placing a final kiss on my other cheek. Then he stopped and become perfectly still.

No! Don't stop, please—! my mind begged. The chasm between what I was longing for and what was actually happening tore at me as Ben sat there, poised over my body, not moving.

Finally, after what seemed like centuries, Ben moved—but only to bring his mouth close to my ear. His breath on my neck sent a new wave of scorching heat rolling down my body. "Let's try *tempting* your subconscious into releasing you," he whispered. "Maybe if we give it a good enough incentive to let you move again…." He reached over and smoothed down my hair. "We could start with a kiss."

Ben's lips brushed across mine, the first in a slow, languorous procession of feathery-soft kisses that fueled the heat inside of me until I was certain I'd catch fire. Finally, the sheer force of my hunger for him grew so strong that my lips couldn't help but answer his. The instant he felt my response, Ben's mouth was on mine in earnest. His tongue teased my lips apart and plunged inside, claiming everything it could reach. I kissed him desperately, pulling myself back from the brink. Ben tangled his hands in my hair as he absorbed my moans and cries.

Inhaling his scent drove me over the edge. My ache for him became so acute that other parts of my body could no longer remain still. Pushing through their paralysis, my arms reached around his back and my nails bit into his shoulder blades. *Oh my God,* I thought. *I'm moving! I'm cured!* But then, with alarm, I realized that I still didn't have control over my body. My need for Ben had taken me over.

Ben climbed onto the bed, straddled me, and tried to sit back. But my arms wouldn't let go of him, and of its own accord, my back arched wildly in an attempt to press our bodies together. I was powerless to stop my legs as they wrapped themselves around Ben's waist and dragged his body closer, trying to force his hips against mine.

Once assured that his intervention had really been a success, Ben made several half-hearted attempts to pull away from me. Then he whispered hoarsely, "I want the same thing you do—more than you know. But now is not the time."

"You don't understand," I whimpered. "I can't control—"

Then I mewled in frustration as Ben slowly unwrapped my arms from around him. He leaned back and searched my eyes. It only took a second for him to grasp the situation. "It's okay," he said. "I've got you." He tucked my hands beneath my hips to keep my arms in check. Then he gently pushed my legs down onto the mattress, keeping a grip on my ankles until my legs stopped kicking against his hold.

Still breathing heavily, Ben asked, "Okay now?"

Slowly at first, then in a rush, I felt my own control flowing through my limbs again. "Yes," I whispered, willing my body to be still, to relax.

Ben's expression eased as though he finally believed what he saw: I was really talking and moving. It looked like he was allowing himself to feel relief for the first time in ages. "I love you, Cate Duncan."

I propped myself up on my elbows and peered at him, giving voice to the tattered remnants of my anxiety. "You mean, you didn't just say that to try to cure my paralysis?"

He frowned down at me. "You know the answer to that."

"Oh," I said as feverishness once again flashed through me. Ben and I: in love. As I tried on the idea, the profound rightness of it surrounded me like a warm, soft sea.

I wanted to close my eyes, nestle into that feeling, and stay there forever. But I couldn't ignore that Ben had opened up and told me how he felt—with no reply from me. "Ben, I don't know what to say…."

He pressed his finger softly against my open lips. "You don't have to say anything. No pressure, no expectations. I wanted to tell you, so I did—and I will continue to."

A wave of emotion swelled in my chest until I thought it might burst through my ribs. "I just feel so much for you, more than I've ever felt for anyone, but I don't… I mean, I have no words…."

"Shhh, Cate." Ben's eyes softened as a wide smile spread across his face. "It's okay. I know how you feel about me. You show me every time you look at me. There's plenty of time for words later."

"Do I hear Cate?" Kai called from the hallway. The door handle jiggled.

Ben ran over to catch the door just as Kai cracked it open. "Give her a minute."

Gingerly, I tested my legs and stood up next to the bed. Finally, my body seemed to be working normally—except that between my heavy breathing, rapid heartbeat, perspiration, and full-body flush, I probably looked as though I had just run a mile. I adjusted my hospital gown and tied it more tightly closed, reluctantly readying myself to receive our visitors.

Meanwhile, Ben was already buckling his belt. "Uh, Cate...."

"What?"

Ben's eyes glinted. He pointed at his chin. "There's a little bit of drool...."

Certifiable bastard, I thought. I quickly wiped my chin on my hospital gown. Heat exploded across my face anew—just in time for all of our friends to rush in, hug me too tightly, and congratulate Ben on working his miracle.

CHAPTER TWENTY

The first thing I did after Dr. Washington medically cleared me was to go back to my room and take another bath. I wanted to feel like myself again, and to wash off the adhesive tape residue and iodine stains. Ben lurked outside the bathroom door, inquiring periodically if I might be feeling weak or need any assistance. But I knew that he was only offering because he knew I'd refuse. The last thing I needed was yet another physical encounter that we both knew wouldn't reach a satisfying conclusion.

Not that I wasn't grateful to Ben for curing me. I'd felt such joy in that moment when I regained control over my body, and I must have thanked him a million times. But I also couldn't help grumbling once or twice about the exasperating technique he'd used to un-paralyze me. Ben simply ignored my complaints. As far as he was concerned, all that mattered was that I was healthy again. He promised that once my training was over and the "no sex" rule didn't apply anymore, he would dedicate himself to making up for any frustration he may have caused me.

Between that enticing promise and Ben's earlier confession of his feelings, I felt like I was floating on a cloud. *Ben loves me.* I repeated the phrase over and over in my mind, trying to convince the parts of me that still couldn't quite believe it.

I soaked in the hot water, reflecting on our post-ritual conversations. Ben had spent some time asking me questions about what happened during the toxic cleansing ritual. Since he wasn't a sensitive, he'd been the only person in the room who hadn't felt the energy vibrations in the air. I tried to explain what they felt like, and to describe how the knowledge of how to use the energy rose up spontaneously inside of me.

Ben nodded slowly. "That goes along with what my mother has learned so far about the kheir. She says that it doesn't give sensitives special powers or anything like that. It just makes you more sensitive to energy, as Vani said, and provides a shortcut to a fuller knowledge of how to use your gifts—like reaching enlightenment without having to spend years meditating."

"Kai said something along those lines, too," I recalled, "and that does sound like a pretty good description of what I experienced during the ritual. One moment I had no idea how to handle the vibrating energy. The next moment, I just knew what to do—and it worked."

"What you experienced does appear to give the myth of the kheir more validity," he murmured.

"Possibly." My skepticism was softening by the day, but it was also an intellectual flotation device of sorts, keeping me from sinking too far and too fast into the unknown. I wasn't quite ready to give it up yet. Ben must have felt something similar because he didn't push the subject any further.

I asked why Pete hadn't been with us during the ritual. Ben said he'd been called into service playing good cop with Jennifer. Apparently, the fact that Pete was a tall, handsome cowboy and not an active duty marine made him a bit less intimidating than the other interrogators.

Jennifer was in the same subbasement we were. Ben asked if I'd like to meet her. I assured him that if I met her I would probably exhibit very poor impulse control, thereby undoing any good-cop progress Pete had made. Ben saw the wisdom in that and agreed that she and I should be kept as far apart as possible.

As my skin began to wrinkle in the tub, I heard someone knock on the door of the room and talk to Ben in urgent tones. When Ben returned to the bathroom door, he said, "Cate, I have to run to a meeting. Are you going to be okay here for a while?"

My mood dipped. "A meeting? I thought we were going to

be able to hang out for a while—you know, now that I can talk and move."

"I know," he said, his voice echoing the disappointment in mine. "I have to work out a couple of things with Kai and Vani. It won't take long. I'll be back in time to pick you up for dinner."

"Ooo," I said in my best seductress voice, "are you taking me somewhere nice?"

"Not tonight, but very soon," he said, and it sounded like a promise. "Are you sure you'll be okay by yourself?"

"Of course. Don't worry," I teased, "if I need assistance getting out of the tub, there are any number of big, strong marines around who can help me."

I could practically *feel* Ben on the other side of the door, and the great effort he was exerting to resist opening it. Finally, his voice came through the door again. "That reminds me, I came up with a nickname for you."

My eye roll was wasted on the empty room. "A nickname? Why? Cate is short and sweet."

"So is Ben, but that doesn't stop people from calling me Rottie," he replied. "It just came to me while we were trying to cure your paralysis."

I sighed heavily. "All right, fine. What is it?"

There was a dramatic pause. "Trouble."

"*Trouble?*" I splashed the bathroom door with water—as if that would accomplish anything.

"You don't like it?" The devilment in Ben's voice told me that the less I liked it, the harder it was going to stick.

"I'll show *you* trouble!" I tried to sound indignant, but I couldn't stop a smile from stealing across my face. "Go away, go to your meeting!"

"Yes, ma'am," he said in a perfect imitation of Pete as he retreated.

Half an hour later, I was dried off and dressed in my yoga pants and sweatshirt when there was a frenetic knock on the door.

Cautiously, I opened it to find Asa and Eve grinning like fools—and no marines anywhere to be seen.

"Oh my gosh," I whispered, "what are you guys doing here? And what did you do with the marines?"

Asa spoke first. "I guess Captain Abbott thinks you're not going to run away anymore. They removed your guard!"

"Yeah," Eve chimed in. "We overheard him telling Ben, so we thought this would be a good time to celebrate!"

My heart jumped a little. "Celebrate how?"

Shrugging apologetically, Asa said, "We couldn't leave the bunker, of course, so we couldn't get anything good like liquor, but we found this super-long hallway with really smooth floors, which means—"

"Oh, just come on," Eve said, tugging at my sleeve. "We'll show you!"

Their enthusiasm was infectious, and my curiosity was piqued. "Wait, let me get my shoes—"

"You won't need shoes!" Eve insisted, pulling me out the door.

Several twists and turns later, we were facing into what was indeed one of the longest hallways I'd ever seen.

"Sock sliding contest!" Asa announced triumphantly.

"Wheee!" Eve exclaimed, spinning in place with her arms outstretched.

"A sock-sliding contest?" I giggled at the absurdity. "How do you know who wins?"

"Distance," Eve explained. "We mark a starting line. Then you run up to it, and from the line, you slide. Whoever goes the farthest is the winner."

"Oh my God, you guys are going to totally kick my butt! I have no balance—plus, I was recently paralyzed, so my coordination…."

Asa interrupted me. "Oh come on, you'll get the hang of it. And no 'I've been paralyzed' excuses. You think *you've* had it bad; I've had my body hijacked by comatose people all week—one of whom was you!"

"Okay, okay, fair enough. Thank you, by the way. And I'm sorry about that," I said, pointing at the protective bracelet he still wore around his wrist. "I didn't mean to shout my thoughts at you. Kai thinks I opened some screwed-up portal to you by accident."

"Oh, I know it wasn't your fault." Asa shrugged. "And I'm just giving you a hard time about the coma thing. I was glad I could do something."

"I thought it was cool that you could shout into his head," Eve said. "It's like you have weaponized, laser-guided thoughts or something!"

"Oh, God," I moaned. "Please don't say that out loud around here. They'll probably lock me up and do experiments on me for the rest of my life."

Asa nodded and slowly looked around. "Wow, you're right, they probably would."

"Creepy!" Eve exclaimed, appearing fascinated by the prospect.

"Okay," I said, forcing a change in subject. "Let's get this thing moving. But you two have to go first and show me how it's done."

Asa had brought a shoe with him, which he placed some distance down the hallway to represent our starting line. Then he and Eve took turns demonstrating their considerable sliding skills. Eve had a clear lead, which Asa chalked up to her lighter body weight and acrylic socks. They leaned against the wall midway down the hall and egged me on. "Come on, Cate! You can do it!"

It occurred to me that if I fell or slammed into a wall, I might put myself into a coma for real. But Eve and Asa were so pleased with their idea, and I was thrilled to be doing something fun—not to mention something physical, which felt wonderfully freeing after having been trapped in my own body.

Since I figured that I might only get in one run before injuring myself, I decided to make it a good one. With all of the energy and speed I could muster, I hurtled myself towards the starting line shoe, then planted both feet on the ground and crouched with my arms outstretched as Asa and Eve had done. Much to my shock, I found myself flying down the hallway at high speed. I must have had socks made of WD-40. I whizzed towards Eve and Asa as they cheered, but as I passed them, their cheers quickly turned into warnings to slow down. I looked up and noticed that the end of the hallway was fast approaching. My heart lurched as I realized that I had no idea how to stop or even reduce speed without throwing myself to the ground.

A scream began to well up from my chest into my throat, but right before it escaped into my mouth, a man rounded the corner: Captain Abbott. For one panicked moment, I thought there was going to be a deadly collision. With reflexes that were much quicker than I would have expected from a tree trunk, the captain hooked an arm around my waist and spun us both in a circle, using my momentum to execute some sort of weird martial arts move until he had slowed me to a stop. There we stood, with me lying back against his arm as though we were dancing the tango and he'd just dipped me. His expression reflected what I was sure he saw in mine: surprise and confusion over what had just happened.

His back stiffened. "Miss Duncan, what exactly is going on here?"

Still cradled in his arm, I stared up at his face, which was even more intimidating from that angle. "Um, we're kind of having a sock-sliding contest. Sir."

"I see." As though I weighed no more than a feather, he lifted me up into a standing position, then steadied me by the shoulders and looked me over, appearing to reassure himself that I wouldn't fall. "And who is winning?"

I looked helplessly over at Eve and Asa, who shrugged. Clearly they were as surprised by his follow-up question as I was. "Eve, I think. She's gone the farthest without slamming into anyone. Or anything."

Captain Abbott gave Eve a thumbs-up sign. "Congratulations, Eve. Keep up the good work."

Eve gave a nervous wave. "Sure thing, Captain."

Captain Abbott looked down at me again. His mouth was turning up at the corners. "All right then, Miss Duncan," he said, "carry on." Then he marched off down the hallway, leaving three astonished individuals with wide-open mouths in his wake.

We all stared at each other.

"Did that actually just happen?" I asked.

Asa said, "I guess he's forgiven you for being… you know."

"A pain in his derriere?" Eve offered.

"I guess he has."

"Ready to try again?" Asa asked.

Eve winced. "Maybe we should prop some mattresses up against the far wall before we give Cate another turn."

I rolled my eyes—then offered to be the distance judge instead of a participant. This idea was met with much enthusiasm from both Asa and Eve. Then the competition really heated up.

• • •

Ben surprised me by agreeing to try eating with the entire MacGregor Group in the mess hall for dinner. It would be the first time that he'd be eating in front of them—except for Pete, of course. But I encouraged him to give it a try, suggesting that being surrounded by tables of marines might dilute his anxiety. I told Ben to think of it as though we were all marines since we were all on the same mission. That had been enough of a psychological fudge to convince his brain that it was worth taking the risk.

The rest of the group had already started eating when Ben and I sat down with our trays. They had enough sensitivity—and warning looks from me—not to say anything about the unprecedented event that was about to take place. They simply carried on eating and talking as usual. Once we were settled, Ben tensed up. For a few seconds he frowned at his tray, and I thought I might have pushed him too quickly. But then I had another light bulb moment. I leaned over so that my lips were practically touching his ear and murmured, "Would you like me to feed you again?"

Ben continued to stare at his food, but his eyebrows slowly raised as he, too, recalled the breakthrough technique I'd used at our first therapeutic meal together. "Yes," he said, "but not right now. I only want you to do that again when I have the freedom to undress you afterwards. Or during."

I suppressed a moan and turned back to my own food. "Then you'd better dig in, you big, tough marine, you."

That was all it took. Soon he was chowing down and jumping into the conversation as though nothing unusual were going on. My heart swelled as I thought about all of the ways in which Ben's seemingly endless courage manifested itself—and how that simple act may have required more of him than anyone would ever know. I was so inspired, and so happy for him. Judging from the secret glances I was getting from our friends, they shared my emotions.

As we were finishing up, Ben announced, "After dinner, Captain wants us all in the conference room for a final briefing."

"A final briefing?" I asked. "Does that mean it's over? Has Sid been released?"

A muscle in Ben's jaw twitched. "I'm not sure where things stand at this moment. Captain Abbott will answer all of our questions in the briefing. But I would imagine that yes, if he's calling this a final briefing, the end of the mission is near. Oh, and by the way." He flashed a knowing smile around the table. "Thanks for not making a big deal out of the fact that I broke bread with all of you."

Everyone but Pete shrugged and pretended not to notice that anything out of the ordinary had happened. But Ben continued, "You all know that I've always had trouble eating in front of other people, but Cate has been helping me with it. She's quite a talented therapist."

The group then chimed in with their encouragement and praise. But all I could see was Ben, giving me a look so full of love and heat that it made my toes curl.

CHAPTER TWENTY-ONE

As usual, Captain Abbott's commanding presence filled the conference room, but I found him less intimidating since our sock-sliding encounter. When I walked in, he even gave me respectful nod, which I returned. The MacGregor Group was present, along with Skeet and a few of the more senior marines, including Hector, Mike, and Nessa. We all exchanged greetings.

As soon as we were all seated, Captain Abbott bellowed, "This will be our final briefing. The mission has been a success. Everyone will be expected to vacate the premises by noon tomorrow."

This news was met by curious glances and a few murmurs, but they were quickly silenced by Captain Abbott's voice. "Tomorrow at 0900, a small group of us will gather in the main hospital lobby to pay our last respects to Dr. Belo before his body is returned to Brazil for burial. If you are to be a part of that group, you will be notified."

I certainly wanted to be a part of that group. I gave Ben an anxious look. He responded with a subtle nod.

"Now to the details. As expected, we were contacted by CIA agent and head of the Deep Sea cell, Anglerfish, asking to make a deal. The four members of the cell, which also included Blackdragon, Lancet, and Daggertooth, were named after different types of deep sea fish, no doubt to highlight their impenetrable stealth." All of the marines in the room chuckled. "As everyone is aware, thanks to the creative and dedicated efforts of the MacGregor Group, we were able to locate and apprehend Blackdragon. In retaliation, Anglerfish called in a false tip to the FBI to pick up Sid, an asset of the MacGregor Group. In short, we had some leverage, and they had some leverage. After some excellent negotiating by members of Yankee Company, a deal was reached."

My leg began to bounce. Ben rested his hand on my thigh and rubbed gently back and forth until the bouncing stilled.

"Anglerfish agreed to call his FBI contact, say that the tip he called in was a case of mistaken identity, and request Sid's immediate release. We have confirmation that this part of the deal has been accomplished and that Sid is home safe."

I wanted to collapse with relief. I held myself up by sheer willpower and the strong desire to not embarrass either Ben or myself.

Captain Abbott continued, "As for our part of the deal, Anglerfish knew there would have to be some consequences. After all, an innocent man is dead, and while Blackdragon didn't give us much, she did help us by identifying the other members of the Deep Sea cell. Their boss at the CIA is one of our close contacts there— one of the people we contacted initially, in fact, when it became clear that there was CIA involvement in Braz's poisoning. Word on the street is that their boss has no love for Anglerfish. Indeed, he was all too happy to learn from us that the Deep Sea cell had been engaged in a secret project that fell so far outside of departmental guidelines. However, as our part of the deal, we agreed to retract the murder allegation. On the record, we told Anglerfish's boss that we were mistaken; Braz had accidentally poisoned himself in his first attempt to make fugu."

I squinted up at the captain. "Fugu?"

"A Japanese delicacy," he explained, "made from pufferfish, parts of which are highly toxic. Only specially trained chefs are allowed to prepare the dish in restaurants. Braz was known to be something of an adventurous cook, especially when he was drinking, so the story is plausible. Their boss assured me that Anglerfish, Lancet, and Daggertooth would be taken out of the field permanently. After being put through one of the CIA's 're-education programs,' they will be reassigned to desk jobs at Langley for the remainder of their careers. That way, the CIA can continue to keep a close eye on them, and they can't do any further harm."

This announcement was met with general sounds of approval from around the room, but I began to feel vaguely nauseous. Braz was dead, and the consequence was *desk jobs?*

"As for Blackdragon—Jennifer—she expressed a desire to leave the CIA altogether," Captain Abbott said. "This presented something of a dilemma for all parties involved. First, she killed an innocent man, although she has yet to confess to this. Second, she knows a lot of secrets that the CIA would prefer remain secret. Third, there is every chance that if she were allowed to leave the CIA without another assignment in place, the other members of her cell would know that she had turned on them and might retaliate against her, putting her life in jeopardy. Fortunately, we have a silver-tongued cowboy on our side." Pete tipped his hat. "After a few conversations with Pete, Jennifer decided that she wants to join the Marine Corps and, ultimately, Yankee Company. Of course, given her history, she will have a several-years-long probationary period and will be under the joint supervision of the CIA and the Marine Corps. But I have to say, since it's usually Langley stealing marines from us, it would be nice to steal one of their agents for a change."

There were more general noises of approval, but bile was rising in my throat. Before I could stop it, my hand shot up.

"Yes, Miss Duncan?" Captain Abbott asked.

I struggled to put my frustration into words. "Sir, I don't mean to sound ungrateful for all of the negotiating that has happened, and that you got Sid released," I said carefully. "But Jennifer—she killed Braz! Shouldn't she go to jail? Shouldn't they *all* go to jail? And if you let her join the Marines—*especially* Yankee Company—how could you ever trust her? She could up and attack someone at any moment with an epi-pen!"

"All valid points and excellent questions, Miss Duncan," Captain Abbott acknowledged in a tone so collegial that it took me by surprise. "Due to the politics, sensitive information, and high security clearances involved, where possible, the CIA prefers to handle internal problems themselves. Part of the agreement we made with them in this case was that we would not push for a public reckoning."

My head was spinning. "But once those agents complete whatever 're-education program' they're doing, couldn't they then just quit their jobs and do whatever they liked?"

"Certainly, but if they quit their jobs at the CIA against the orders of their superiors, there would be a high probability that they'd meet with sudden, 'accidental' deaths." His matter-of-fact tone made me shudder. He continued, "As for Jennifer, she killed Braz under direct orders from her superior. Now, technically speaking, she has become a whistle-blower herself—just the type of person Yankee Company was formed to protect. These situations are rarely black and white, Miss Duncan. In fact, they're usually murky, and questions of justice must sometimes be set aside in order to achieve the best possible outcome, which we believe we have done here. Given what you told us about Braz's wishes, we think he would agree—and he is, after all, the most aggrieved party in this case."

Well, that part was true. Braz had wanted them to let Jennifer off lightly—but not the other three agents! And were the Marines really going to trust Jennifer to protect vulnerable people?

As though he'd read my mind, Captain Abbott added, "As touched as I am by your concern about the wellbeing of the members of Yankee Company, rest assured that we know how to take care of ourselves. Believe me, Jennifer's every move will be monitored for years before we even *think* about letting our guard down. And if she comes at any of us with a—what did you call it, an 'epi-pen'—she will not live to tell about it."

His last few words were spoken in a tone that made a chill slide down my spine—but it was a chill that I found oddly reassuring. I felt sure that Captain Abbott would see to it that Jennifer never harmed anyone else.

"Does that answer your questions, Miss Duncan?"

Not satisfactorily. The whole thing still made me ill. But it was clearer than ever that I was dealing with a world I knew nothing about—a world that ran according to entirely different rules than the ones I was used to. Sid was safe; at least I could hold on to that. "Yes, thank you, sir."

"Good," he said. "Any more questions?"

After a few moments of silence, Captain Abbott declared the briefing over and the room began to buzz with various conversations. All I could do was look down at my hands.

Ben put his arm around my shoulders and slowly rubbed his hand up and down my arm. "Messy, isn't it?"

I rested my head against him. "It just feels all wrong."

"I know," he said. "That's one of the reasons I like being in charge of things and calling the shots—not having to take orders anymore. I can manage gray areas if I have to, but I don't like it. And I don't like having to compromise."

"You don't say."

Humor flashed in his eyes. "You noticed?"

I suppressed a smile. "But you're not really in charge at the MacGregor group, are you? I mean, you still work for your *mother*."

He didn't even come close to taking the bait. "Yes, but since she and I are basically the same person, there's no conflict."

I knew that to be almost entirely true—almost. But I decided to let that sleeping dog lie. As I sat there with Ben's arm wrapped around me and my head cradled against him, I was hit by another sudden wave of exhaustion. "Can we call Sid and then go to bed?"

"Go to bed, yes. But call Sid?"

"I know Captain Abbott said he's home safe, but I won't believe it until I can talk to him." Ben was frowning, so I added an argument that I knew he would find compelling. "I feel incredibly guilty about what happened to him, and I feel responsible for making sure that he's okay."

Sure enough, Ben nodded. "I'll see if we can use the captain's office for a few minutes. Just remember to make it short and sweet, and don't give away any sensitive information."

But I was too tired to remember what was sensitive information and what wasn't. "Will you make the call with me? I'm afraid I'll screw it up otherwise. After all, I'm just a civilian," I quipped.

He smiled and tucked a stray strand of hair behind my ear. "Sure thing. But then it's time for you to get some sleep."

• • •

ParaTrain Internship, Day Five

Fittingly, it was raining. A small group of us had gathered under a makeshift roof of umbrellas to witness Braz's coffin being transported from somewhere inside the hospital to the hearse waiting in the driveway—the same driveway where I had followed Braz's instructions to catch a cab. It felt as though years had passed since then.

Ben and Pete stood on either side of me, holding umbrellas over the three of us. Dr. Washington was there, as well as Skeet, Captain Abbott, Kai, and Asa. The captain was striking in his dress blues. The rest of us had dressed in the best civilian clothes we had, which unfortunately in my case was yoga pants and Ben's sweatshirt. I felt disrespectful, but I was also relatively certain that Braz would forgive me.

I lost track of how long we had been waiting, but it didn't matter. Time seemed meaningless as we all stood there, frozen in place. My mind drifted back to the phone call Ben and I had placed to Sid the night before. Sid had been his usual, easy-going self, pretending— for my benefit, no doubt—that he'd taken his detention by the FBI completely in stride. I knew better, having connected to him through our portal, but I let him believe that I was buying his act.

I apologized profusely, but Sid said that after he found out they were holding him because of something having to do with *me*, he felt much better. "Although I recently learned that you live a secret life of mystery and intrigue, you are also possibly the most harmless person I've ever met," he'd said. "At least then I knew it must be some kind of misunderstanding, and that it would get sorted out sooner or later."

Ben and Sid had then engaged in some businesslike conversation about the situation. Ben checked to make sure Sid had been treated properly and asked if he needed anything else, while Sid thanked Ben for making sure he'd been a VIP prisoner from the outset and for protecting his family. I was surprised at how congenial their interaction seemed given the circumstances, but both men seemed to be going out of their way to be pleasant.

Although I wouldn't feel fully at ease until I saw Sid in person and in one piece, my relief at hearing his voice had been enough for the moment. I had collapsed into sleep shortly afterwards, and although Ben practically had to drag me out of bed for Braz's send-off, I'd made it in time. The rain softened the world around us as we waited.

We all turned when Braz's casket was wheeled out onto the sidewalk. There was an orderly at each corner of the metal cart. Once it reached us, Ben and Pete gave me their umbrellas to hold. Then they joined Skeet, Captain Abbott, and Dr. Washington in serving as pallbearers, lifting the casket and helping the hearse driver place it in the back of the vehicle. Before they closed the back doors, Captain Abbott said, "If anyone wants to say goodbye, now's the time."

Not even sure what I was doing, I walked to the back of the hearse and handed the umbrellas back to Pete and Ben. I pressed my fingertips to my lips, then to the edge of the casket. "Bye, Braz," I whispered. "I'm sorry we couldn't keep you longer."

I stepped back. No one else stepped forward, so after a respectful period of time, the driver closed the back doors. Skeet spoke briefly to the driver and handed him an envelope before the man got in and drove slowly away. "Making sure Braz gets the royal treatment," Skeet explained as he rejoined our group.

None of us moved as we watched the hearse pull around the driveway. I couldn't help thinking of my mother, and although Ben's expression was implacable, I knew that the whole scene must have been bringing up some difficult memories about his father. I slid my arm around his waist and pressed myself against the cool length of his wool suit.

He wrapped his free arm around my shoulder, leaned down, and placed a soft kiss on the top of my head. "You okay?"

"Yeah," I whispered back. "You?"

"Fine," he said, but he couldn't smooth all of the tension from his voice.

Suddenly, I saw four familiar-looking marines quick-march out of the lobby doors accompanied by a small, dark-haired woman. My breath left me in a *whoosh*.

My head spun around as I looked first at Skeet, then at Captain Abbott—but they were watching her, too. I turned to Ben. "That's her!"

A dark emotion clouded his expression. "I know."

I looked back at Jennifer. The hearse driver had parked and was opening the back doors. She practically fell on top of the coffin while the marines stood at attention nearby.

Anger erupted inside of me. I pulled my arm from around Ben and lurched forward, prepared to run across the driveway to her— and do what, I didn't know. But I knew it was wrong that she should be allowed to pay her last respects to the man she had murdered—a man who had cared so much for her, and who was such a better human being than she was.

But Ben was quick. He caught me in his arms as I tried to run, holding me close to him and murmuring in my ear: "She has a right to say goodbye."

"No she doesn't!" I tried to wrest myself from his embrace. "She *murdered* him!"

Pete came around the other side of me, and he and Ben lifted me by the elbows and practically carried me back towards the lobby doors. "Let go of me!" I demanded, but they seemed not to hear. I cast a desperate glance back towards the hearse just in time to see Jennifer pull herself away from the coffin and wipe her eyes on her sleeve.

Before I knew it, Pete, Ben, and I were in an elevator going down. I knew I was glowering, but I felt completely justified. Ben and Pete exchange a knowing glance, and rivulets of tears once again began to flow down my cheeks.

The elevator doors opened, and Ben held out his elbow. Because there was absolutely nothing else for me to do, I took it.

"Hang in there, sis. I'll see you guys later," Pete said.

"Will do," Ben replied. We turned and began walking down the hall.

Once we reached our room, I threw myself facedown on the bed. I was a boiling cauldron of emotions: grief over Braz and my mother; concern for Ben and his grief over his father; and outrage that Jennifer was allowed to get anywhere near Braz's coffin. I was also sick and tired of being captive in a subbasement, and being told what to do and what not to do.

"Why did you stop me?" I yowled at Ben.

"You know why." He sat on the edge of the bed and began rubbing my back.

"But she's...."

"I agree with you. But that wasn't the time or the place."

I knew he was right, but still I didn't like it. His backrub was calming me, but I couldn't decide whether to let him continue or to push him away and return to my volcano of righteous outrage. I turned my head to look at him as my tears began to abate. "I'm so sick of this, all of it. Can we please go home now?"

He pulled out a handkerchief and dabbed the last of the tears from my cheeks. "I'll tell you what," he said gently. "We're all packed, so yes, we can leave. But Skeet wants to take us out to lunch. After that, we can go home. Do you think you can manage a while longer?"

"Oh, hell." I buried my face in the pillow.

"What is it?"

I leaned up on my elbows. "I just... I don't know. I guess I was hoping to go straight home. Plus, I've been meaning to talk to you about Skeet."

Ben's eyebrows shot up. "Oh?"

"Yeah," I began. "How well do you know him?"

"Not very. As I told you, we work with him on occasion, treating some of his research subjects. We talk about cases to coordinate care, but that's the extent of our contact. My mother is good friends with him, though. They went to college together."

"Oh, they *did*?"

"Yes. I would have mentioned it before if I'd thought it was important."

"No, it's okay. I guess I'm glad to hear that, actually. I had a conversation with Skeet that made me a little bit uncomfortable, but if your mother trusts him, then…."

"Uncomfortable, how?"

I told him about how Skeet had offered me first a job, then a position as a paid guinea pig in his research projects.

Ben's body tensed like a mousetrap that had just been set.

"I told him no—about the job, anyway." I grabbed his hand and kissed the tip of his thumb. He relaxed slightly.

"Well, I'm glad to hear that." He rolled me onto my side so that I was facing him. "What about the research? Did it interest you?"

"I'm not sure." I clenched and unclenched my hands. "It's interesting, yes, and sounds like it has some potentially good applications—but also some potentially bad ones. And I while *think* Skeet means well, I can't be sure. I don't want to be a part of something that could end up hurting people down the line."

Ben rubbed his jaw. "I think most research into paranormal gifts has the potential to cut both ways. There have always been powerful groups interested in how those gifts could be used for spying, interrogation, or worse. And while I don't know where Skeet stands on any of that, I'm sure that to be the head of the Paranormal Division at NIMH, you have to have a certain amount of moral flexibility, or at least a tolerance for it. If you don't trust him completely, maybe it's because you were picking up on some of that."

"Oh God!" I slammed my fist into the mattress. "So he could be as bad as Anglerfish!"

"No, come on, Cate. You were there; you saw that he was just as horrified as the rest of us by what Anglerfish intended to do with Braz's work." Ben took my hands in his. "Look, I think it's safe to say that you and I are on the conservative end of an ethical continuum. It's possible that Skeet is a bit further down that continuum that we are, but that doesn't mean he's anywhere close to Anglerfish. If he were, I can tell you for certain that my mother would have cut ties with him years ago."

"I guess that's true." That thought was somewhat comforting. I suddenly realized that I was clenching my hands again, and my fingernails were digging into Ben's palms. I took a deep breath and ordered myself to relax. "Do you think it's okay for me to talk to your mom about all of this?"

Ben raised my hands to his mouth and kissed each of them in turn. "I'm sure she'll be happy to tell you exactly what she thinks. You know she won't pull any punches."

He had a point. Dr. MacGregor was famously blunt. "Okay. I wanted to talk to her anyway, about the whole kheir thing."

"Great idea." Ben glanced at the clock. "Right now, though, Skeet wants to take us out for a thank-you lunch—the whole group of us, Yankee Company and all. At a nice restaurant, I'm told. My mother will be joining us as well. Maybe the two of you could set up a time to talk. If you'd rather go straight home, I understand completely. But if there's any chance you'd be willing to accompany me…." One of his eyebrows rose like a question mark.

Having talked through some of my concerns about Skeet, I was feeling a little better equipped to face the outside world. And Ben's second mention of the word "lunch" elicited a loud grumble of protest from my stomach. Although Yankee Company had better food than I had expected, I was longing for a really good meal. It also occurred to me that it might be rude and unprofessional to decline, especially with Dr. MacGregor coming.

However, I hadn't packed any clothes suitable for a *nice* restaurant, especially not D.C.-style. I knew Ben might think it was silly concern, but I decided to raise it in the event that it got me out of going. "I don't have anything to wear."

His smile held a hint of victory, as though he had known he'd be able to convince me. "It's taken care of. Vani and Kai said they didn't have anything to wear either, so the three of you are going shopping. We'll meet you at the restaurant."

I knew he was lying about Vani and Kai not having anything to wear, since they both had been quite nicely dressed for our entire stay. However, my body was practically clawing to get out of the clothes I'd been wearing through the whole ordeal. I wanted to say yes, but it had been quite some time since I'd been in a large crowd of people, and the idea was somewhat intimidating. "Honestly, I'm just not sure I have the emotional energy to go shopping."

"Don't worry. Vani has it all arranged, some kind of private shopper thing at Saks. And since it's a work-related event, all expenses will be paid by the MacGregor Group. Apparently you three will get your own room, and they'll bring the clothes to you. You won't have to mix with the unwashed masses."

I gave him the most reproachful look I could muster. However, private shopping *did* sound like something I could manage—even if it also sounded totally bizarre compared to my usual bargain rack hunt. "Well, okay. Since Vani went to all of the trouble of arranging it…."

"Excellent! I'll go get her."

CHAPTER TWENTY-TWO

The limo ride to the restaurant after our private shopping session made me feel like we were on our way to prom. Vani looked regal in a fitted shift of turquoise-and-silver brocade. Kai was resplendent in an asymmetrical silk color-block dress that dramatized his angular frame. I definitely felt a little down-market in my outfit, particularly because they were both wearing five-inch Jimmy Choos, and I had opted for two-inch, no-name slingbacks. But I was determined to be comfortable, goddammit—and also *not* to fall over sideways like a felled tree as soon as I tried to take a step.

I tried to keep my head from leaning against the window or the seat, since my visit to Saks's onsite "blowout bar" had created big, gently swinging curls that I was afraid of crushing. Vani and Kai had embraced the whole makeup treatment, including having foundation air-brushed onto their faces like a coat of paint on a car. True, they looked fabulous, and I was sure that their makeup would remain in place through the apocalypse if necessary. But I had managed to prevent the makeup artist from doing anything that might make me feel like a cake being iced.

I had to admit that it was a pleasure to feel like the most attractive version of myself possible after having spent so many days in such a grim atmosphere where the only thing about me that seemed to matter was my utility to the mission. And although it wasn't as fancy as the other dresses, I really liked the plum-colored wrap dress I'd chosen. It was comfortable, flattering, and hadn't cost a fortune.

Vani and Kai had each accepted some fine jewelry pieces from Saks on loan, but I opted out. I was certain that if I borrowed something, it would get lost or broken. I'd forced the personal shopper to take me to the costume jewelry section, where she practically held her nose as I chose a pair of understated silver earrings that I thought went nicely with my protective pendant.

The conversation consisted almost entirely of Kai and Vani admiring each other. Since we finally had cell phone reception again, I took the opportunity to text Simone that things had gone well on my "getaway" with Ben and that I'd be home the next day—and then spent the next several minutes dodging her questions about *exactly* how well the getaway had gone. Eventually I managed to satisfy her with promises that I'd tell her more about it when I saw her in person.

When I put my phone away, Vani said, "That was a long text. Everything okay?"

"Yeah, just checking in with a friend," I said with a smile. "So, does anybody know where we're going?"

Kai said, "I'm not sure, but I think we're in Capitol Hill."

"I hope they have steak," I murmured, and my stomach growled loudly in agreement.

"Not a chance," Vani scolded. "You're vegetarian for another week at least. Program rules. Or had you forgotten?"

I turned and stared out the window. I'd come out of paralysis for him; the least Ben could do was give me was a nice steak—even if it did "muck up" my aura, as Vani claimed it would.

Vani and Kai shared a conspiratorial glance, then Kai turned to me and said in a low voice, "So, are you going to tell us how Ben un-paralyzed you? Because he is being ridiculously tight-lipped."

Thank God, I thought, sending a silent pulse of gratitude to Ben, wherever he was.

"Yeah," Vani said, "he told us that if we wanted to know, it was up to you whether you wanted to tell us."

"I'm sorry," I said. "Nothing personal, but not in a million years."

Vani blinked innocently. "Not even for science?"

I rolled my eyes, but fortunately I was spared having to reply. We had reached our destination. Kai was right; we were in Capitol Hill, and right near the White House by the looks of things.

The limo driver let us off in front of the elegant entrance to a restaurant called The Oval Room. As we entered, the maître d' seemed to recognize Kai. "You are here for the private party?"

Kai nodded. The maître d' said, "You're in the Blue Room. Follow me."

I eyed Kai nervously. "Good grief," I whispered as we weaved through a short maze of hallways. "All of this playing dress-up, and now we're a private party? How fancy *is* this lunch?"

He exchanged a smile with Vani. "Relax," he murmured. "If you can't figure out which fork to use, just watch me."

"Fine," I grumbled, silently cursing Skeet for taking us somewhere so upscale that I knew I would feel out of my element—and cursing Ben for having gone along with the plan.

The maître d' opened a set of double doors and waved us in. "Your party is waiting."

Kai gestured for me to step in first. It did appear as though everyone from the subbasement was there, and all together in one room, we were quite a sizeable group. There were huge flower arrangements as centerpieces, and all of the chairs and tables were draped in blue and green silks. Ben came to greet me, looking impossibly delicious in a dark blue suit and a white shirt with a mandarin collar. His collar was held closed by a black pin, which I guessed was the closest he would ever get to wearing a tie.

Ben also smelled so damn good that I wanted to grab him by the hand and run out of the restaurant and down the street to the nearest hotel. But the gold flecks in his eyes were glowing with mischief, and I could tell that he had something else planned. His pupils dilated slightly as his gaze traveled from my blown-out hair down to my shoes and back. "You look beautiful," he murmured as he took my hand and tucked it into his elbow, then turned us around to face the room.

Skeet walked over from where he had been standing nearby, his face alight. "Here she is, everyone!" He announced to the room. "Our MVP!"

A few seconds later, everyone had turned towards us and broken into applause.

"Your *what?*" I whispered to Skeet.

"Most valuable player! Don't be embarrassed," Skeet murmured, then again turned to the others. "As you know, this luncheon is to celebrate a mission that turned out to be as much of a success as it could possibly be. Thanks to all of your hard work and dedication, the mystery behind Braz's murder has been solved, and his death will not be in vain." Skeet bowed his head for a moment and the room was silent. Then Skeet slid his hand around my arm. "As you all know, Captain Abbott and I would like to offer a special thanks to Miss Cate Duncan, whose courage and skill overcame the key obstacles to a positive resolution. Thank you, Cate."

There was another round of applause. I could feel every beat of my heart pulsing in my cheeks, and I realized that I must have turned bright red. I also had to force myself to close my mouth, which had fallen open at some point. Mercifully, Skeet noticed my distress and cut the moment short. "Everyone, please enjoy the *hors d'oeuvres* and open bar. I'm told the main course will be served shortly."

I tried to catch my breath as the rest of the guests returned to their conversations. Skeet turned towards me, concern etched in his expression. "Cate, I'm so sorry if this made you uncomfortable. That was not our intention. We just wanted to acknowledge your extraordinary efforts, and we thought you'd enjoy a *pleasant* surprise for a change."

The truth was that I hated surprises in general; it didn't matter if they were good or bad. But I was touched that Skeet—and especially Captain Abbott—had thought enough of my work to single me out, and I didn't want to appear less than gracious. I forced myself to smile brightly. "Not uncomfortable," I said, "just surprised—you succeeded there! And thank you so much for honoring me, but I was just grateful to be able to help Braz."

"I know," Skeet said as his tension eased. "And you did help him, Cate, and us, more than you'll ever know. We just wanted to let you know that." Skeet produced a smallish square gift box from his suit pocket and handed it to me. "That's from Braz," he said softly. "Before he died, he asked me to make sure you got it. It belonged to Pedra."

"Oh!" I exclaimed as a pulse of grief throbbed in my chest. "Thank you." My cheeks began to ache from forced smiling.

Ben tucked my hand into the crook of his arm again and gave it a squeeze. When I looked up at him, I felt the portal between us open. His love flowed into and around me, calming me a bit. He turned to Skeet, "Do you mind if I take her away for a moment? I think she could use a sit-down and a glass of water."

Skeet nodded. "Certainly. You two enjoy yourselves."

Ben steered me toward the front of the room. My legs were still a little rubbery from the shock, so I leaned on him as we walked to an empty table. I carefully laid down the wrapped box. While we sat, the rest of the guests stood around socializing. Servers circulated around the room carrying trays of drinks and what looked like canapés. I looked around in wide-eyed wonder, trying to take it all in. Ben handed me the promised glass of water. "Was that MVP announcement an okay thing to do? When Skeet asked me, I told him I thought it would be all right."

I took a few sips of water. The sensation of the cool liquid filling my mouth and traveling down my throat grounded me a bit. "It's fine, and I do appreciate the sentiment. It's just that—and you had no way of knowing this, but for future notice—I'm not big on surprises. And I'm even less enthusiastic about being the center of attention."

Ben seemed to relax a bit. "Oh, okay. Well, just so you know, Kai and Vani were in on it, too. The shopping trip was their idea." I looked over at Kai and Vani, who waved and gave me thumbs-up signs.

Ben slid his cell phone out of his pocket and appeared to be reading a text. "There's someone waiting to see you outside. Come on, I'll take you."

"What? Who?" I asked as he led me to the doors. "And why outside?" But as the doors to the room shut behind us, I spotted a familiar figure walking towards us down the hallway. My eyes widened. I turned back to Ben. "*Sid?*"

"Of course," Ben said as his gaze traveled behind me. "Sid, over here," he called out. "Glad you could make it."

Sid was dressed in one of his more formal suits. Before I knew it, I was squeezing the life out of him. "Sid!" My heart did a jig: he really *was* fine and all in one piece! I pulled away. "I'm so glad you're okay! What are you doing here?"

Sid extended his hand to Ben, who shook it firmly. "Thank you for calling me."

My eyes widened as I looked up at Ben. "*You* invited him?"

"Of course," Ben replied, taking in both Sid and me with a magnanimous smile. "I knew you wouldn't be satisfied that he was all right until you saw him in person. I'm glad you could make it, Sid. Can I bring you something from the bar?"

I couldn't quite believe how comfortable Ben was acting—and I wondered how much of it was acting.

"No, thank you. Unfortunately, as I mentioned, I can only stop long enough to say hello. Family business; you understand."

"Absolutely. We'll talk more later. It's nice to meet you." Ben turned to me. "I'll see you inside?"

I gave Ben a questioning look. He inclined his head in Sid's direction. I took the hint and grabbed Sid's arm. "I'm sorry you can't stay. Let me walk you out."

Ben headed back into the Blue Room. As Sid and I meandered toward the restaurant entrance, I whispered, "You're *sure* you're okay? I'm so sorry about everything."

"Please don't apologize," he said. "I'm fine. I was furious at first, of course. But once I learned that I was essentially doing you a favor, I started to enjoy my confinement. The FBI is going to have quite a room service bill, not to mention pay-per-view."

"I'll still never forgive myself, ever." I squeezed his arm. "Do you really have to leave? We both know you don't have any family business. You're just afraid of Ben."

"I most certainly am," he murmured. "You are aware that he's a trained killing machine, right? But that's not why I can't stay. I wasn't exactly invited to the luncheon itself. Apparently you have to have a security clearance to get into that room, and it would be rude of me to keep you away from your party for too long. But your marine thought it might be good for you if we saw each other, and knowing you and your penchant for worry, I agreed. I respect him for asking me to come. He's much more generous than I would be under the circumstances."

"So you like him?" I asked, hopeful. In spite of our unusual relationship, Sid had become one of my closest friends, and his opinion mattered a lot to me.

"Yes. He seems like a stand-up guy," Sid replied. "And you may not be aware of this, but you're glowing, my dear. If he makes you happy, that's all I really care about. Still, I have no intention of ever getting on his bad side—any more than I must already be, by default. Surely you've sensed the steel beneath that charming exterior of his? He sure puts it into his handshake."

I glanced back at the doors to the Blue Room. "Yeah," I muttered, "I know about the steel."

"Good," he said. "I might be worried if I weren't so confident that you could handle him."

I rolled my eyes. "I don't think he's exactly what you'd call 'handle-able.'"

Sid chuckled. "You're a perfect match, then."

"What's *that* supposed to mean?"

As we reached the doors to the outside, he turned and put his hands on my shoulders, holding me at arm's length. "It means that you're quite a handful yourself—a delightful handful, of course," he added, grinning as he dodged a poke in the ribs. "I can tell, though, by the way he looks at you, he would do anything to make you happy. Including calling me here, which was quite big of him. But I'd better be going. I don't want to be seen as taking advantage of Ben's leniency."

I smirked to let Sid know exactly what I thought about the

concept of Ben extending leniency. Then I gave him another huge hug. "I'll never be able to thank you enough."

"You're welcome," he said, hugging me back. "Now get back to your marine. You know where to find me if you need anything—a Persian rug, an FBI patsy...."

I groaned and shoved him away from me. "Go home already!"

Sid's eyes shone with real emotion as he said, "Bye, my dear. Don't be a stranger."

"Never," I called after him with a catch in my throat as he turned and walked out the door.

CHAPTER TWENTY-THREE

Ben was waiting for me when I got back. Looking very pleased with himself, he offered me his arm again. I gave him a sideways glance as we walked.

"That was very thoughtful of you," I murmured.

"Of course. I wanted you to feel at ease about Sid's wellbeing. I also respect the way he handled everything he's gone through on our behalf this week."

"So you were killing three birds with one stone: thanking Sid, reassuring me that he's okay—*and* showing him in person how Marine-y you are."

"Marine-y?" Ben arched an eyebrow.

"Yes, and job well done," I said dryly. "He's duly intimidated."

"Hm." He brushed an imaginary piece of lint off of his jacket sleeve. "I don't know why. I thought I was perfectly polite."

As I tried to think of a pithy comeback, Skeet brought Dr. MacGregor over to our table. It was a little disorienting to see Skeet out of his lab coat and wearing a suit. He looked pretty dashing for a research scientist. Meanwhile, Dr. MacGregor was elegant in a light blue dress covered with a layer of white lace. Judging from their comfort and ease with one another, I could see that they were indeed old friends.

"You doing okay over there, Cate?" Skeet asked.

"Fine now, thanks," I said.

He smiled warmly and nodded at Dr. MacGregor. "I hope you realize what an amazing boss you have."

She waved Skeet's compliment away as Ben returned and sat a

tray of champagne glasses on the table. He placed one in front of me, whispering, "Sparkling cider. Program rules."

It seemed completely unfair that I should be expected to adhere to ParaTrain's dietary rules at a party where I had been honored. But before I could object, Dr. MacGregor cut in. "Congratulations. Skeet tells me that you were an extraordinary help this week. I knew you were a good hire." She smiled affectionately—an expression of hers I hadn't seen before. "And it's lovely to see you and Ben together like this. The ring suits you, by the way."

"Thank you," I said, touched by her words. "I love the ring. I guess I have you to thank."

"You're most welcome, but you only need to thank Ben. It was always his to do with as he pleased." She gestured towards the box. "It seems you have an unopened gift, there."

"Yes, of course." I had wanted to wait until I was in private to open it, but thanks to Dr. MacGregor, all eyes were on me. My hands trembled slightly as I picked up the box, untied the bow, and carefully removed the wrapping paper. I lifted the lid off of the small white box. There was glint of metal surrounded by tissue paper. I reached in and pulled out a delicate gold bracelet. Each end of a snake chain was fastened to a beautifully ornate anchor charm. With the bracelet draped over my fingertips, all I could do was stare.

There were *oooh*s and *ahh*s around the table. Ben slid his arm around my waist and leaned in close. His nearness relaxed me. "An anchor," he murmured. "I wonder what it means?"

"He said that about Pedra," I whispered. "He said she was his anchor."

"Mmm." Ever so subtly, Ben brushed his lips across my temple, sending a shiver of pleasure through me. "Would you like me to put it on for you?"

I bit my lip. It felt odd to wear a bracelet that belonged to a woman I'd never met (in life, that was), gifted to me by a friend who had just recently died. But as I thought about Braz and his vigorous love of life, I knew that he would think such considerations were silly, and would encourage me to embrace his gift. I held out the bracelet and nodded.

With a surprising agility given his man-sized fingers, Ben managed to operate the clasp and close the bracelet neatly around my wrist. I blinked back tears as I thought of what the symbol meant to Braz, and why he would have wanted me to have it. I knew that he thought Ben was a good anchor for me, or a "tether" to the earth, as he'd called it. As I leaned against Ben and inhaled his scent—a scent I had already begun to crave—I thought that maybe Braz was right.

All at once, it felt as though the sun was rising right in the middle of my chest. I smiled a genuine smile this time and held out my wrist to show the others. The emotions around the table were strong as everyone admired the bracelet.

Dr. MacGregor came over to take a closer look. "It's lovely. I don't think I've ever seen an anchor styled quite like that."

"Me either. I'd like to do a little research into the design and find out where it originated." I figured it was as good a time as any to set up a meeting with her. Unsure whether Skeet knew about her involvement in the kheir research, I was carefully vague. "Speaking of research, Dr. MacGregor, I'd love to talk to you more at some point about your work with the Smithsonian."

Dr. MacGregor's eyebrows flew upwards. "My, my," she said, looking from me to Ben and back again. "So our people have been filling you in on some things, Cate. I'll certainly be happy to talk to you about it. Tomorrow afternoon, perhaps? I'd be happy to make lunch for you and Ben."

After our work on his phobia, Ben had managed to eat a meal in front of his mother. I was sure she was eager to repeat the experience. I glanced over at him. "Ben?"

He nodded. "Sounds perfect."

She squinted over my shoulder. "Excellent, but I think some people over there are trying to get your attention."

I followed her gaze. The other members of the MacGregor Group were waving at us from another table. Vani was with a date—Hector from Yankee Company. Clearly, some things had been going on in the subbasement to which I had not been privy. Captain Abbott was at another table with a few of the other marines, along with Dr. Washington. The rest of the marines filled out the other tables in the room.

We waved back at our friends, but visiting would have to wait; our entrées had arrived. Ben had ordered the salmon for me. Fortunately it was delicious, which made up somewhat for the fact that it wasn't a huge slab of prime rib. Meanwhile, Ben hadn't been given a meal—at his request, I assumed. While he had managed to eat in front of a crowd in the mess hall, he would probably have to work up to eating in a fancy restaurant. I slid my hand under the table and rested my hand on his leg. He reached down, taking my hand in his, and stroked the back of it with his thumb. It was nice to be able to do things like that without worrying who was watching.

Since I had arrived later than everyone else, after lunch, Ben and I walked from table to table and said our hellos. The more walking and standing I did, the more relieved I was that I'd given the Jimmy Choos a pass.

When we reached Nessa and Kevin's table, they both practically crushed me with bear hugs. Nessa took a moment to admire the bracelet. "You get all the nice jewelry," she said with a wink.

"I keep tellin' ya, Red," Kevin said, "all you gotta do is say you'll marry me and I'll give you so much jewelry you'll need to buy a storage space just to hold it all!"

There was an outbreak of laughter. Ben shook his head. "I can't believe you're still trying after all these years."

Kevin resolutely folded his arms across his chest. "You laugh, but I think I'm wearing her down!"

"Yeah, what's that you always say?" Nessa asked him. "Persistence wins the day?"

"Damn right!" Kevin exclaimed with a broad grin.

"Then keep at it, big guy!" Nessa gave him an affectionate thump on the back.

This prompted another round of laughter. Then Nessa addressed Ben and me. "Listen you two, don't be strangers, okay?

We went too long without seeing you this time. Good friends are hard to find."

"We promise," Ben said.

I reached out my hand, and she took it. "Thank you for everything," I said softly.

"I have no idea what you're talking about, but you're welcome." She gave me a warm smile and then waved us off. "You'd better get going. Your people over there are looking restless."

The MacGregor Group's table was our final stop. We pulled up chairs, smiling as Vani and Hector tried to take their eyes off of each other long enough to greet us. Everyone admired my bracelet. We had a bittersweet conversation about what an extraordinary person Braz was, and what a large hole his absence had created.

The table fell silent for a while. Then, with prompting from Kai, Pete stood up and said he had something important to tell us.

"What is it?" I asked, fascinated to see the confident cowboy looking at the ground and shuffling his feet back and forth.

"Well." He looked at Kai, who gestured for him to continue. He glanced up at Ben and me. "We just wanted to let you know that there's gonna be a wedding."

"What?" I gaped at them. "You're *engaged*?"

Kai beamed and nodded vigorously, then nudged Pete. "Tell her what happened!"

Pete pushed his hat back and rubbed his hairline. "Lydia called."

My hands flew up to cover my wide-open mouth. Lydia was Pete's little sister. He hadn't been allowed to speak to her in years, ever since he came out of the closet and his parents disowned him. "Are you serious? When?"

"Last night." A look of pride crept across his face. "She's a freshman at college now, eighteen years old and livin' away from home, and she managed to track me down. Gol darn stupid and bull-headed as always, she called Marine Corps headquarters and kept buggin' people until they patched her through to me." In spite of his harsh words, he beamed with pride. "So Lydia said she never cared who I dated, and she thinks our folks are backwards rednecks.

I yelled at her for bein' disrespectful, of course. But then she said she wants to come out and meet Kai."

Unable to contain himself any longer, Kai jumped in. "We're having her out here for a few days during her Thanksgiving break, and she said she's going to work on his parents, too—try to bring them around. Isn't that incredible?"

"Truly!" I flung myself at Pete, hugging him tightly, and did the same to Kai. Ben embraced them both as well. The excitement around the table was palpable.

Pushing his hat back down, Pete added softly, "Even if my folks don't come around, at least I'd have *some* family at the wedding. Plus, Lydia said some of my cousins might come, too. So Kai and me, we decided to just go ahead and do it."

Pete wrapped his arm around Kai's shoulders as they exchanged an intimate look that spoke volumes.

"By the way, Ben, I'm already working on designing my ring," Kai said, "and it's not going to be cheap, so you'd better give Pete a raise."

Pete grimaced, and the whole table laughed—except for Kai, who looked perfectly serious.

"Consider it done," Ben said with a firm nod.

After a bit more mingling, the high level of emotion flowing through the room began to overwhelm me. Even though it was all positive, I felt as though I'd hit an energetic wall. I pulled Ben aside and confided in him. "I feel so bad. Skeet went to all of the trouble to plan all of this this, and you arranged for our shopping trip and everything…. I know this is horrible, but I just… I don't know how much longer I can last."

To my surprise, Ben folded me into his arms and held me for several moments. I allowed my body to relax into his. He placed a kiss on the top of my head, sending tendrils of warmth all the way down to my toes. Then he leaned down and whispered in my ear, "You've been a champion today. I'm impressed that you've lasted this long. Let's slip out. I'll have my mother make our apologies."

"No," I objected, pulling away slightly. "We can't just slip out!

241

That would be rude. We at least have to say goodbye to everyone, and thank Skeet...." But even as I said the words, I doubted whether I would have the stamina.

Ben looked down at me, his eyes sparkling like the stone in my ring. "You don't get it yet, do you? All I care about is you—*all* I care about." He again enfolded me in his arms. "These are all people who love us. They'll understand. They'll probably stay for a few more hours drinking; they won't even notice we're gone. Let's go. The limo's outside."

I gritted my teeth. "I don't know."

In spite of my words, though, I must have looked relieved. Ben murmured intently, "You pretend you're going to the ladies' room, but instead, go outside and get in the limo. I'll have a quick word with Skeet and my mother and meet you there."

I couldn't help myself; I smiled. "Okay."

"Good. The coast is clear. Go!"

I tossed my blown-out waves and tried to look casual as I headed for the double doors. Kai waved me over, but I mouthed "bathroom." He nodded and turned back to the conversation at the table. Outside, the limo was waiting as promised. I hopped in the back and kicked off my shoes. My heart was beating against my ribs like a wild bird in a cage, but I couldn't stop smiling. Ben had said that I was all he cared about. Although I knew that wasn't true, as long as I was somewhere near the top of his list, I really couldn't ask for more.

Minutes later, Ben burst in, slammed the door, and knocked on the divider between our compartment and the driver's.

"Yes sir?"

"Baltimore, please. The lady would like to go home."

"Yes, sir," the driver replied and discreetly closed the divider.

Still troubled, I peered over at Ben. "Was Skeet okay with this?"

Ben gave me a wry half-smile. "He said, and I quote, 'You two kids have some fun.'"

I moaned, slapping myself on the forehead. "It sounds like he thinks we're going to get *up* to something!"

I yelped in surprise as with a loud growl, Ben leaned over, grabbed me, and pulled me onto his lap. "What a great idea," he said in a low, seductive rumble. "By the way, your MVP gift from me isn't quite ready yet, but we should be able to pick it up in a few days."

"My *what?*"

"Braz isn't the only one who's allowed to give you presents, is he?"

I threw my head back and laughed. "Oh my God, Ben, please tell me you're joking. An MVP gift? You just bought me this dress, for goodness' sake—"

"The MacGregor group paid for that dress—which I think you should wear every day from now on, by the way, as long as there are no other men around." He settled me into his lap so he could get a firmer grip. "If it makes you feel any better, your next gift is for my benefit as well as yours."

What did that mean? Had he custom-ordered some lingerie or something? But my curiosity was momentarily overshadowed by my embarrassment. I didn't know if constant gift giving was a part of normal relationships or just a Ben thing, but already there was no way I could match his generosity. I balled my hands into fists and shoved them into my lap to keep from biting my nails.

Ben leaned over and peered into my eyes like he was looking at me through a microscope. "What is it?"

"It's just…." I shrugged, looking down at my hands. "You keep giving me gifts, and I haven't given you any. And I *can't*—not like the ones you've given me, I mean."

Ben splayed his fingers across my cheek and pressed my head against his shoulder, kissing a trail along my hairline. I shivered with pleasure. "You're coming to work for the MacGregor group," he murmured. "We're together. You're healthy and safe. Those are gifts of limitless value, Cate. You've already given me more than I ever could have wished for."

A riot of butterflies loosed themselves in my stomach. I didn't know whether what I was feeling was joy, terror, or both. As my whole body flushed with heat, I tried to squirm away from Ben, just to feel the relief of some cool air between us. But within seconds, he pulled some kind of tricky hand-to-hand combat move, using my motion to shift our bodies again until I was cradled tightly in his arms, our faces mere inches apart.

"What are you doing?" I stammered, as a mighty blush burst across my cheeks like a red brushstroke.

"Examining you." Ben looked me over carefully, his face a solemn mask of concern. He smoothed a perfectly styled lock of hair away from my temple and rested the back of his hand against my forehead. "I'm a little worried," he murmured. "You seem feverish."

I made one last attempt to pull away from him before admitting defeat. I collapsed against him with a sigh. "That's because I'm blushing, you moron."

"Hmm." He nodded sagely. "I know how to make that worse."

I squinted up at him. "Did you say *worse?*"

"I did. Come here, Trouble." Ben covered my mouth with his, swallowing my startled cry. He pulled me even more tightly against his body. Then, true to his word, he proceeded to deepen my blush, brazenly and determinedly, all the way home.

THE DESOLATE KISS

Your tongue ran like a stream
across parched earth, filling in cracks,
opening all that was closed and locked,
your lips lending their passion to mine
to speak again, to cry out.

Yours were the painstaking fingers
untying all the knots so tightly wound,
touching each of the human needs
my body had forgotten, breathing fire
back into this warrior's limbs.

We were forged together,
a double helix, as inseparable
as the building blocks of life,
tumbling and roaring through the city,
then sleeping in the dream we made.

So bitter it is to dream.
Better to be blank and empty,
sleepwalking through each day, than to know
the foul taste of dreams torn away
by the same lovers who gave them life.

This beaten dog's pure and hopeless hope
is kept alive by my subversive heart:
somewhere in your mansion of black rooms
there is one devoted to me, and to regret.
Like a mystic, I sicken and die with this faith.

If you or someone you know needs help, you may find information and resources, including links to immediate help, on the following website from the U.S. Department of Health and Human Services:
www.mentalhealth.gov

The National Suicide Prevention Lifeline has trained crisis workers available to talk 24 hours a day, 7 days a week:
1-800-273-TALK (8255)
www.suicidepreventionlifeline.org

If you are outside of the U.S., a database of international resources can be found on the website of the International Association for Suicide Prevention:
www.iasp.info

Connect with Anise Eden at her website:
www.AniseEden.com

Thank you for reading *All the Wounds in Shadow*. Our sincere thanks to all of the bloggers and reviewers who take the time to get the word out about books they love!

For more of the Healing Edge series, look for *All the Broken Places* (Book One). And keep an eye out for *All the Light There Is* (Book Three) coming in 2017 from Diversion Books!

Author's Note: The poet Lewin Lima referenced in this book is a fictional character. The poem, "The Desolate Kiss," was written as part of *All the Wounds in Shadow*.

9 781682 302873